Postcolonial Travel Writing

Postcolonial Travel Writing

Critical Explorations

Edited by

Justin D. Edwards

and

Rune Graulund

palgrave
macmillan

First published 2011 by
PALGRAVE MACMILLAN

Palgrave Macmillan in the UK is an imprint of Macmillan Publishers Limited, registered in England, company number 785998, of Houndmills, Basingstoke, Hampshire RG21 6XS.

Palgrave Macmillan in the US is a division of St Martin's Press LLC, 175 Fifth Avenue, New York, NY 10010.

Palgrave Macmillan is the global academic imprint of the above companies and has companies and representatives throughout the world.

Palgrave® and Macmillan® are registered trademarks in the United States, the United Kingdom, Europe and other countries.

ISBN 978–0–230–24119–0   hardback

This book is printed on paper suitable for recycling and made from fully managed and sustained forest sources. Logging, pulping and manufacturing processes are expected to conform to the environmental regulations of the country of origin.

A catalogue record for this book is available from the British Library.

Library of Congress Cataloging-in-Publication Data

Postcolonial travel writing : critical explorations / edited by Justin D. Edwards and Rune Graulund.
     p. cm.
Includes bibliographical references and index.
ISBN 978–0–230–24119–0
1. Travelers' writings, Commonwealth (English)—History and criticism.
   2. Travelers' writings, English—History and criticism.
   3. Commonwealth prose literature (English)—History and criticism.
   4. Travel in literature. 5. Postcolonialism in literature. I. Edwards, Justin D., 1970– II. Graulund, Rune.
PR9080.5.P73 2011
820.9'32—dc22   2010033939

10 9 8 7 6 5 4 3 2 1
20 19 18 17 16 15 14 13 12 11

Printed and bound in Great Britain by
CPI Antony Rowe, Chippenham and Eastbourne

Table of Contents

Contributors

William Dalrymple is a travel writer and novelist who was born in Scotland and brought up on the shores of the Firth of Forth. His first travel book, *In Xanadu* (1989), won the *Yorkshire Post* Best Book Award for the Best First Work and a Scottish Arts Council Book of the Year Award; it was short-listed for the John Llewellyn Rhys Memorial Prize. His second book, *City of Djinns* (1993), a book on Delhi published six years after he had moved to the Indian capital, won the 1994 Thomas Cook Travel Book Award. His other travel books and novels include *From the Holy Mountain* (1997), *The Age of Kali* (1998), *White Mughals* (2002) and *The Last Mughal* (2008).

Justin D. Edwards is Professor of English at Bangor University, Wales. He is the author of several books, including *Postcolonial Literature* (2008), *Understanding Jamaica Kincaid* (2007), *Gothic Passages: Racial Ambiguity and the American Gothic* (2003), *Gothic Canada: Reading the Spectre of a National Literature* (2005), and *Exotic Journeys: Exploring the Erotics of U.S. Travel Literature* (2001). He is also the co-editor of *Other Routes: 1500 Years of African and Asian Travel Writing* (2005) and *Downtown Canada: Writing Canadian Cities* (2005).

Rune Graulund is a Carlsberg Postdoctoral Fellow and teaches in the Department of Arts and Cultural Studies and the Department of English, Germanic and Romance Studies, University of Copenhagen. He has published on travel writing, postcolonial theory and contemporary American fiction and is currently completing a book titled *Drifting Horizons: Travel Writing, Nature Writing and the Idea of the Desert*.

Tabish Khair is Associate Professor of English at Aarhus University in Denmark, where he teaches, among other things, postcolonial literature and culture. He is the co-editor of *Other Routes: 1500 Years of African and Asian Travel Writing* (2005) and the editor of *Amitav Ghosh: A Critical Companion* (2003). Khair is also the author of *Babu Fictions: Alienation in Contemporary Indian Fiction* (2001) as well as several books of poetry and fiction, including two novels *The Bus Stopped* (2004) and *Filming: A Love Story* (2007) both published by Picador.

Claire Lindsay is Senior Lecturer in Latin American Literature and Culture at University College London. She is the author of *Locating Latin*

American Women Writers (2003), co-editor of special issues on *Studies in Travel Writing* (2003) and *Tesserae* (2006) on travel writing and is currently completing a book titled *Contemporary Travel Writing of Latin America* for Routledge.

María Lourdes López Ropero teaches English at the University of Alicante in Spain. She has published widely on contemporary postcolonial writing, including the book *The Anglo-Caribbean Migration Novel: Writing the Diaspora* (2004). She has written numerous articles on contemporary Caribbean writers such as Caryl Phillips, Austin Clarke, Fred D'Aguiar and Paule Marshall.

Pankaj Mishra is a travel writer, novelist and essayist who was born in North India and studied in Allahabad and Delhi. His first book, *Butter Chicken in Ludhiana: Travels in Small Town India* (1995), was one of the first travelogues to trace the social and cultural changes in India in the new context of globalization. Mishra's novel *The Romantics* (2000) contains many narratives of travel and desire and his recent book, *Temptations of the West: How to be Modern in India, Pakistan and Beyond* (2006), describes his travels through 'Bollywood', Afghanistan, Kashmir, Tibet, Nepal and other parts of Asia.

Zoran Pećić teaches literary and cultural studies at Roskilde University in Denmark. He recently completed a doctoral dissertation at the University of Wales on the queer narratives of the Caribbean diaspora. His research focuses on displacement and sexuality in the writing of, among others, Dionne Brand, Shani Mootoo and Jamaica Kincaid.

Richard Phillips is Reader in Geography at the University of Liverpool. He has formerly published the monographs *Sex, Politics and Empire: A Postcolonial Geography* (2006) and *Mapping Men and Empire: A Geography of Adventure* (1997) and is currently involved in the research project 'Postcolonial Human Rights and Sexuality Politics'. This project examines the complex negotiations of identity and power that produce and are produced by interventions by Western activists in sexuality politics in developing countries, particularly former colonies.

Bidhan Roy completed his PhD at Goldsmiths College, University of London on the influence of globalization on Anglophone writing. He has published articles on Hanif Kureishi, contemporary South Asian fiction, and the effects of globalization on Muslim identity. He currently lives in Los Angeles, CA, where he is Assistant Professor in Literature at California State University, Los Angeles.

Anne Schroder is completing her PhD on zombification in contemporary Caribbean and US literature at the University of Essex. Her dissertation explores the zombie as a paradigmatic figure of Otherness. Theorizing the shifting signifying potential of the zombie by drawing on the critical discourses of postcolonialism, posthumanism and globalization theory, the thesis examines the categories of agency, consumerism and commodification and interrogates the state of the human under capitalism. She has presented her research on Jean Rhys, Don DeLillo and Erna Brodber at several colloquia and conferences in the UK.

Paul Smethurst is Associate Professor in the School of English, University of Hong Kong, where he teaches travel writing and contemporary fiction. He is the author of *The Postmodern Chronotope* (2000), and *The Reinvention of Nature in Scientific, Picturesque and Romantic Travel Writing 1768–1840* (forthcoming), and editor (with Steve Clark) of *Asian Crossings: Travel Writing on China, Japan and South-East Asia* (2008), and (with Julia Kuehn) of *Travel Writing, Form and Empire: The Politics and Poetics of Mobility* (2008).

Acknowledgements

Thanks to our international contributors, this book has travelled a great deal. From London to LA, Copenhagen to Hong Kong, north Wales to north India, we thank our authors for their patience, professionalism and keen insights. We would also like to thank Rose Lewis for her impeccable copy-editing of the volume and Linda Jones for preparing the index.

An earlier version of María Lourdes López Ropero's chapter appeared in *Atlantis* 25.1 (June 2003). Thanks to the journal for allowing it to be reprinted here.

Introduction: Reading Postcolonial Travel Writing

Justin D. Edwards and Rune Graulund

1. Critical Borders

In the field of postcolonial studies, travel writing has often been demonized. Critics have, at times, aligned travel narratives with other textual practices associated with colonial expansion – mapping, botany, ethnography, journalism and so on – to suggest that travel writing disseminated discourses of difference that were then used to justify colonial projects. The literary critic David Spurr (1993), for instance, writes that such texts perpetuated 'the rhetoric of empire' by offering information to colonial administrators about what was happening in Kenya or Canada or Kashmir, while also depicting the colony for a general readership. Within this context, travel writing allowed Europeans to conceive of areas outside of Europe as being under their control, as an extension of land through ownership. Other critics have supported Spurr by arguing that travel writing contributed to the construction of modern conceptions of identity. Douglas Ivison (2003) writes that:

> travel and travel writing are determined by and determine gender, racial identity, economic status and a host of other interrelated markers of status and privilege. The genre of travel writing ... was the cultural by-product of imperialism, often written by those actively involved in the expansion or maintenance of empire (explorers, soldiers, administrators, missionaries, journalists), and dependent upon the support of the institutions of imperialism in order to facilitate the writers' travels. (200–1)

Here, Ivison points to the ways in which travel writing – particularly 19th-century texts – formulated discourses of difference and contributed

1

to the politics of colonial expansion. Indeed, it would be hard to argue that the depictions of African cannibalism and brutal violence in, for example, Henry Morton Stanley's *In Deepest Africa* (1890) are not open to such readings or critiques. Stanley's work, which sold 150,000 copies in the first few weeks of publication, was inspired by an expedition funded by King Leopold II of Belgium who hoped to acquire the Sudan and build up a trading company in east Africa (Carr, 2002: 71).[1]

Such approaches to the genre of travel writing have been fruitful and influential. But more recently a new generation of cultural and literary critics has begun to identify alternative representations of travel and to challenge Eurocentric understandings of the genre. Inderpal Grewal (1996), for instance, notes that travel writing can unsettle assumptions about the 'consolidation of stable unitary identities of nation, class, sexuality or gender, and suggest forms of Selfhood that evade such consolidations' (3). Other critics like Abu-Lughod (1989) and Avtar Brah (1996) see travel writing as offering possibilities for exploring transnational movements such as the Atlantic triangle and the phenomenology of diaspora and other forms of enforced migration. *Postcolonial Travel Writing: Critical Explorations* is part of this critical trajectory, for our contributors examine how postcolonial travel texts resist the gravitational pull of metropolitan centrality and cosmopolitanism by articulating experiences and ontologies that are often removed from dominant European or North American productions of knowledge.[2]

Part of the problem is that 'travel' has so often been conflated with 'European(ized) travel'. Even postcolonial critics well-versed in the politics of travel still say things like, 'to a certain extent ... travel writing is inevitably a one-way traffic, because the Europeans mapped the world rather than the world mapping them' (Clark, 1999: 3). What is often forgotten in such critiques, however, is that the world was 'mapped' by non-European peoples as well, and that many of these peoples also left behind travel accounts. For instance, Tabish Khair's Introduction to the anthology *Other Routes: 1500 Years of African and Asian Travel Writing* (2006) addresses this erasure by demonstrating how some Asian and African travellers drew textual and visual 'maps' sometimes used by European travellers to 'discover' the world (11–12). 'There is hardly any denying', writes Khair, 'the extensive – and overlooked – textual and cartographic evidence of vast parts of the world being navigated and traversed by Asians and Africans before, during and after Europeans set out on their post-Enlightenment voyages' (12). And yet by the 20th century, human movement in the past came to be seen as a predominantly European activity, an imagined trope connoting modernity, technological advancement and power.

Postcolonial Travel Writing builds on this research by analysing texts that continue to articulate a growing sense of decentring Europe, North America, globalization and other contemporary forms of Empire through representations of travel. Postcolonial writers as diverse as Jamaica Kincaid, Caryl Phillips, Amitav Ghosh, V. S. Naipaul, Charlotte Williams, Pico Iyer, Jan Morris and others have used the genre to engage in cultural critique and explore a range of personal conflicts from questions about home and belonging to displacement and diaspora. In fact, the critics Patrick Holland and Graham Huggan (1998) refer to the writers who take up the genre's potential for cultural critique as 'countertravelers' – travel writers who resist the tendency to indulge in exoticism or demarcate clear borders in order to differentiate or separate national and cultural identities. We seek to extend the 'countertravelers' paradigm by arguing that postcolonial travel writing is not just oppositional or a 'writing back'; it offers frames of reference that exist outside the boundaries of European knowledge production.

2. Producing Knowledge: Postcoloniality and Travel

The contemporary Indian novelist Amitav Ghosh offers an illustrative example of the way in which fictions of colonial authority and the subsequent production of knowledge can be undermined via travel writing. In his 1992 book *In an Antique Land*, Ghosh intertwines the story of Abraham Ben Yiju, a Middle Eastern merchant of the 12th century, and his Indian slave, Bomma, with Ghosh's own journeys through Egypt during the 1970s and 1980s. The book's subtitle is 'History in the Guise of a Traveller's Tale', and it is told in the first person by a traveller who finds himself in Egypt doing anthropological research. The author/narrator highlights the fact that he is an Indian traveller in Egypt and, as a result, he is seen to lack the cultural authority held by European and American travellers in the region. In this, he exposes the artificial construction of structures of difference, while also calling attention to the fact that he employs a very different gaze from European or American travellers in Egypt: he is not identified by the Egyptians as coming out of a culture of material wealth and technological advancement, and Egyptians treat him as irrational and ignorant, a foreigner without authority.

In an Antique Land is, among other things, a sharp critique of a classic quest – exoticist, anthropological, orientalist – for pure traditions and discrete cultural differences. When he first travels to Egypt, the narrator expects to find in that 'antique land' a settled group of people. However, he soon realizes that everyone in the village has, at some time or other, engaged in extensive travel, and that this tradition of mobility has gone on for centuries. Travel, then, is not just an activity of cosmopolitan privilege, for in Ghosh's text 'the anthropologist is not a worldly traveler visiting local natives, departing from the metropolitan center to study a rural periphery'. Instead, his ancient and settled field site opens him up to complex histories of dwelling, travelling and home.

Ghosh, in short, subverts the colonial travel narrative, uprooting it from its recent past as a tool of Empire. This project is further developed in his 2006 travel text about his visit to Angkor Wat, in which Ghosh writes that, for him, the most successful travel writing is that which does 'not assume a universal order of reality'; nor does it structure the journey into a narrative that 'correspond[s] to teleologies of racial or civilizational progress' (Foreword: ix). Instead, the most interesting travel narratives are, he suggests, those that express 'openness to surprise' and 'acknowledge ... the limits of the knowingness of the witness' (ix). To illustrate his point, he recounts the story of visiting the Cambodian monument Angkor Wat in 1993. Upon reaching the monument, Ghosh tells of how he recalls the account of Henri Mouhot (1826–61) 'discovering' Angkor Wat in 1860: the Frenchman had parted the 'veil of greenery' surrounding the ancient temple and 'found' the abandoned structure that had lain dormant since it was raided by the Thai army in 1431 (x). Ghosh writes:

> The tale he told was entirely at odds with the tale of [Mouhot's] exploration [and] discovery of Angkor Wat ... Monks had [in fact] lived in Angkor Wat for centuries before Mouhot's discovery ... It was only after the monument's 'discovery' by the French that it was truly abandoned: when archeologists took possession of the complex, they forced the monks to move their shrine out of the temple's interior. (xii)

Ghosh's description of visiting the Cambodian temple illustrates, among other things, how narratives of travel are linked to power and the production of knowledge. 'So to whom was the monument "lost"?', Ghosh asks. 'Certainly the Buddhist Sangha was well aware of its existence, as were the ruling powers in Thailand and Cambodia ... It was only to Europeans, then, that Angkor was a "discovery"' (xii). Here Ghosh reveals that in 1860 the European colonial administrators rewrote the complicated narrative of the monument's past. The French travellers and explorers composed a travel account focusing on an abandoned site – a lost temple – that Mouhot 'discovered' and brought back to life. But Ghosh points out that the European 'discoverers' also tried to recast the actual structure of the temple to fit into their own version of the tale. Thus, the archaeologists in 1860 attempted to purge the building of all traces of recent human life, forcing the monks out of the temple and compelling them to inhabit the surrounding areas. Life was altered to correspond to the official narrative of Mouhot's travels.

3.   Dislocating Empire

We invoke Ghosh's texts in our Introduction to *Postcolonial Travel Writing* to demonstrate how the impetus for our project comes out of a need to analyse contemporary travel writing within a range of specific locations and subject positions, while also studying contemporary travel writing from a global point of view – a perspective that encompasses texts about Indian travellers in Egypt or a globalized tourist industry that has impacted Angkor Wat and, by extension, Cambodian culture and society. Such work, within fluidly globalized conceptions of space and place, allows for new, insightful and cutting-edge analyses of the relationship between travel, cultural exchange and Empire.

But why *postcolonial* travel writing? Some readers might consider the term 'postcolonial' to be inappropriate now that some critics have begun to question its validity. According to Suman Gupta's recent *Globalization and Literature* (2009), we must pay heed to the possibility that the very idea of the postcolonial is 'not necessarily the only, or even the dominant, axis for understanding globalization processes' (120–1). The impact of the postcolonial may be read as being, if not irrelevant, then at least of secondary, or perhaps even tertiary, importance in the face of far more powerful processes governing our increasingly global world. As for the term itself, we may question whether there is any critical currency left in the theoretical paradigms accompanying a postcolonial approach. By extension, we might even ask if 'the postcolonial' has become too embedded in European and North American institutions (particularly universities) for it to be an effective political and analytical frame of reference.

We can begin to address these questions by recognizing that 'the postcolonial' has always been – and will continue to be – an unstable and contested critical term. In fact, it is the contested nature of the word that has generated such lively and productive scholarly debate.

Our topic – indeed, our very title – includes a series of tensions, strains and stresses that, for us, generate a critical energy for investigating complex theoretical concerns alongside close readings and the textual analyses of case studies. The word 'postcolonial' imparts potential for dislocation, disjuncture and even rupture when it is combined with a genre – travel writing – that has been harshly critiqued within postcolonial circles. Thus, we seek to shake the reader's complacency through the unmapping of mapped critical areas and decentring dominant theoretical territories.[3]

By focusing on contemporary travel writing, we seek to avoid the pitfalls of an ahistorical critical practice that ignores the complex material determinations of imperialism's history and, in so doing, conflates all forms of Empire with capitalist expansion. A particularly striking example of this problem exists in the writing of Michael Hardt and Antonio Negri: their books *Empire* (2000) and *Multitude* (2004) have sparked debates about the limits of 'the postcolonial', perhaps best summed up in *Multitude* when they argue that the nation-based strategies of postcolonial politics are ineffective as 'the nation-state is declining … and a supranational level is forming a new sovereignty, a global Empire' (7). Indeed, for Hardt and Negri, Empire is neither a figure of speech nor a form of imperialism. Rather, it is a decentred and deterritorializing apparatus of rule that progressively incorporates the entire global realm inside its open, expanding frontiers. Within this definition of Empire, 'postcolonialist theories may end up in a dead end' because they are restricted to regional, national or local concerns and, as a result, 'postcolonialist strategies that appear to be liberatory would not challenge but in fact coincide with and even unwittingly reinforce the new strategies of rule' (*Empire*, 137–8).

However, we might wonder if Hardt and Negri reproduce a colonial modernist mode of knowledge production. Perhaps by adopting a Eurocentric ontology, they incorporate a teleological concept of history, narrative and philosophy (a trajectory that runs from Spinoza to Marx to Foucault to Deleuze and Guattari to, well, them) and inadvertently adopt an assumption that 'the universal Idea is the driving force of social life' (Rofel, 2002: 183). We might well ask: do Hardt and Negri assume a 'master imperial logic' that places Europe at the centre of thought, history and being? Perhaps their theorization of globalization does not decentre the rule of European supremacy or provincialize Europe but in fact assumes a political unconscious in which Empire/ *Empire* is the European subject looking out. Their pursuit of Empire as a concept requiring a philosophical approach and their focus on Europe and Euro-America ignores, as Lisa Rofel suggests, 'the rest of the world and tells a Eurocentric tale of everyone else's histories' (184). According to this paradigm, Europe is the only place that is 'theoretically knowable'; all other places and histories are 'matters of empirically fleshing out the European theoretical subject' (184). Maybe it would be more productive for contemporary critiques of Empire (and economic globalization) to leave behind the European discourses of modernity and form a critique that focuses on the cultural production of capitalism and the transformations currently taking place in this production. It might be better to emphasize the culturally, geographically and historically specific and uneven manifestations of these processes. We might also treat 'discourses of global capitalism and globalization as, themselves, elements within this cultural production that require critical scrutiny not only regarding their accuracy but also, more importantly, regarding the kinds of work to which they are being put' (185).

Let's be clear about this: we do not seek to revitalize the nation-based politics of postcolonialism. But we do want to reflect on the complexity of space/place relationships that have informed the rise of interest in postcolonial travel writing. Travel might lead to a reflection on home and belonging but it can also lead to a sense of homelessness through a disintegration of nation-based notions of identity. In a postcolonial context, we might say – however hesitantly – that the cessation of one identity (through national independence) without a sufficient connection between citizen and space being 'in place' leads to an experience of being out-of-place. This is one reason why 'the postcolonial' (however it is defined) lends critical currency to theories of global travel: globalization is, among other things, a way of producing knowledge that, like the travel writer, is not always contained within or restricted by borders, boundaries, regions, nations or languages.

4.   From *Empire* to 'Empire'

One year before Hardt and Negri published *Empire*, the contemporary travel writer Pico Iyer published a piece titled 'Empire' in *The Global Soul* (2000). Here, Iyer describes himself and an unnamed Indian friend leisurely overlooking the backs of the Cambridge colleges, watching the punts on the River Cam. This scene is the setting for a conversation in which Iyer's friend stresses that the British Empire was always (and continues to be) an idea – an idea that was fluidly disseminated in figurative language and narratives across borders and boundaries. 'The thing is', he states, 'I admire the idea of England, but I can't stand the reality of it ... I always thought that England meant fairness and free choice and all that kind of thing, that this was the centre of decency' (236). This would seem to suggest that the British Empire shared similarities with Hardt and Negri's definition of contemporary Empire: the British Empire was a concept – an Idea – that circulated (and continues to circulate) fluidly and freely, regardless of borders and boundaries. In the context of the British Empire, though, abstractions are circulated in stories rather than in the free flow of capital within a globalized financial system. Both lack foundations in material reality; but for Iyer's friend the British Empire is still described as the centre of something, if only an imagined decency that inspired him to move to England years before.

Empire might well be an idea without a stable grounding in materiality, but it motivates people to travel. It is this combination of conceptual and material forms of Empire that is so vital to Iyer's piece. For he suggests that the new forms of Empire have not necessarily erased the pull or influence of the ideas associated with the British Empire. Rather, the two exist alongside one another: Britain in the year 2000 might have been 'a suburb of the International Empire' but it still motivated travel from the former colonies based on the 'enthralling', albeit old-fashioned, narratives of Britain as a centre of 'civilization' (239, 246). 'Our ideas of the Englishman in the flesh were very different from our ideas of his civilization', writes Nirad Chaudhri, who, according to Iyer, moved to north Oxford to 'berate the English for not being English enough, and to assert the force of an England that mostly existed, if it existed at all, in Indian memory, and in copies of Wodehouse' still found in country railway stations across the subcontinent (251). In this, the British Empire is not over: it lingers on in ideas, stories and texts.

What we want to suggest here is that Iyer's text – and postcolonial travel writing more generally – has the potential to merge the ideas of Empire with the material conditions of the places in which the writer travels. We are not suggesting that the traveller can articulate the essence or truth of a particular location. Rather, that there is a convergence – an interlocking – of the conceptual and the material. For instance, Iyer ends 'Empire' with a walk through London's Trafalgar Square. Flanked by the National Portrait Gallery and the centuries-old buildings marked 'Suid Africa', 'Uganda' and 'Canadian Pacific', he reflects on the 'centre' of an Empire that was always as much an idea as a physical reality. Circumnavigating Nelson's Column, Iyer notices a smaller monument (beside St Martin-in-the-Fields Church) upholding an imperial lion and a Christian cross. Inscribed above is the dedication 'For King and Country', surrounded by the words 'Humanity', 'Devotion', 'Fortitude' and 'Sacrifice' (264). These symbols of a former Empire, he reflects, have motivated travel in the past; but they also inspire journeys in the present. In fact, as he circles the square, Iyer describes the plurality of people who have been drawn to this place: Muslim protestors, Jewish Socialists, Lesbian Avengers, Women of Iran and the Islamic Labour Party alongside football hooligans, Irish Catholic girls, tourists and Hare Krishnas (262).

While Hardt and Negri are thus conceivably correct in claiming that the postcolonial in isolation is becoming increasingly inadequate as a tool for deciphering 'contemporary global power' (2000: 218), this does not mean we can simply abandon the term. As the literary critic Revathi Krishnaswamy (2008) has pointed out, while 'many theorists of globalization see little sense in thinking of anything outside or beyond capital', we need to realise that even if Empire in the old, nation-based sense of the term has become far less evident, the new 'imperiality is not simply imperialism without territory' (13). The impact of the 'global' and the 'transnational' are unquestionably forces we cannot afford to ignore, but it does not follow that we have somehow transcended the national or the colonial. 'Imperiality is also post-Communist, post-Cold War, postmodern, and, above all, postcolonial (but not postcapitalist, postpatriarchal, or postracist)' (13).

The continued presence of Empire is witnessed in the regulation and categorization of travellers at border crossings into one of the former colonial centres. But this is also seen in those motivated to cross the borders in the first place. People are still influenced by Empire to travel, people still migrate because of Empire and people are still hampered in their travels by Empire. This power, this pull, continues to shape the territories travelled as well as the people travelling in them. Empire is, in other words, still in place, literally as well as figuratively.

5. The End and the Beginning of Travel

Postcolonial travel writing has critiqued, and continues to critique, the notion of 'real' and 'authentic' travel by posing the question: 'Authentic to whom?' The supposed deterioration of travel as first identified by Claude Lévi-Strauss and taken up by Paul Fussell in *Abroad: British Literary Travelling Between the Wars* (1980) is challenged in postcolonial travel writing. As Fussell and many others have lamented, tourism and global capital have undermined the last vestige of 'real' travel. 'Travel writing, it seems', writes Kasia Boddy, 'has reached an impasse in which the writer's characteristic response is either to repeat or to parody experiences of previous generations' (1999: 246). Yet as Boddy points out, 'not all writers are willing to go down these paths nor do they want to reject the relationship between travel and writing as exhausted. Rather than abandoning that relationship, they say, we simply need to redefine it' (246).

This, too, has been the intent of this collection, albeit in a different vein. We suggest that instead of constantly chasing forms of the 'new' or the 'real' or 'authentic', travel is an ongoing activity with no terminal point, no objective way of assessing it in terms of 'better' or 'worse'. Instead of seeing travel as a mode of experiencing the world that is devalued by the minute, we are better served with travel as a constant renegotiation of different and equally valid modes of mobility; an activity that is not any worse, or better, than it was a hundred or a thousand or two thousand years ago. It is simply different.

Travel will never grow old or obsolete. But this will not stop some people, including the former colonial masters, from worrying about *one* particular mode of travel. As the social geographer Doreen Massey points out, the 'regulation of the world into a single trajectory, *via* the temporal convening of space, was, and still often is, a way of refusing to address the essential multiplicity of the spatial' (2005: 71). There is consequently no need to worry about, as Boddy concludes, 'the end of either travel or travel writing' (251). The original mode of Eurocentric questing for 'authentic' experiences of otherness may be on the decline (although there does seem to be an inexhaustible stream of recently 'discovered' tribes in the Amazon or New Guinea), yet all the better if it is. Such a decline might offer more room for alternative versions of travel, accounts that do not take Europe or the authentic as a foundation but recognize that 'space is always under construction' (Massey, 2005: 9).

Graham Huggan suggests in *Interdisciplinary Measures: Literature and the Future of Postcolonial Studies* (2008) that 'Postcolonialism's more immediate future surely lies in a patient, mutually transformative dialogue between the disciplines rather than in triumphal announcements of the imminent end of disciplinarity *tout court*' (13). Postcolonial travel writing, we suggest, may be one such transformative dialogue, one that is rooted in one place but that opens up to other places for the future. The following chapters are written in this vein. For instance, the first piece is Claire Lindsay's 'Beyond *Imperial Eyes*', which traces the impact of Mary Louise Pratt's seminal study *Imperial Eyes: Travel Writing and*

Transculturation (1992) and re-evaluates the critical reception of the study in order to assess its usefulness for discussions of contemporary travel writing. In her analyses of the critical response to *Imperial Eyes*, Lindsay suggests we move 'beyond' the study, not in the sense that we expand on what has rightly been a highly influential study, but by augmenting and developing Pratt's central terminology, Lindsay advises that we take on the lessons of canonical works like *Imperial Eyes*. Consequently, Lindsay offers a thorough and thought provoking introduction to theoretical thinking on travel writing of the past 20 years and provides us with a model for the continued use of older critical insights combined with the most recent contributions to the field of travel writing studies. In addition, 'Beyond *Imperial Eyes*' enables us to think about travel writing differently, both in terms of genre and territory. Lindsay's reassessment of travel writing in terms of its 'literary' qualities poses pertinent questions about the state of a genre increasingly understood as being under the siege of fiction; her focus on Latin America (via Pratt) points to an omission in critical studies that needs to be remedied. It is about time, Lindsay suggests, that we start to move away from a Eurocentric definition of travel writing in order to recognize that other regions of the world, such as Latin America, are also rich and fertile producers of travel writing.

Bidhan Roy's contribution, 'Disturbing Naipaul's "Universal Civilization": Islam, Travel Narratives and the Limits of Westernization', also takes its point of departure from *Imperial Eyes* in order to destabilize the seemingly Eurocentric basis of travel writing. Roy uses Pratt's study as a tool to pry open a debate on Islam. In analysing the travel writing of V. S. Naipaul, Roy examines constructions of 'universal civilization' vis-à-vis Islam's 'fraught' relationship with modernity to show that a rejection of 'universal' Western values does not necessarily mean a rejection of modernity. Writers like Naipaul, Roy argues, are often seen to epitomize the Eurocentric position that 'universal' means 'Western', thus presenting a hegemonic discourse that suppresses dissident voices that might possibly oppose such a belief. Roy challenges this interpretation as overly simplistic. Reconsidering arguments proclaiming the inevitable triumph of Western values as exemplified in the writings of Francis Fukuyama, Roy suggests that we should not read Naipaul as presenting a straightforward affirmation of the hegemonic position and inevitable triumph of the West. Rather, his travel writings should be read as presenting Islam as an alternative epistemological centre to Western global modernity. Roy's deconstructive analyses of a supposedly pro-Western, neo-imperialist writer like Naipaul demonstrates that it is possible to identify a subtler strand – a 'disturbance' – traced in the discomfort with the globalizing tendencies of political Islam. This strand belies the otherwise confident tone of the superiority of the West, whether it is in the condemnation of the past (Naipaul), the predictions of the future (Fukuyama) or comments on the present (Paul Wolfowitz).

Rune Graulund's piece 'Travelling Home: Global Travel and the Postcolonial in the Travel Writing of Pico Iyer' investigates the impact of globalization on postcolonialism and travel. Analysing Pico Iyer's *Video Night in Kathmandu: And Other Reports from the Not-So-Far East* (1988) and *The Global Soul: Jetlag, Shopping Malls and the Search for Home* (2000), Graulund charts how Iyer's early conflation of globalization with Americanization in *Video Night* transforms into a more nuanced and polycentric view of globalization in *The Global Soul*. Iyer's texts, he argues, reflect a shifting outlook on globalization at large and a change in the relationship between travel and global cultural exchange. By focusing on the concept of 'home', Graulund's reading investigates the ways in which travel can inspire us to reconceptualize our notions of belonging in a particular place.

In this, Graulund's chapter speaks to María Lourdes López Ropero's contribution on Caryl Phillips, which argues that the postcolonial travelogue is a prolific and innovative textual form that must be distinguished from 18th- and 19th-century European travel writing. For her, the postcolonial travel writer's movements explore the socio-political changes in postcolonies. But they also document complex and multivalent ideas about home and dwelling places. Caryl Phillips's travel narratives, she suggests, extend contemporary travel accounts to powerful instruments of cultural critique and the voicing of an independent subject-orientation through the themes of displacement and belonging.

Richard Phillips's essay 'Decolonizing Travel: James/Jan Morris's Geographies' intervenes in a vital critical debate in travel writing: the position of the travelling subject. In a nuanced reading of James/Jan Morris's sex change, Phillips charts the elision from a masculine and primarily imperial outlook in James Morris's early travel writing to the later and less assertive position of Jan Morris's travel texts. The gender shift destabilizes and reinvents the previous travelling subject and signals a change in perspective. In a reading of the entire oeuvre of James/ Jan Morris's travel writing, Phillips makes clear that rather than cementing the traveller's subject position (a charge often levelled at the genre) travel writing may also lead to ambivalence: an ambivalence that can be used to challenge terms like 'the imperial' and 'the colonial', 'centre' and 'margin', 'male' and 'female', 'other' and 'self'. By recognizing this ambivalence, we can begin to acknowledge that travel writing is not necessarily a move into the past in pursuit of a belated authenticity. Instead, it can also open up trajectories and perspectives in the present and the future.

Justin D. Edwards's chapter on Denis and Charlotte Williams is the first critical assessment of *Sugar and Slate* (2002) as a postcolonial travel text. Drawing on Denis Williams's theories of cross-culturality, catalytic interaction and filiastic tendencies, Edwards suggests that Charlotte Williams's *Sugar and Slate* incorporates travel writing's potential for cultural critique by exploring her movements between Wales, Africa and the Caribbean. Charlotte Williams, he argues, pushes the envelope of Denis Williams's theories of cross-cultural creativity and cultural syncretism by depicting postcolonial travel as a continuous process and an activity of becoming.

Similarly, Anne Schroder's contribution illustrates how postcolonial travel writing presents a multiplicity of avenues for exploring the dialectics of place and self. She suggests that the contemporary travel text approaches its subject material with (and through) the realization that the act of writing about a place is a simultaneous production of the self and its range of identifiable speaking positions. Focusing on Jamaica Kincaid's now canonical travel text *A Small Place* (1988), Schroder documents how Kincaid's appropriation of the genre follows the postcolonial injunction to disrupt and redirect the currents of imperialist discourse by problematizing the construction of Otherness through travel. In this, Schroder argues that *A Small Place* is a multivocal travel text that interrogates the sites and speaking positions on a continuum of vocalization that spans and transcends the categories of autobiography, performance and ventriloquism.

In 'Floral Diaspora in Jamaica Kincaid's Travel Writing', Zoran Pećić examines Kincaid's more recent travel texts. Focusing on *Among Flowers: A Walk in the Himalaya* (2005) and, to a lesser extent, *My Garden (Book)* from 1999, Pećić examines how these works provide both the theory and the practice for understanding Kincaid's travels through postcolonial spaces. Spatial theory and notions of global mobility, Pećić suggests, offer access routes into how Kincaid utilizes the genre of the travel narrative to expose (through the language of travel and horticulture) the effects of material and figurative forms of colonial transplantation. Central to Pećić's argument is his reading of Kincaid's journey through the Himalayas as an ambivalent narrative: the desire to see and experience the visual pleasure of travel is combined with uncomfortable feelings of frustration, alienation and displacement. This ambivalence, then, leads to a multivalent experience of travel in which Kincaid invokes the language of Empire, but also turns it into a weapon directed at asymmetrical power relations and the exploitation of spaces, places, regions and nations.

Paul Smethurst's 'Post-Orientalism and the Past-Colonial in William Dalrymple's Travel Histories' explores the themes of hybridization, transculturation and boundary-crossing in Dalrymple's travel writing. Smethurst examines Dalrymple's subject position as a (Western) traveller as well as the (Western) armchair travellers for whom Dalrymple is writing. For Smethurst, though, texts like *City of Djinns: A Year in Delhi* (2005) disorientate and de-occidentalize the readership by challenging historical narratives through which the West has identified itself rationally against its others. This, then, extends the postcolonial political paradigm to the decolonization of the colonizer's ontology. Dalrymple's travel writing, Smethurst argues, works towards the reconciliation of colonizer and colonized through the recovery and accentuation of historical crossings, while also challenging historical divisions and cultural differences.

The travel writers have the final word, for the ultimate contribution is Tabish Khair's interview with William Dalrymple and Pankaj Mishra. In a series of questions raised by the essays in this volume, the interview revisits the central concepts of 'postcolonialism', 'globalization' and 'travel writing'. The dialogues that emerge here explore and reflect on these terms from the travel writer's perspective. By focusing on the shifting position of the travel writer in a postcolonial and globalized world, Dalrymple and Mishra examine the past as well as the future of travel writing. And, most importantly, they offer their own views on the limitations and possibilities of the genre.

Works Cited and Consulted

Abu-Lughod, Janet (1989) *Before European Hegemony: The World System AD 1250–1350*. Oxford: Oxford University Press.

Ashcroft, Bill, Gareth Griffiths and Helen Tiffin (1989) *The Empire Writes Back*. London: Routledge.

Behdad, A. (1994) *Belated Travellers: Orientalism in the Age of Colonial Dissolution*. Durham: Duke University Press.

Boddy, Kasia (1999) 'The European Journey in Postwar American Fiction and Film' in Jas Elsner and Joan-Pau Rubiés (eds) *Voyages and Visions: Towards a Cultural History of Travel*. London: Reaktion Books, 232–51.

Brah, Avtar (1996) *Cartographies of Desire: Contesting Identities*. London: Routledge.

Carr, Helen (2002) 'Modernism and Travel (1880–1940)' in Peter Hulme and Tim Youngs (eds) *The Cambridge Companion to Travel Writing*. Cambridge: Cambridge University Press, 70–86.

Clark, Steve (ed.) (1999) *Travel Writing and Empire: Postcolonial Theory in Transit*. London: Zed Books.

Clifford, James (1997) *Routes: Travel and Translation in the Late Twentieth Century*. Cambridge, MA: Harvard University Press.

Clifford, James (1991) 'The Transit Lounge of Culture' *Times Literary Supplement* 3, May, 7–8.

Fussell, Paul (1980) *Abroad: British Literary Travelling Between the Wars*. New York: Oxford University Press.

Ghosh, Amitav (1992) *In an Antique Land*. London: Granta.

Ghosh, Amitav (2006) 'Foreword' in Tabish Khair, Martin Leer, Justin D. Edwards and Hanna Ziadeh (eds) *Other Routes: 1500 Years of African and Asian Travel Writing*. Oxford: Signal Books, ix–xii.

Grewal, Inderpal (1996) *Home and Harem: Nation, Gender, Empire, and the Cultures of Travel*. Durham: Duke University Press.

Gupta, Suman (2009) *Globalization and Literature*. Cambridge: Polity Press.

Hardt, Michael and Antonio Negri (2000) *Empire*. Cambridge, MA: Harvard University Press.

Hardt, Michael and Antonio Negri (2004) *Multitude: War and Democracy in the Age of Empire*. New York: Penguin.

Holland, Patrick and Graham Huggan (1998) *Tourists with Typewriters: Contemporary Reflections on Contemporary Travel Writing*. Ann Arbor: University of Michigan Press.

Huggan, Graham (2008) *Interdisciplinary Measures: Literature and the Future of Postcolonial Studies*. Liverpool: Liverpool University Press.

Hulme, Peter and Tim Youngs (2002) *The Cambridge Companion to Travel Writing*. Cambridge: Cambridge University Press.

Ivison, Douglas (2003) 'Travel Writing at the End of Empire: A Pom Named Bruce and the Mad White Giant', *English Studies in Canada* 29(3–4): 200–1.

Iyer, Pico (2000) *The Global Soul: Jetlag, Shopping Malls and the Search for Home*. London: Bloomsbury.

Kaplan, Caren (1996) *Questions of Travel: Postmodern Discourses of Displacement*. Durham: Duke University Press.

Khair, Tabish (2006) 'Introduction' in Tabish Khair, Martin Leer, Justin D. Edwards and Hanna Ziadeh (eds) *Other Routes: 1500 Years of African and Asian Travel Writing*. Oxford: Signal Books, 1–27.

Korte, Barbara (2000) *English Travel Writing from Pilgrimages to Postcolonial Explorations*. Basingstoke: Macmillan – now Palgrave Macmillan.

Krishnaswamy, Revathi (2008) 'Postcolonial and Globalization Studies: Connections, Conflicts, Complicities' in Revathi Krishnaswamy and John C. Hawley (eds) *The Postcolonial and the Global*. Minneapolis: University of Minnesota Press, 2–21.

Massey, Doreen (2005) *For Space*. London: Sage.

Mills, Sara (1991) *Discourses of Difference: An Analysis of Women's Travel Writing and Colonialism*. London: Routledge.

Phillips, Caryl (2000) *A New World Order*. London: Vintage.

Pratt, Mary Louise (1992) *Imperial Eyes: Travel Writing and Transculturation*. New York: Routledge.

Rofel, Lisa (2002) 'Modernity's Masculine Fantasies' in Bruce Knauft (ed.) *Critically Modern: Alternatives, Alterities, Anthropologies*. Bloomington: Indiana University Press, 176–86.

Spurr, David (1993) *The Rhetoric of Empire: Colonial Discourse in Journalism, Travel Writing and Imperial Administration*. Durham, NC: Duke University Press.

Notes

1. Recent critics have also argued that travel writing contributed to the construction of national and regional identities, fuelling nationalisms as well as Eurocentric ideologies that cast Europe as progressive in relation to the 'foreignness' of other peoples or places. Most influential here has been Mary Louise Pratt's *Imperial Eyes: Travel Writing and Transculturation* (1992). In her study, Pratt examines how travel and exploration writing has 'produced Europe's differentiated conceptions of itself in relation to something it became possible to call the rest of the world'. For Pratt, those travel writers who romanticize – not demonize – distant locations and who published anti-conquest narratives are still gazing at the foreign place through the filter of an imperial eye. The contact zone might be a space of transculturation, but it is represented by the 'seeing man' who looks out at the world from (and for) the domestic subject of Euro imperialism (5).

2. The works of Inderpal Grewal, Abu-Lughod, Avtar Brah as well as many of the essays in this volume are influenced by the pioneering study of women's travel writing and colonialism. Sara Mills's *Discourses of Difference* (1991), for instance, demonstrates how women's travel texts took a 'less authoritarian stance' and developed narrative voices with unique relationships to power and hierarchical structures (21).

3. We are conscious of how the language of travel and location is present in our critical discourse. Caren Kaplan (1996) writes cogently about the symbols and metaphors of travel in theory's 'colonial discourses' and their continuing presence in the liberatory critical practice of poststructuralism and feminist theory. 'The production of postmodern discourses of displacement in modernity', Kaplan argues, 'calls attention to the continuities and discontinuities between terms such as "travel", "displacement", and "location", as well as between the particularized practices and identities of "exile", "tourist", and "nomad"' (4). Throughout this study, we seek to avoid symbols and metaphors of travel that obscure key differences of power between nationalities, classes, races and genders. But because the writers we engage with in this book are travellers (writing about their journeys), the language of travel is present throughout.

1
Beyond *Imperial Eyes*

Claire Lindsay

> 'To travel is to move into new spaces with eyes already
> written over, and in the encounter of strange worlds
> and familiar paradigms the direction of disturbance …
> may move in unpredictable ways, unsettling as much
> as confirming the cognitive structures that sustain the
> authority of critics and their culture.'
>
> (Ferris, 1999: 468)

> 'The demand in the present has altered.'
>
> (Scott, 2005: 391)

The influence of Mary Louise Pratt's 1992 study, *Imperial Eyes: Travel Writing
and Transculturation*, has been far reaching. That Pratt was persuaded to
update and expand her original book in a recently published second edition (2008) is indicative of its canonical status. That a number of the book's
key tenets and terms – such as the 'contact zone', 'autoethnography' and
'anti-conquest' – have been widely appropriated in anthropology, geography, history, philosophy, cultural and literary studies, further testifies to
its authority. Nevertheless, while certain ideas articulated in *Imperial Eyes*
have proved especially attractive to scholars of travel writing, some of its
central propositions have been contested in other quarters: whether it be
the particular interpretation of Alexander von Humboldt and more general
'naturalization' of the colonial traveller, the apparently 'misplaced' assertion of a Linnaean watershed, or the absolutist character of some of the
book's theoretical vocabulary. In addition to its recent re-edition and the
broad dissemination of its distinctive terminology, therefore, the volume
and breadth of such (re)interpretations are a further significant indication
of the study's impact. This chapter considers the reach and implications

of this dissension with what remains a path-breaking book for the study of travel writing in (and outside) Latin America. It is in this initial respect that this chapter engages with the 'beyond' of *Imperial Eyes*: in the focus on critical responses to the study elaborated across a range of disciplines as in its own illustration of some (still overlooked) tensions that emerge from the application and recalibration of its main ideas in contemporary Latin America particularly. The aim is not to suggest an outright renunciation of Pratt's paradigms, however. It is on this level that a second sense of my title, germane to the usage of Ania Loomba and others in their volume, *Postcolonial Studies and Beyond* (2005), operates. Loomba et al. explain that their invocation of this preposition is not about a utopian hope for a complete methodological and theoretical transformation of that field: rather, it is about 'renewing engagements with analytical models developed by older anticolonial thinkers [and] positing new forms of critique that will address the ideological and material dimensions of contemporary neo-imperialism' (Loomba et al.: 4). My endeavour here is similar: in reading critically Pratt's justifiably canonized work *and* a representative selection of her detractors, the purpose is not to dismiss *Imperial Eyes* or its myriad recensions; rather, through their examination and by thinking through the critical conversation that emerges between them, this chapter seeks to advance a more subtle and appropriate method for the continued study of travel writing (in Latin America especially), which is commensurate with the issues at stake in the contemporary period, and thus to augment methodological debates in travel writing studies more generally.[1] The chapter is in three parts: the first deals with Pratt's encoding of the colonial traveller in *Imperial Eyes*, the second with issues pertaining to the book's conceptual vocabulary, while the third considers in brief one contemporary case study of the recalibration of its central ideas.

I

One of the central planks of Pratt's foundational study is her analysis of the journey narratives of Alexander von Humboldt, which, for a number of critics, is precisely the part of her work which 'leaves something to be desired' (Godfrey, 1993: 542). In essence, there is disagreement with her readings of the Prussian scientist, his precursors and heirs on at least three counts. First, with what is perceived to be a specious delineation of transformations in the 18th-century travel narrative; second, with an oversimplification of Humboldt as a traveller and 'travel writer'; and third, an occlusion of the implications of the interplay between form and ideology in his work.

In respect of the last of those contentions, for example, Ina Ferris argues that the fixation on the encoding of 'imperial eyes' in travel writing has blinkered scholars so that what she calls the 'chronotope of the random passage' and the potentially suggestive implications of the travel account's structural errancy have often been underestimated or even erased entirely. That those imperial eyes were 'mediated through prolix, irregular texts', Ferris argues, in fact 'rendered more difficult than we sometimes credit the totalling view that informed and was often explicitly sought by the travel writers' (Ferris: 458). As a specific case study she considers the 'traveller-seer' Humboldt, whose 30 volumes in 30 years are cast on 'an epic scale' in Pratt's book. While that critic identifies an ideology of colonial complicity underpinning and consolidating his voluminous works, by contrast Ferris observes that 'contemporary eyes were overwhelmed by the sheer quantity and inchoateness' (Ferris: 459) of the 30 volumes of his *Personal Narrative* (1799–1804). Drawing on reviews published between 1814 and 1825, Ferris illustrates how what received particular notice then was the sprawling nature of the author's output and his 'habit of association' which 'produced a disconnected text and a distracted reading'. As such, any sense of a whole or all-encompassing view is undermined: the 19th-century experience of reading Humboldt's *Personal Narrative*, Ferris claims, contrary to Pratt's thesis, generated 'a sense of thickness rather than wholeness' and what became obvious was 'the "textiness" as opposed to the transparency of travel writing' (460).

Historian Aaron Sachs also takes issue with Pratt's ideological critique of Humboldt – which in his view eclipses his important contribution to science – as well as, more generally, with the idea that all Euro-American elites are 'always-already in an exploitative relationship with the people and natural resources of the developing world' (Sachs, 2006: 111).[2] The failure of postcolonial studies like Pratt's to look beyond Humboldt's apparent collusion in imperial structures results in what Sachs sees as an inverse process of 'othering'. While Pratt sees Humboldt as beholden to the Spanish crown, for example, Sachs acknowledges that the scientist may well have come to arrangements with European monarchs and leaders – in order, say, to gain safe passage to Spanish America – but that he did so with his liberal beliefs intact: the self-financing and independent planning of the trip are advanced as evidence of a relative degree of 'independence' from political interference or contagion. In support of this view, Sachs also draws attention to passages in Humboldt's *Political Essays on the Kingdom of New Spain* (1811) where he criticizes Spain's appropriation of land, violence against nature and native peoples as well as its slave system. Furthermore, Sachs asserts a much more radical perspective on Humboldt's scientific endeavours in the region. In *Imperial Eyes*, Pratt sees Humboldt's reinvention of South America as nature, if not as an analogous form of possession to processes of European expansion and annexation, then certainly as a contributing factor in their implementation. His 'godlike, omniscient stance' prefigures a broader erasure of human life from his journey accounts, she claims, which codified the 'new continent' as primal nature (especially in terms of the portrayal of vast tropical forests, snow-capped mountains and seemingly endless interior plains) (Pratt: 124). By contrast, Sachs reinterprets Humboldt's emphasis on the enormous scope of nature in the continent as part of what he calls a 'socially conscious ecology', one which he sees as akin to the project of present-day environmentalists (Sachs: 118). The Prussian scientist's emphasis on nature's ability to overwhelm humanity was, he says, part of a broader effort to raise the consciousness of his fellow citizens regarding the impact of their actions in far-off places, especially on the continent's native inhabitants. Indeed, according to Sachs, '[Humboldt's] withering attack on colonialism reads as though it were written in the twenty-first century by a left-leaning expert on international environment and development issues' (128).[3]

Another contradiction to the Humboldt portrayed in *Imperial Eyes* – although along quite different lines – is expedited by James Dunkerley who, in a recent article, also seeks to address the image of that traveller 'as a kind of intellectual advanced guard for European capitalist despoliation' (Dunkerley, forthcoming: 8). It is in this respect that the 'disciplinary fault lines become [most] apparent' in *Imperial Eyes*. In essence, Dunkerley builds on Pratt's recognition of Humboldt's fusion of affect and science, although he disputes the claim, made in the first edition of *Imperial Eyes*, that the scientist's homosexuality was widely acknowledged during his lifetime. Dunkerley focuses on the circumstances of Humboldt's inclusion of the young Ecuadoran Carlos Montúfar in his 1802 expedition, during which the famous ascent of Chimborazo took place, to the exclusion of the 'difficult but brilliant' Francisco José de Caldas, as well as on the matter of the Prussian scientist's erasure of the entire incident from his *Personal Narrative*. In contrast to Pratt, Dunkerley proposes a more sympathetic, transactional exegesis of this episode. Reconsidering the question of his swift expulsion of Caldas in favour of Montúfar, Dunkerley conceives of Humboldt's relationship with the latter as a form of *sensucht* or 'longing ... a particular type of yearning and desire that confers both anguish and emancipation from the dullness of present experience'. Critically, Dunkerley also proposes that Humboldt's 'alternative sexuality' was 'a form of being that sought a creative and fulfilling combination of sensuality and sensibility with science' (Dunkerley, forthcoming: 19).

If Pratt has been found to play down the complexity of Humboldt's subjectivity as well as the subtleties of his journey accounts, not to mention the magnitude of his geographical and scientific contributions, her periodization of the 18th-century travel narrative has also come under scrutiny. Pratt proposes that journey texts of that century can be demarcated by the event of the classification of nature by the Swedish biologist Carl Linnaeus. Following the dissemination of his *Systema Naturae* (1735), which, she avers, inspired a 'secular, global labour that ... made contact zones a site of intellectual as well as manual labour', travel and travel writing were transformed; natural history came to be embedded in any subsequent expedition to non-European parts of the world, whether it claimed to be scientific or not (Pratt: 27). Whereas in the early 18th century the portrayal of the quotidian experience of the contact zone was possible, after the so-called Linnaean watershed something of a 'massive textual depopulation' takes place in the travel narrative, which turns its attention thereafter to the flora, fauna and landscape as the terrain 'is prepared for colonial expansion' (Huigen, 1998: 68). Siegfried Huigen takes issue with this idea, however, in his consideration of two travellers to South Africa, Robert Gordon and Peter Kolb, who in different ways complicate the rather neat dichotomy set up in *Imperial Eyes*. The German astronomer Kolb's *The Present State of the Cape of Good Hope* (1731), of which Pratt has (to Huigen's mind) only seen a partial translation, testifies to a significant interest in nature in a pre-Linnaean period: Kolb's work, he claims, is as taxonomically ordered as the Swedish scientist's later natural history. Meanwhile, the Dutchman Gordon's accounts of his later journey to the country (1773–1775) attest to a refusal to submit to the 'dehumanising natural-historical discourse' (Huigen: 74) by which Pratt characterizes the period, primarily because of his interest in indigenous cultures ('the landscape is anything but depopulated', Huigen: 73), the greater influence of the empiricist George Louis Leclerc de Buffon, as well as his own criticism of existing understandings of the region. 'There seems little reason to insist on a Linnaean watershed in the middle of the eighteenth century,' Huigen concludes: indeed, 'in neither case does the presence or absence of taxonomic intention preclude the sympathy of the authors with the indigenous population' (76).

Like Huigen, Matthew Brown (2006) seeks to complicate the archetype of the foreign traveller in Latin America consolidated in *Imperial Eyes*.

In his work on Richard Vowell, a British adventurer to South America in the 1820s, Brown argues that travellers of Pratt's 'capitalist vanguard' – who were 'mainly British and mainly travelled and wrote as advance scouts for European capital' (Pratt: 146) and whose travel memoirs were 'part-financed by their business contacts in order to encourage further interest and speculation in the contact [zone]' (Brown: 99) – were by no means representative of the many thousands of British and Irish travellers who went to the continent in the first decades of the 19th century. Among that number were also numerous migrants from humble origins who then subsequently settled into a post-independent Latin America: as such, Brown contends, 'These people ... were as much missionaries of capitalism as they were missionaries of Protestantism, which is to say, not at all' (99). Indeed, Brown avows, Vowell's novelistic output about the region – which deploys 'a range of narrative voices and perspectives from diverse social and economic and caste backgrounds' (120) – attests to a closer association with the independent women travellers examined in *Imperial Eyes* (Maria Graham and Flora Tristán) who, according to Pratt's analysis, exploit heteroglossia rather than the monovocal forms of discourse adopted by the capitalist vanguard. That Vowell also fought in military campaigns which brought independence to Gran Colombia is seen as further testimony to a material as well as an imaginative ability to 'see outside the blinkers imposed by [the imperialistic gaze]' (120–1).

In articulating their dissension from Pratt's encoding of Humboldt as well as her delineation of other travellers of the period, Brown, Huigen and others are not, of course, making apologist attempts to vindicate colonialism or attempting to elide from history recurring processes of conquest and invasion. Rather, as Jessica Dubow puts it, their projects are about 'thicken[ing] and extend[ing] its implications' (Dubow, 2000: 101). As such, their work is more than a barometer of the impact of *Imperial Eyes*: it is indicative of a broader reassessment of postcolonial scholarship which has been executed from both within and outside the confines of that relatively young field. For Dubow, therefore, Pratt's othering of Humboldt is part of a widespread tendency in postcolonial studies to 'take its "subject" for granted ... to perform on the coloniser its own brand of naturalising operation' and thus, paradoxically, to 'delimit [its] own imperiums' (Dubow: 92). In consequence, and in a move which effectively crystallizes the foregoing positions, Dubow urges a departure from postcolonialism's emphasis on the spectatorial position of 'the colonizer' (to which of course the very title of Pratt's study alludes) in favour of exploring the phenomenology of colonization, 'the experiential aspects of "being in" and of seeing in a new country'. Focusing on the processual nature of the colonizer's *coming-to-be* and *coming-to-be-located*, Dubow foregrounds the 'lived reciprocity of subject and space', drawing particular attention in her case to the idea of the picturesque, an aesthetic that occurs with frequency in representations of colonial settlement (Dubow: 93).[4] She contends that 'the colonial subject's desire to inhabit' might be seen to rest on the need for a place where vision and reciprocal recognition may occur: the picturesque becoming in this sense 'a kind of spatial speech act' (Dubow: 98).

That such studies point up the Manichaean structures underpinning Pratt's own critical position in *Imperial Eyes* is significant. To reproduce conceptual and ideological binarisms of the sort identified by her critics, is, as David Scott writes, 'not only misguided but indeed [possibly even] complicit with [colonial] power', which 'drew a sharp dichotomy between colonizer and the colonized as a function of the requirements of rule' (Scott, 2005: 395). Nevertheless, such revisions of Pratt's renderings of Humboldt and others have in turn their own deficiencies. Insofar as many of them offer a welcome 'thickening' or complicating of the colonial experience – for example, by painting a more complex picture of the fascinating and already well studied Humboldt – they also continue to privilege the scrutiny of that experience from the point of view of the metropolitan European subject. Compelling though such critiques of *Imperial Eyes* on this level may be, therefore, in their insistence on revisiting already canonized works and in focusing repeatedly on the colonial subject, they are limited in the extent to which they advance a truly more expansive account of the (post)colonial period. Perhaps the most significant shortcoming of such studies in this respect is that they effectively shore up the occlusion of the journey accounts and other cultural expressions of indigenous inhabitants of the world's formerly colonized regions. While, for example, a welcome reinterpretation of the category of the adventurer and, given the range of Vowell's activities, including his settlement in and soldiering on behalf of South America, an illuminating study of the complexity of the very categories of 'foreign' and 'native', Brown's work is symptomatic of this tendency, although his work on that British traveller (rather than on Humboldt, say) does bring to light more 'peripheral', even 'hybrid' works of interest in this respect. Given that Pratt's chosen corpus of works as well as that of many of her critics 'remains bound within the covers of European travel texts', however, the need to move beyond the 'usual suspects' in the study of travel writing and postcoloniality in this and other parts of the world is both long overdue and urgent (Butler, 2008: 7).

II

While critical reassessments of Pratt's work have involved in part providing a more nuanced if still problematic picture of the colonial subject, other developments in postcolonial studies have entailed reconsideration of the implications of its theoretical engagement and reach. In this respect, the aim has been to address a pervasive misconception of colonialism, which tends to fix it historically and geographically, and which ultimately risks ignoring its contemporary manifestations as well as disempowering those people who were and may continue to be colonized. As such, an examination of the ways in which key concepts and terms from *Imperial Eyes* have been challenged proves to be illuminating.

In the vast array of scholarly literature on postcolonialism, it is commonplace to come across reference to the 'contact zone', a term Pratt uses in *Imperial Eyes* to refer to the space of colonial encounters. According to Pratt, the contact zone is a 'social space where disparate cultures meet, clash, and grapple with each other, often in highly asymmetrical relations of domination and subordination – like colonialism, slavery, or their aftermaths as they are lived out across the globe today'. In the contact zone relations between colonized and colonizer are treated 'not in terms of separateness or apartheid, but in terms of copresence, interaction, interlocking understandings and practices' (Pratt: 4, 7). While an attractive and well-used concept, the contact zone, like Pratt's other theoretical terms, has been found by some scholars to be wanting. Although it avoids the ideological connotations of conceptions such as 'the colonial frontier', for example, the very lack of specificity of the contact zone proves to be unsatisfactory for Brian Godfrey. He points out that the 'basic spatial question as how to delimit [it]' is not addressed by Pratt anywhere in *Imperial Eyes*; and precisely because of its lack of nuance, it cannot hope to incorporate or distinguish regional differences in economic, cultural or environmental terms. As a corollary, Godfrey writes, in Pratt's interpretation of the ideological reinvention of America in the early 19th century (in his view, the most successful part of *Imperial Eyes*), 'One is left to wonder ... how the Creole elites in the southern cone differed in outlook from those of the Andean countries' (Godfrey, 1993: 543).

Liz Stanley (2000) also takes issue with the notion of the contact zone, but from an entirely different perspective. If for Godfrey the notion is too expansive and abstract, for Stanley it is too reductive. For her the problems with this concept are not geographical but temporal: the contact zone is weakened by its confinement to 'the historical juncture of "then and there"' and by its failure to take into account the politics of present-day rereadings of the experiences of, and in, such territories. In her analysis of Olive Schreiner's *Trooper Peter Halket of Mashonaland* (1897), therefore, Stanley proposes expanding the idea of the contact zone to include the moment of '"now" as we look back on "then"' (Stanley: 200). Stanley's valuable point is that the contact zone does not stop but is '*still* acting as a way in which trajectories of people and minds continue to intersect around the always interactive and improvisational dimensions of colonial encounters' (214). Nevertheless, insofar as the contact zone persists, it does not mean that the 'here and now' is necessarily postcolonial or post-imperial. As Stanley observes, it is not only that the vestiges of colonial structures endure in the contemporary period but also that 'colonial' is itself a complex term which has taken different forms in different times and places. Indeed, what it meant in the context of her own case study – South Africa – changed in a relatively short period. In drawing attention to the complex epistemology and phenomenology of the 'colonial', then, Stanley also points out that colonized groups performed as '*agents* within these changes and upheavals, not supine victims' (215, original emphasis), and that, as such, colonialism and imperialism were activities not exclusively confined to white Europeans.[5]

Stanley's insistence on the dynamic, transactional nature of the colonial experience is acknowledged elsewhere in Pratt's study, however, in the process she calls transculturation, a phenomenon intrinsic to the contact zone. Extrapolating from 'transculturation', a term coined by the Cuban anthropologist Fernando Ortiz, Pratt uses it to refer to 'how subordinated or marginal groups select and invent from materials transmitted to them by a dominant or metropolitan culture'.[6] Although, as she points out, subjugated peoples cannot control what material emanates from a dominant culture, 'they do determine to varying extents what they absorb into their own [culture], and what they use it for' (Pratt: 6). On one level the idea of transculturation provides a corrective to unilateral processes of change (as implied in concepts such as 'acculturation') as well as to what Godfrey describes as 'the passivity attributed to the colonial periphery by many working in the tradition of "dependency theory"' (Godfrey: 543). Nevertheless, if the contact zone suffers from a lack of specificity, then transculturation is in turn circumscribed by what still appears to be too much like a one-way process, albeit in the obverse direction, from periphery to metropolis. It is also weakened in Pratt's case, Godfrey claims, by a lack of empirical verification. As such, transculturation transpires to be as monolithic a term as the contact zone in that it too 'implies a certain uniformity throughout large regions of the global periphery' (543).

Of the number of 'promising' but clearly also contentious concepts introduced in *Imperial Eyes*, but perhaps 'the least developed and most suggestive' of them all, in James Buzard's view, is that of autoethnography. Pratt uses this category to refer to 'instances in which colonised subjects undertake to represent themselves in ways that *engage with* the coloniser's own terms' (Pratt: 7, original emphasis). She distinguishes this form from the more familiar category of ethnography: if ethnographic works provide a means for European subjects to represent themselves to their subjugated others, she says, autoethnographic texts are 'those the others construct in response to or in dialogue with those metropolitan representations' and thus they inevitably involve 'partial collaboration with and appropriation of the idioms of the conqueror' (7). In a fascinating reading of Charles Dickens's *Bleak House* (1852–53), however, Buzard sees a contradiction in Pratt's elaboration of this idea: for insofar as she 'limits the application of her concept to the reactive products of the colonised', he writes, '[Pratt's] model remains trapped in just the kind of undeconstructed metaphors she seeks to avoid: those of the Voice, of Letting the Silenced Speak or of Talking Back to Power' (Buzard, 1999: 9). That is, Pratt's argument is for Buzard part of a broader tendency to read ethnography and culture as always part of an aggressive, hegemonic project, 'nothing but [a] gadget for turning others into The Other', so that any other possible (and productive) associations of the ethnographic are entirely precluded. Buzard casts his own critique of Pratt within a wider consideration of the ways in which postcolonial theory tends to oversimplify earlier periods of globality in comparison with the contemporary era as well as to underestimate the complexity of the process of negotiating identities, 'even for seemingly confident colonisers' (10).

By calling time on the oversimplification of ethnographic voices from the 'centre', Buzard's work is symptomatic of those attempts mentioned earlier to have what David Scott calls 'one all-embracing analytical frame of reference, namely, "empire"' (Scott: 394). Moreover, Buzard and others – with the exception of Stanley perhaps, who transforms our perception of the contact zone, if not its lexical terms – still largely fail to provide viable alternatives to the paradigms established in *Imperial Eyes*. There is too another (dubious) tendency that emerges from the bulk of the work of Pratt's detractors discussed here: namely, the implicit proposal in such rebuttals of *Imperial Eyes* – whether in terms of the codification of the colonial traveller or the glossary of conceptual terms – of an inferred entrenchment, rather than traversal, of disciplinary boundaries. That is, one of the corollaries of the 'thickening', 'textiness', or depth offered by this kind of work appears to be a sharpening of demarcations between different fields of study. Notwithstanding the shift towards multi- and inter-disciplinarity, therefore, and mindful of the pitfalls of the manoeuvres that that entails, such responses have similar implications as those observed by Pablo Vila in another, comparable context.[7] In his robust critique of postmodern theories emerging from and in respect of the Mexico–US borderlands, the very idea of *crossing* borders, Vila writes, requires caution, since '[that] fragmentation of experience can lead to the *reinforcement* of borders instead of an invitation to cross them' (Vila, 2003: 307, my emphasis). Brown's persuasive study of Vowell is, once again, for me emblematic of this tendency, coming up short in terms of its overly instrumental approach to that traveller's novelistic output. Brown suggests, for example, that Vowell's impromptu collection of sketches and anecdotes into a novel 'serves to reveal his thinking and workings about a Hispanic America which he had little interest in colonising or conquering' and that he chose to publish 'in order to pass on to his readers some deeper understanding of the significance of the events that he had been involved in' (108, 109); comments which rest upon a disregard of both the performative aspects of and unconscious motivations at stake in the authorship of literary texts. Elsewhere, Pratt's own 'literary approach' is frequently invoked by historians as if it were a nasty infection one should avoid at all costs. On the reach of the theoretical vocabulary of *Imperial Eyes*, which, as we have seen, is 'increasingly shared across disciplinary lines', Godfrey, for example, in a protectionist and paternalistic tone, warns against the 'limitations of that kind of sharing for professional geographers and historians' (Godfrey: 542). Elsewhere, notably in Dunkerley's and Liebersohn's work, the literary seems to operate as a pejorative synonym for the unempirical. Such repudiations and simplifications evince a wider scepticism often articulated by scholars of history in relation to postcolonial studies; that, as Loomba et al. put it, '[it] functions as a carrier … of other perspectives, such as poststructuralist thought, critical race theory and next-wave feminism, that may destabilize the core of their discipline' (30). Given the hybrid character of travel writing itself, the study of which ought to encourage rather than eschew interdisciplinarity, the implications of these manoeuvres are troubling as well as fundamentally at odds with the very object of study.

III

If the literary is a dirty word for historians and one which provokes a retreat behind those 'disciplinary fault lines' mentioned by Dunkerley, it is also a problematic one in terms of its implicit delimitation of generic boundaries. Here, however, the culprit is once again Pratt, rather than her critics. In an additional chapter of the recently revised *Imperial Eyes*, Pratt engages with contemporary forms of mobility in the 'neocolony'. Although a welcome amplification of the first edition into the more recent period of (late) modernity and globality, this supplementary work manifests one further shortcoming to those already discussed. This emerges specifically in Pratt's preference for the discussion of contemporary forms of mobility in works of literary fiction from Latin America rather than in or in addition to the so-called non-fictional travel book. In the course of that new chapter, Pratt cites Horacio Quiroga's collection of short stories, *Los desterrados* ('The Exiles') (1926), as a pertinent example of a text written from the perspective of the 'travellee'. Pratt sees this fictional work as even more significant because it posits Misiones, a frontier region on the Argentine–Brazilian border in which the stories are set, 'not as a location, but as a destination, a terminus ... a place with the power to disrupt the circular paradigm of departure and return that produces travel literature' (Pratt: 225). Quiroga's Misiones thus evinces the predicament of the neocolonial position: for Pratt it is 'a tragicomic version of ... peripheral modernity' (225). Pratt then goes on to draw on a range of other literary examples – from writers as diverse as Ricardo Piglia, José María Arguedas, Gabriela Mistral, and Mário de Andrade – in the course of her discussion of the 'unfreedom' of the neocolony, before concluding her consideration of contemporary modes of mobility with a number of material examples, which include border crossings from Mexico to the United States and the transnational journeys of the Virgin of Zapopan. While she acknowledges the reconfiguration of enduring narratives and tropes of travel in those brief case studies, there is no mention or examination of any 'non-fictional' journey narratives of the kind ordinarily associated with the category of 'travel writing'.[8] This is disappointing, for such works are not only in print and in circulation in Latin America (and elsewhere) but, significantly, they also attest to those 'new forms of citizenship and belonging ... [and] often permanent "awayness"' (226) mentioned by Pratt in the new chapter which are indicative of the region's more recent experience of neoliberal globalization. This privileging of the literary is, in my view, analogous to the 'Eurocentric' manoeuvres of *Imperial Eyes* and its detractors, in the sense that it constitutes a recrudescence of another form of elitism in the contemporary context, this time of a generic, rather than geographical character. On one level, such a focus resounds with an epistemology which regards 'travel writing' as being only of documentary value, its stylistic or aesthetic qualities somehow secondary, and decidedly second best, to its counterpart of 'travel liter-ature'. On another level, to talk about contemporary travel writing in Latin America in relation only to literary texts, without taking into account 'non-fictional', empirically observed narratives is a seriously truncated endeavour, one which is at odds, too, with the rest of Pratt's book. Indeed, Dennis Porter's assertion that 'One of the positive results of the poststructuralist critique ... has been that we no longer fetishize so-called creative writing as something essentially separate from and superior to writing of other kinds' is an especially timely reminder in this respect (Porter, 1991: 19).[9]

What can we learn, then, for the continued study of travel writing from the evident imperfections of *Imperial Eyes* and the limitations of its own recensions? What do they mean for the analysis of material about travel in contemporary Latin America especially, the region in which so much of the discussion of Pratt's book is located, and in respect of which its paradigms have been so pervasive and yet equally so tested? Dane Kennedy's more measured approach to the interplay of literature and history proves to be instructive in formulating an answer to that question. In his consideration of the effects of literary approaches to postcolonial studies, Pratt in fact provides Kennedy with some cause for celebration:[10] she is invoked as one of a small number of scholars who in his view distinguish between 'history as a text and history as a tool, between its presence as a discursive product and its use as an ana-lytical practice' (Kennedy, 1996: 352). His own choice of metaphors is telling, shifting from a self-consciously aggressive military formulation at the beginning of his article (to describe how '"literary invaders" have claimed squatters' rights over imperial history's unclaimed provinces' (346)), to rest finally on a linguistic one in which he encourages a dia-logue between literary and historical scholarship 'that exposes areas of difference and delineates points of convergence' (359).[11] Taking issue, as have others, with any tendency to abstract the Other, 'as an undiffer-entiated, unknowable category', (359) as well as with the constraints of the canon itself, it is significant that Kennedy sees further opportunity to enrich the field of postcolonial studies in the greater engagement with the work of non-Western writers. Although the upturn in travel writing studies promises one means of advancing knowledge in that area, he admits 'the abiding limitation of this genre [is] its Eurocentric character' (356).

The circumspection of Kennedy's forecast notwithstanding, his invitation to postcolonial studies to 'open its inquiries to a wider range of voices, especially from colonial and ex-colonial territories' has been taken up with particular energy in Latin American and hemispheric American studies, in which areas the findings and insufficiencies of *Imperial Eyes* have a particular conceptual, geographical, and historical resonance (Kennedy: 356).[12] Recent studies by Shannon Butler, Miguel Cabañas, and Thea Pitman, for example, all of which consider 19th and 20th-century travel accounts of the region in Spanish, in different ways address the hitherto missed opportunity to explore 'direct contestation of European representations of Latin American culture in the travel texts of Latin Americans themselves' (Butler, 2008: 7). In his argument for a broadening of theoretical models in this context, for example, Cabañas draws attention to the limitations of Pratt's analyses in terms of their operation within a European/Other dichotomy: 'by changing the axis of research from East to West to North to South and by broadening the scope to include travellers from both poles,' he proposes in his study, 'a more transnational and complex model which avoids falling into reductive "Eurocentrism"' (Cabañas, 2008: 11). Significantly, these kinds of engagement with Latin American travellers' texts in countries such as Mexico and Peru are inclusive of 'non-fictional' travel accounts rather than only those contemporary literary expressions favoured by Pratt in her book's second edition.[13] In studies such as these, then, Latin Americanists are doing important work to contest the notion that, as Steve Clark puts it, 'travel writing is inevitably one-way traffic' as well as to complicate the idea that the travel encounter is always about 'simple relations of domination and subordination' (Clark, 1999: 3). These works also attest to what is at stake in the encounter between postcolonial and Latin American studies more generally which, as Loomba et al. observe, 'means more than just recognising new linguistic or geographic territory; it means a continual and reciprocal reshaping of key concepts [and] intellectual practices' (Loomba et al.: 6). I want to conclude this chapter, therefore, with one representative case study of such work which testifies to this shift and to the formulation, within an interdisciplinary framework, of an attenuated if still abbreviated vocabulary for the analysis of the region's contemporary travel narratives.

José David Saldívar, in his study of contemporary cultural production of the US–Mexico frontier, reformulates Pratt's idea of the contact zone in order to invoke what he calls the 'heterotopic forms of everyday life whose trajectories cross over and interact' at this site (Saldívar, 1997: 14). In bringing into dialogue the specificities of this geopolitical border with currents and ideas elaborated in British and US cultural studies, he observes that 'some terms and concepts ... require additional defining' (13). In consequence, Saldívar devises what he calls the '*transfrontera* contact zone' to refer not only to the 2,000 mile long border between the United States and Mexico but also to other frontiers, 'such as Raymond Williams's border zone between Wales and England'. Like Pratt's space, this is a zone of subaltern encounters, but one which is a 'Janus-faced border line in which peoples geographically forced to separate themselves now negotiate with one another and manufacture new relations, hybrid cultures, and multiple-voiced aesthetics' (13–14). Given the apparent necessity and urgency of this recalibration of one of Pratt's central ideas to correspond to the particularities of border sites, it seems anomalous that in his later analysis of interventions into what he (once again) determines as US–Mexico border writing, Saldívar takes at face value other categories inherited from *Imperial Eyes*. This emerges most obviously in the organization of his discussion of a number of cultural representations of Tijuana around the category of 'autoethnography', as well as in relation to Pratt's influential but, as we have seen, perhaps rather undiluted suggestion that travellers including 'their postcolonial heirs ... are "intertextually" part of the imperial infrastructure' (130).[14] From what is at first an affirmative appreciation of autoethnography, Saldívar, in his analysis of Luis Urrea's *Across the Wire* (1993), accuses the Mexican–American writer of 'imperial complicity' for his affiliation with a Baptist charity and for failing to acknowledge the issues of power traditionally bound up in the positions of missionary and travelling ethnographer in that work. What is at stake in such an accusation – and in Saldívar's insistence on the denomination of Urrea's work as 'autoethnography' – is that the 'difference' and specificity for which he so persuasively argued in terms of his conception of the '*transfrontera* contact zone' is undermined, if not collapsed. That is, while on the one hand Saldívar admirably brings to attention contemporary examples of what Buzard earlier dismissed as 'the reactive products of the colonised', on the other hand, he remains in thrall to the uniform character of 'autoethnography' as he (and Buzard) receives it – unquestioningly – from Pratt.[15] To put it bluntly, can we really consider Urrea an autoethnographer of the same degree as the 17th-century Andean Guaman Poma de Ayala invoked in *Imperial Eyes*? In effect, such a classification of Urrea and his work reveals a fixation with the Mexican-American's apparently transparent spectatorial position as traveller, while it largely ignores the 'persuasive art' of that narrative form. In short, it disregards not only Urrea's complex, transcultural positionality but also the more subtle formal properties of his work which, as I have argued elsewhere (to some extent in concert with Ferris's line of argument), evinces an 'ethico-fictive' quality which exonerates him from that damning and rather excessive indictment.[16] If Buzard laments the ways in which, in terms of ethnography, postcolonial theory oversimplifies the colonial subject, then we ought to be equally vigilant about similar reductions in respect of the contemporary traveller. In sum, not unlike Stanley, Saldívar is right to reconfigure and territorialize the idea of the contact zone for his purpose. That his project is essentially 'incomplete', however, and in fact veers towards a deterritorialization of sorts, pulls into focus the need to continue recalibrating the parameters of both the study and vocabulary of the narrative of travel in contemporary Latin American geographies, in which neocolonial context the critical terminology relating to the operation of this inherited category (which extends beyond the realm of writing, of course) requires ongoing refinement.

Works Cited and Consulted

Borm, Jan (2004) 'Defining Travel: On the Travel Book, Travel Writing and Terminology' in Glenn Hooper and Tim Youngs (eds) *Perspectives on Travel Writing*. Aldershot: Ashgate, 13–26.

Brown, Matthew (2006) 'Richard Vowell's Not-So-Imperial Eyes: Travel Writing and Adventure in Nineteenth-Century Hispanic America', *Journal of Latin American Studies* **38**: 95–122.

Butler, Shannon Marie (2008) *Travel Narratives in Dialogue: Contesting Representations of Nineteenth-Century Peru*. New York: Peter Lang.

Butz, David (2009) 'Autoethnography as Sensibility' in D. DeLyser, S. Aitken, S. Herbert, M. Crang and L. McDowell (eds) *Handbook of Qualitative Geography*. London: Sage, 295–335.

Buzard, James (1999) 'Anywhere's Nowhere: *Bleak House* as Autoethnography', *The Yale Journal of Criticism* **21**(1): 7–39.

Cabañas, Miguel (2008) *The Cultural 'Other' in Nineteenth-Century Travel Narratives: How the United States and Latin America Described Each Other*. Lewiston: Edwin Mellen.

Clark, Steve (1999) (ed.) *Travel Writing and Empire: Postcolonial Theory in Transit*. London: Zed Books.

Dubow, Jessica (2000) '"From a View on the World to a Point of View in It": Rethinking Sight, Space and the Colonial Subject', *Interventions* **2**(1): 87–102.

Dunkerley, James, (forthcoming) 'Wo ist Carlos Montúfar?' Scenes of Sensibility in the Scientific Life of Alexander von Humboldt', in Claire Lindsay (ed.) *Traslados/ Translations: Essays on Latin America in Honour of Jason Wilson.*

Ferris, Ina (1999) 'Mobile Words: Romantic Travel Writing and Print Anxiety', *Modern Language Quarterly* 60(4): 451–68.

Godfrey, Brian J. (1993) 'Imperial Eyes: Travel Writing and Transculturation', *Annals of the Association of American Geographers* 83(3): 542–4.

Guelke, Leonard and Jeanne Kay Guelke (2004) 'Imperial Eyes on South Africa: Reassessing Travel Narratives', *Journal of Historical Geography* 30: 11–31.

Gruesz, Kirsten (2002) *Ambassadors of Culture: The Transamerican Origins of Latino Writing.* Princeton: Princeton University Press.

Huigen, Siegfried (1998) 'Natural History and the Representation of South Africa in the Eighteenth Century', *JLS/TLW* 14(1–2): 67–79.

Joseph, Gilbert M., Catherine C. LeGrand and Ricardo G. Salvatore (eds) (1998) *Close Encounters of Empire: Writing the History of US–Latin American Relations,* Durham: Duke University Press.

Kennedy, Dane (1996) 'Imperial History and Post-Colonial Theory', *Journal of Imperial and Commonwealth History* 24(3): 345–63.

Liebersohn, Harry. (1996) 'Recent Works on Travel Writing', *The Journal of Modern History* 68(3): 617–28.

Lindsay, Claire (2010) *Contemporary Travel Writing of Latin America.* New York: Routledge.

Loomba, Ania, Suvir Kaul, Matti Bunzi, Antoinette Burton and Jed Esty (eds) (2005) *Postcolonial Studies and Beyond.* Durham: Duke University Press.

Moraña, Mabel, Enrique Dussel, and Carlos E. Jáuregui (eds) (2008) *Coloniality at Large: Latin America and the Postcolonial Debate.* Durham: Duke University Press.

Pitman, Thea (2008) *Mexican Travel Writing.* Bern: Peter Lang.

Porter, Dennis (1991) *Haunted Journeys: Desire and Transgression in European Travel Writing.* Princeton: Princeton University Press.

Pratt, Mary Louise (1992) *Imperial Eyes: Travel Writing and Transculturation.* New York: Routledge.

Rowe, John Carlos (1998) 'Post-Nationalism, Globalism, and the New American Studies', *Cultural Critique* 40: 11–28.

Sachs, Aaron (2006) *The Humboldt Current: Nineteenth-Century Exploration and the Roots of American Environmentalism.* New York: Viking.

Saldívar, José David (1997) *Border Matters: Remapping American Cultural Studies.* Berkeley: University of California Press.

Scott, David (2005) 'The Social Construction of Postcolonial Studies' in Ania Loomba, Suvir Kaul, Matti Bunzi, Antoinette Burton and Jed Esty (eds) *Postcolonial Studies and Beyond.* Durham: Duke University Press, 385–400.

Spitta, Silvia (1995) *Between Two Waters: Narratives of Transculturation in Latin America.* College Station: Texas A&M University Press.

Stanley, Liz (2000) 'Encountering the Imperial and Colonial Past through Olive Schreiner's *Trooper Peter Halket of Mashonaland*', *Women's Writing* 7(2): 197–219.

Thomas, Nicholas (1994) *Colonialism's Culture: Anthropology, Travel and Government.* Cambridge: Polity Press.

Vila, Pablo (2003) *Ethnography at the Border.* Minneapolis: University of Minnesota Press.

Notes

1. Indeed, Loomba et al., in the introduction to their volume, single out Latin America as an exceptional case, a triangulation of models of West-rest geography which 'reanimates the debate around alternative modernities' (Loomba et al.: 6).
2. For Brian Godfrey, Pratt's ideological critique also succeeds in overshadowing the importance of Humboldt's contribution to science, especially his work on the vertical zonation of agriculture and ecology in tropical America (Godfrey: 542).
3. Elsewhere Harry Liebersohn takes issue with Pratt's description of Humboldt as 'a member of a national elite' in an era when there was no German nation-state. He also takes her to task for locating the scientist's studies at Frieburg's School of Mines rather than in the Bergakademie Freiburg, where Humboldt registered as a student in 1791 (see Liebersohn, 1996: 624).
4. Comparing it to a synonymous concept captured visually in René Magritte's famous 1933 painting *La condition humaine*, Dubow proposes that: 'the picturesque enacts nothing less than the notion of present sight as "seeing through" a surrounding referent: a view of nature recognised via a background stock of perceptual knowledge' (Dubow: 96).
5. This is a critical point in respect of the position of the creole elites in Latin America's own experience of colonialism. For more on this see Moraña et al. (2008).
6. As Silvia Spitta explains, Ortiz's notion of transculturation, regardless of his own proposal that it could explain any encounter between two cultures, needs to be seen as a 'specifically Cuban theory'. Although transculturation can be useful, therefore, in codifying cultural contact, Spitta underscores the necessity of redefining it for specific geographical and geopolitical contexts. See Spitta, 1995: 1–28.
7. In respect of the risks of interdisciplinarity, Nicholas Thomas warns: 'It would be a pity if the spectacle of intellectual plurality fostered a relativist permissiveness that acknowledged the fertility of diverse agendas and refused to discriminate between them' (Thomas, 1994: 19).
8. Although these terms need to be held under erasure, given the troubled relation in the form between factual and fictional discourses, Jan Borm's definition of the travel book is useful here for what I have in mind: '*any narrative characterised by a non-fiction dominant that relates (almost always) in the first person a journey or journeys that the reader supposes to have taken place in reality while assuming or presupposing that author, narrator and principal character are but one or identical*' (original emphasis) (Borm, 2004: 13).
9. For more on this see Lindsay, 2010: 8–10.
10. While acknowledging its necessary reinvigoration of imperial studies more generally, Kennedy also considers the shortcomings of postcolonial scholarship of the literary kind. These include its theoretical promiscuity (although, as he sees it, much of it is 'less engaged in developing a body of theory than in making gestures of obeisance to it', Kennedy, 1996: 347), its tendency to essentialize the West, its privileging of canonical authors, not to mention its frequent disavowal or even dismissal of history. Scholars of colonial

discourse such as Edward Said, Homi Bhabha and David Spurr are seen to be the most egregious examples in this respect.

11. Pratt, of course, draws from that same discipline in her elaboration of the 'contact zone'.

12. It is striking that scholars working to advance hemispheric studies of the Americas often invoke paradigms made commonplace by *Imperial Eyes* in their imaginings of how this comparative field ought to operate. For example, Joseph et al. explain their concern with the deployment and contestation of power in terms of the contact zone (Joseph et al., 1998: 5); Juan Carlos Rowe proposes adoption of the same theoretical model in order to articulate his version of a Comparative American Studies (Rowe, 1998: 18); while Kirsten Gruesz also appeals to Pratt, but in respect of her typology of travellers, such as the navigator and scientific explorer-collector, in order to distinguish a set of what Gruesz calls 'American [cultural] ambassadors' (Gruesz, 2002: 19).

13. Such journey narratives may well deploy figurative strategies, rest on, and create fictions of their own, but they are based nonetheless in large part on empirical journeys undertaken by their very authors. Obviously we should recognize that that term must in any case be held under erasure, especially in the context of a form with such a troubled relationship with factual and fictional discourses.

14. Saldívar states that it is Pratt's emphasis on the refashioning of traditions through cross-cultural contact, whereby 'colonised subjects undertake to represent themselves in ways that engage with the coloniser's own terms', which informs his own deployment of autoethnography.

15. For more on the complications of this term, see Butz 2009, who delineates five main types of autoethnography.

16. See Lindsay, 2010: 92–114.

2
Disturbing Naipaul's 'Universal Civilization': Islam, Travel Narratives and the Limits of Westernization

Bidhan Roy

In her seminal book *Imperial Eyes* (1992), Mary Louise Pratt argues that European colonial travel writing tells us more about European society than it does about the places the travel writers are visiting. For Pratt, contact between European travel writers and the outside world not only represents the projection of colonial identity outward onto 'the rest of the world' but also shows how European identity is produced from the outside in (5). Thus the barbarity of new exotic cultures becomes crucial to the European sense of self as civilized, the irrationality of this Other constitutive of European rationality. Colonial travel narratives in other words are not only narratives about other cultures, but narratives that help Europe manufacture a sense of self. Pratt calls this process 'transculturation': the reciprocal but unequal exchange between Europe and its colonies. The story of global integration that emerges from such travel narratives is a world history defined in European terms that provides 'multiple ways of legitimizing and familiarizing the process of European expansion' (Pratt, 2001: 150). At the same time, such narratives are themselves made possible by colonialism which, as Rob Nixon puts it, enabled Victorian travel writers to write with 'the supreme imperial confidence that came, quite literally, from being on top of the world' (1992: 51).

Following Pratt, numerous postcolonial critics have argued that more recent travel narratives written in English re-inscribe a mutually supportive relationship between Western global power and representations of the non-Western world (see Lindsay, Chapter 1). For many recent postcolonial critics, chief amongst the contemporary exponents of neocolonial travel narratives is V. S. Naipaul, who, according to Nixon, is considered a 'lackey of neo-colonialism' by Third World critics (4). The conception of Naipaul as a 'lackey of neo-colonialism' not only offers a particular reading of his travel writing but also makes the assumption of equating contemporary globality with neo-imperialism: that is that 'nations who may have gained their independence ... are still subject to domination by European or US capitalism and culture' (Nixon, 1992: 4; Green and Bihan, 1996: 306). However, recent theorists of globalization challenge the theoretical and empirical validity of conceiving of globalization in this way. For example, John Tomlinson exposes how the idea of cultural imperialism locates power in a specific national space, reasserting the legitimacy of national boundaries and national cultures, both of which have been widely contested in recent years (Tomlinson, 1999: 89–93). Similarly, Marxist theorists like Antonio Negri and Michael Hardt argue that despite stressing the historical continuity of global capitalism, contemporary multinational capitalism demands new ways of thinking about how global networks of power operate (Hardt and Negri, 2000: 6). If, as these theorists maintain, contemporary globality is indeed a dispensation that cannot be accounted for as a process of neocolonialism, then critics who conceive of Naipaul's travel writing in such terms appear to miss a more complex relationship between travel narratives written in English and global power that globalization has produced.

The tension between Islam and the 'West, or universal civilization' in Naipaul's travel writing is a particularly fruitful point from which to explore this more complex relationship between travel narrative and contemporary globality (Naipaul, 1981: 168). This is not only because Muslim countries and Islam more broadly have been the focus of much of Naipaul's travel writing, leading him to become regarded as an 'expert on Islam' (Nixon: 152), but also because of recent geopolitical and cultural conflicts between Muslim societies and Western liberal secular societies that raise a number of important issues and nuances in the debate as to whether globalization is best understood as a process of neocolonialism. It is against this complex set of issues that I will discuss Naipaul's representation of Muslims and political Islam in *Among the Believers* (1981) and *Beyond Belief* (1999). The focus of my analysis is the relationship between Naipaul's choice of narrative form in these books and global power. I intend to show that on the one hand, Naipaul positions *Beyond Belief* in the preface to the book as an objective account of the places he visits and people he meets by claiming that it 'IS A BOOK [sic] about people. It is not a book of opinion. It's a book of stories' (Naipaul, 1999: xii). I argue that the underlying assumptions of this claim, as well as the stylistic choices that Naipaul makes to create the impression of objectivity, re-inscribe the relationship between global power travel narratives that Pratt identifies in colonial literature. In this respect, *Beyond Belief* is a book that seems to confirm the widely held view amongst postcolonial theorists that Naipaul's travel narratives reinforce an understanding of 'the West' as the 'universal civilization'. On the other hand, Naipaul's encounters with Muslims at times also challenge his assumptions of the universality of the West. At such moments Naipaul's subjectivity as a travel writer intrudes upon the narrative and undercuts the 'objective' style that he outlines in the preface and which predominates throughout the book. The significance of such narrative intrusions, in light of Bobby Sayyid's theoretical conception of global Islam in *A Fundamental Fear* (2003), is that they expose the challenge that global Islam represents to westernization. Consequently, these moments reveal the incompleteness of westernization rather than its 'final triumph', as critics such as Fukuyama claim, by exposing how global Islam refuses to be represented within a Western narrative of global modernity.

Naipaul, Travel Narrative and the 'Universal Civilization'

Beyond Belief is Naipaul's second book about Islam, following *Among the Believers* which chronicled his 1981 visit to Iran, Pakistan, Malaysia and Indonesia in the wake of the Iran revolution. In *Among the Believers*, Naipaul advances the idea of 'The West, or universal civilization' that he argues the Islamic 'fundamentalists' he visits reject, but are also 'parasitic upon' because of their dependency upon its technology, economic prosperity and intellectual ideas (Naipaul, 1981: 168). The claim that political Islam rhetorically rejects modernity but nevertheless remains dependent upon it rests upon Naipaul equating 'the West' with 'the universal civilization.' Hence, to reject Western culture and ideas, while accepting the benefits of the technological innovations it has produced, represents a profound hypocrisy that Nixon explicates in the following way:

> When discussing the 'universal civilization,' Naipaul is fond of making smug allusions to 'the visitor' and the 'living, creative civilization'; in so doing he soft pedals any suggestion that such universality might often be imperial in its expansiveness. Seen against this backdrop, his quarrel with Muslims (of all persuasions) is straightforward: their relationship to the West will remain contradictory and self-destructive as long as they continue to use the visitors' technologies while denouncing

Western ideologies, that is, as long as they refuse to recognize those technologies as the fruit of the disparaged ideologies. (Nixon: 148)

Travel narrative in *Among the Believers* offers Naipaul a way of exposing this hypocrisy in Muslim societies by demonstrating how Islamist rhetoric contradicts the 'reality' of the places he visits. For instance, while visiting Pakistan, the death of Maulan Maudoodi, 'the saint of the Islamic fundamentalists in Pakistan', gives Naipaul the opportunity to show how the rhetoric of Islamism that Maudoodi advances in Pakistan is undercut by his personal biography (Naipaul, 1981: 168). Thus, while Maudoodi had 'campaigned for Islamic laws' in Pakistan, Naipaul exposes that at the end of his life he 'had gone to a Boston hospital to look for health; he had at the very end entrusted himself to the skill of the civilization he had tried to shield his followers from' (168). Instances such as these are enumerated throughout *Among the Believers* in order to demonstrate that Islamism's rejection of the West is compromised by a dependency upon the material and technological contribution the West has given the world.

The effect of Naipaul's binary division between Islamism's refusal of modernity (and the West's monopoly of it) is that whether the rhetoric of political Islam acknowledges it or not, we live in a world in which progress is defined by Western modernity. In Naipaul's estimation, there is no alternative to westernization because, as his travel experiences throughout the 'Muslim world' repeatedly reaffirm, once 'the West, or universal civilization' is rejected, what ensues is violence, chaos, poverty and disease. For instance, in attempting to find a new Islamic legal 'methodology' following decolonization, Naipaul's experiences in Pakistan lead him to conclude that 'Pakistan had undone the rule of law it had inherited from the British, and replaced it with nothing' (Naipaul, 1981: 169). It is not, therefore, that the Islamist revival that Naipaul encounters in his travels represents an alternative to the 'universal civilization' but that it simply obfuscates the extent to which Muslim societies are dependent upon the West.

A formal narrative decision that Naipaul must make in establishing this representation of Islam as 'parasitic' upon the West is what Nixon calls 'dilemmas of voice' that are common to all 'discourses of cultural description' (Nixon: 72). Nixon explains this dilemma facing the travel writer as follows:

what level of subjectivity will boost the observer's authority and credibility, and at what point does this fade into egocentrism or subjective whimsy? This fundamental quandary is coupled to a second formal decision: how to reconcile through narrative, the traveller's or ethnographer's often random experience of the observed culture with the desire to give a representative sense of that culture. (Nixon: 72–3)

In order to establish the book's broad claim of Islamism as 'parasitic' upon Western civilization then, Naipaul must continually manage the presence of his persona as a travel writer in the narrative and shape the particularity of his travel experiences to support the book's general thesis about political Islam. With respect to the first of these decisions, Naipaul's own subjectivity frequently influences his representation of Muslims and Islam. For instance, upon meeting his translator after arriving in Tehran, Naipaul comments 'I didn't like him' and 'I didn't trust him' (Naipaul, 1981: 3). This sense of distrust and dislike of Muslims is reiterated throughout the book, reinforcing the general antipathetic tone towards Islam and the idea that political Islam is a project of 'bad faith' (Nixon: 147).

With respect to the second formal decision, Naipaul's presence as a travel writer repeatedly intrudes upon the narrative in order to make connections for the reader between his personal experiences and the generalized version of Islam that he is trying to represent. Thus, after meeting a limited selection of Islamist advocates in Pakistan, Naipaul confidently concludes that:

> I felt after this, that there were no Islamic experiments for me to see in Pakistan, that it was as Mr. Deen had said right at the beginning: the Islamic experiments were things people were waiting for other people to start. The great Islamic enterprise of Pakistan existed, but only as an ideal, at once an expression of the highest faith and an expression of the political insecurity in which Muslims lived in the Muslim homeland. (Naipaul, 1981: 118)

By explicating what he 'felt' after meeting a handful of Islamist leaders in Pakistan then, Naipaul makes sure that his authority as an experienced travel writer and 'expert on Islam' legitimates broad claims about 'the great Islamic enterprise of Pakistan'.

Writing in the immediate aftermath of the Iranian revolution, Naipaul's need to explicitly affirm the universality of Western modernity is a response to the perceived threat that the spread of political Islam throughout the 'Muslim world' represents. Naipaul makes specific reference to this threat by citing Khomeini's global ambitions, which proclaim that 'Islam will be victorious in all the countries of the world, and Islam and the teachings of the Koran will prevail all over the world' (Naipaul, 1981: 8). Against this claim, *Among the Believers* forcefully asserts the impossibility of such a project by refuting that 'the teachings of the Koran' can function as an alternative epistemological centre to Western global modernity. In order to underscore this point, Naipaul ends *Among the Believers* by concluding that:

> The life that had come to Islam had not come from within. It had come from outside events and circumstances, the spread of the universal civilization. It was the late twentieth century that had made Islam revolutionary, given new meaning to old Islamic ideas of equality and union, shaken up static or retarded societies. It was the late twentieth century – and not faith – that could supply the answers – in institutions, legislation, economic systems. (Naipaul, 1981: 429)

The need to sum up his personal experiences travelling throughout Iran, Pakistan, Indonesia and Malaysia in this way reveals the extent to which the perceived threat of political Islam shapes Naipaul's travels in these countries, as well as the synthesis of his travel experiences into a generalized argument about the 'Muslim world.' The result is that *Among the Believers* reports back from the 'Muslim world' to its Western readership, reassuring the readers that despite the revolutionary rhetoric of political Islam, the Muslim world remains dependent upon the West for its ideas and 'answers' (Naipaul, 1981: 429). In making this point, the effect of Naipaul's authoritative intrusions within the narrative is to create a highly polemical tone in the book that, in light of Pratt's work, serves to reaffirm that the West is 'the universal civilization' in the face of an emergent global political Islam.

Following *Among the Believers*, *Beyond Belief* advances Naipaul's belief in the universality of Western civilization. But while *Among the Believers* is intent upon showing how evidence of Muslim dependency upon Western technology undermines the rhetoric of Islamist anti-westernization, the thematic focus and narrative voice of *Beyond Belief* are different. Thematically, *Beyond Belief* sets out to show how the spread of Islam around the world is an act of Arab imperialism. Naipaul writes:

> Islam is in its origins an Arab religion. Everyone not an Arab who is a Muslim is a convert. Islam is not simply a matter of conscience

or private belief. It makes imperial demands. A convert's worldview
alters. His holy places are in Arab lands; his sacred language is Arabic.
His idea of history alters. He rejects his own; he becomes, whether he
likes it or not, a part of the Arab story. (Naipaul, 1999: xi)

This shift in emphasis means that Naipaul's travels in Islamic societies
are no longer preoccupied with searching for evidence of Western
modernity in the Muslim countries he visits, but of exposing 'the theme
of conversion' that had 'always been there'; a fact 'he had not seen' in
Among the Believers.

This thematic shift has important implications for the formal narrative
decisions that Naipaul makes in *Beyond Belief* and the extent to which his
role as a travel writer and advocate for the 'universal civilization' intrudes
upon the narrative. Consequently, Naipaul's tendency to make broad
polemical claims about the countries he visits in *Among the Believers*
gives way to a narrative mode that claims to let the stories of the people
he meets during his travels speak for themselves. Naipaul articulates
this approach to travel narrative in the preface to *Beyond Belief* in the
following way:

> So in these travel books or cultural explorations of mine the writer
> as traveller steadily retreats; the people of the country come to the
> front; and I become again what I was at the beginning: a manager of
> narrative. In the nineteenth century the invented story was used to
> do things that other literary forms – the poem, the essay – couldn't
> easily do: to give news about a changing society, to describe mental
> states. I find it strange that the travel form – in the beginning so far
> away from my own instincts – should have taken me back there, to
> look for the story; though it would have undone the point of the
> book if the narratives were falsified or forced. There are complexities
> enough in these stories. They are the point of the book; the reader
> should not look for 'conclusions'. (xiii)

In contrast to the tone of *Among the Believers*, the narrative voice that
Naipaul chooses in this second journey through 'the Muslim world'
assumes a 'neutral' 'objective' tone in order to create the impression
that 'the writer as traveller steadily retreats; the people of the country
come to the front' (xii). Consequently, Naipaul's presence as a travel
writer is very much in the background of the places he visits; not
as a literary personality or an expert on Islam, but as a conduit for
the people he meets and the facts of Islamic history – a 'manager of

narrative' as he puts it. The effect of the shift in style is to create the impression of a disinterested account of the 'Muslim world' in which the authorial intrusions and overt polemics that characterize *Among the Believers* are notably absent. It is a style that would seem to strengthen the claims of Naipaul's literary supporters, such as Bruce King who argues that Naipaul 'does not choose sides, he observes what happens' (King, 2003: 195).

One way to read this stylistic shift in *Beyond Belief* is as an indicator that the threat of global political Islam that Naipaul identified in *Among the Believers* has receded. From this perspective, the narrative style of *Beyond Belief* and the fact that Naipaul no longer needs to explicitly affirm the universality of the Western civilization suggests that, almost twenty years after the Iranian revolution (and ten years after the fall of the Berlin Wall), the globalization of Western modernity is complete – that political Islam does not represent the threat to Western universalism that it did in 1979. Consequently, Naipaul's adoption of the persona of travel writer as objective witness – a 'man of science' who reports the 'naked truth' of places he visits – suggests a return to the sorts of travel narrative that Pratt identifies in 19th-century travel writing (Pratt, 1992: 87). The possibility of adopting such a persona is predicated upon an unswerving confidence in modernity that enables the 'seeing man' to 'look out passively and possess' safe in the knowledge that his world-view is universal (Pratt, 1992: 7).

Support for reading Naipaul's style of travel writing as a re-inscription of 19th-century colonial travel narratives can be found in Francis Fukuyama's essay 'The End of History' (1989), in which, following the fall of the Berlin Wall, Fukuyama claims that:

> The triumph of the West, of the Western *idea*, is evident first of all in the total exhaustion of viable systematic alternatives to Western liberalism. In the past decade, there have been unmistakable changes in the intellectual climate of the world's two largest communist countries, and the beginnings of significant reform movements in both. But this phenomenon extends beyond high politics and it can be seen also in the ineluctable spread of consumerist Western culture in such diverse contexts as the peasants' markets and color television sets now omnipresent throughout China, the cooperative restaurants and clothing stores opened in the past year in Moscow, the Beethoven piped into Japanese department stores, and the rock music enjoyed alike in Prague, Rangoon, and Tehran.
>
> What we may be witnessing is not just the end of the Cold War, or the passing of a particular period of postwar history, but the end

of history as such: that is, the end point of mankind's ideological evolution and the universalization of Western liberal democracy as the final form of human government. This is not to say that there will no longer be events to fill the pages of *Foreign Affair's* [sic] yearly summaries of international relations, for the victory of liberalism has occurred primarily in the realm of ideas or consciousness and is as yet incomplete in the real or material world. But there are powerful reasons for believing that it is the ideal that will govern the material world *in the long run.* (Fukuyama, 1989)

In the world that Fukuyama describes, a world in which there are no legitimate alternatives to global Western modernity, the need to affirm the West's universality to the extent that Naipaul does in *Among the Believers* becomes less pressing. Consequently, unlike *Among the Believers* in which Naipaul explicitly (and repeatedly) draws the conclusion that Islam is parasitic on Western civilization, the contention that readers 'should not look for conclusions' in *Beyond Belief* might be understood as evidence of the renewed confidence that the triumph of Western liberalism has become historical fact. Significantly, Fukuyama reads the 'triumph of the West' as a return to the universal acceptance of Western liberalism with which the century began, corroborating the claim that *Beyond Belief* represents a re-inscription of the Western travel narratives of that earlier period.

An important way that Naipaul's narrative style in *Beyond Belief* reinforces Fukuyama's contention that there is no alternative to Western liberalism is by representing Islam as irrational in contrast to the book's own 'objective' perspective. Therefore, while Naipaul reports the 'facts' in his pared-down prose style, Muslims are unable to perceive the world with his clarity because Islam obfuscates the world through its irrational belief system. Throughout *Beyond Belief* Naipaul reinforces this representation of Islam as irrational on two levels. The first is on a personal level in which individual Muslims are shown to be misguided in the analysis of their own lives as a result of their beliefs. For example, in Indonesia Naipaul makes the following observation of the head of an Islamic school, Mr Wahid:

It was the perfection of the 'value system' of his Islam. It was curiously circular. It was – adapting his preacher's analogy – like a very smooth and easy treadmill, rather than a car: it kept him busy and went nowhere. Even if you said to him that people in Iowa had been kind to him when he was in need, he was prompted to say nothing about the people. Their kindness was simply another tribute to his faith: God, he said, loved him very much. (1999: 47)

This representation of Mr. Wahid's personal Islamic world-view that 'misreads' the world around him is reinforced by a second narrative level that shows Islam to misread the world within a broader social and historical context. For example, when Naipaul gives his 'objective' account of the history of Islam in Indonesia he writes:

> Here, as elsewhere in Indonesia, where Islam was comparatively recent, the various layers of history could still be easily perceived. But – this was my idea, not Mr. Wahid's – the peaantren (Islamic boarding school) ran all the separate ideas together and created the kind of mishmash I had seen. (1999: 23)

These two levels of narrative – the individual story of Mr. Wahid and the layers of history in Indonesia – work to support each other and Naipaul's thesis of Islam outlined in the preface to the book. Namely, that Islam is an imperialist religion that imposes Arab culture and history on non-Arabs, and that the effects of this Arab conversion prevent individual Muslims from seeing their lives, as well as the world, more broadly, with the clarity that Naipaul is able to. Islam, therefore, muddies perception on a personal level because it obfuscates acts of human kindness, and on the level of Naipaul's rationality because it relies on a circular logic. It is, in short, a world-view that contrasts with Naipaul's own 'objective' traveller's gaze; which, as he contends in his preface, represents people and places as they are.

Naipaul's positioning of himself as a neutral conduit who impartially 'observes what happens' is supported by his use of flat, pared-down language. In contrast to his fiction, the language here is devoid of self-conscious literariness. This is an attempt to screen his role as a mediator between the stories of the people he meets, the places he visits, and the reader. For instance, consider Naipaul's description of one entrepreneur/ Islamic teacher in Indonesia:

> The supernatural power that some had attributed to him had blessed him with further great success. He had a supermarket now; a car-hire business; a garment factory; a bank, a computer rental service. These things attached themselves to him, grew around him. He remained as he had started: a teacher. A foundation set up by disciples looked after the business side. All this had been achieved in three years.

It was the success in which other – and Budi now as well – saw the divine hand. (1999: 117)

Naipaul's short simple sentences, the lack of modifiers, as well as the matter of fact tone of his writing, support his claim in the preface that the stories in *Beyond Belief* are not 'forced or false' (Naipaul, 1999: xiii). In this, the writing echoes a journalistic style – or what King has called, 'a form of sociology through story-telling' (King, 2003: 177). The effect of representing Islam in this way is a more powerful rhetorical disavowal of political Islam and endorsement of the 'West' than the universal civilization that Naipaul achieves in *Among the Believers*. This is so for two reasons.

First, by representing Islam as culturally imperialist and irrational, Naipaul establishes Islam as culturally particular in contrast to the universality of the West. Unlike *Among the Believers*, *Beyond Belief* does not explicitly affirm the 'West' as the 'universal civilization' but rather embeds it in the form of the narrative. Thus, Naipaul's positioning of himself as an 'objective witness' in the text obfuscates the possibility that his own world-view, as a spokesperson for the 'universal civilization', might itself be culturally particular. Consequently, while *Beyond Belief* exposes contradictions in Islamic thought, revealing it to be grounded in irrational cultural beliefs (such as 'the divine hand'), the idea that the West might also be rooted in its own set of culturally informed beliefs is never raised. This strategy is more effective in naturalizing the West as the 'universal civilization' than polemically asserting this claim, because it tacitly implies that only a Western world-view is above and beyond cultural particularity and, therefore, that there is no legitimate alternative to Western-led global modernity.

Second, the distinction between the cultural particularity of Islam and the universality of the West serves to legitimate Western interventions around the world on the grounds of universalism and progress. This idea is underscored by Naipaul's penchant for meeting postcolonial subjects in *Beyond Belief* who lament the departure of the British because of the technological benefits that colonialism brought. For instance, one such subject comments: 'My father used to say that the British were better than these governments. It was not injustice in this form. My father used to say that in the British days there were little kerosene lanterns on the street. But now we have no streetlights' (345). Similarly, Naipaul represents the more recent effects of Western-led globalization equally positively by showing how the everyday lives of individuals, such as 'Budi' and his father in Indonesia, are better off when employed by a multinational 'computer company' (113) and 'foreign oil company' (111) respectively. In this way, Naipaul represents westernization as a narrative of progress by showing how the influence of the 'the ineluctable spread of consumerist Western culture' (Fukuyama, 1989) and business interests around the world improve the everyday lives of Third World citizens.

A Fundamental Fear of Naipaul's 'Universal Civilization'

Given the evidence presented thus far, it is not difficult to see why Naipaul's travel writing is read as neo-imperialist by numerous postcolonial critics. Certainly, the idea of the 'West' as the 'universal civilization' is the dominant narrative that Naipaul sets out to tell in *Beyond Belief.* However, also evident in the text is a more subtle aspect of the narrative that reveals the disturbance that political Islam produces in Western discourse and suggests the limits of westernization rather than its universalization. The work of Bobby Sayyid is useful in laying bare this second aspect of *Beyond Belief's* narrative by offering a theoretical framework that conceives of a very different relationship between political Islam and global modernity.

Contrary to the world-view articulated by Naipaul and Fukuyama, Sayyid argues that contemporary globality has not resulted in the 'Triumph of the West' but rather a contested space in which political Islam positions itself as a legitimate global alternative to westernization. Sayyid makes this claim for three reasons. First, despite the privileged position of Western countries within contemporary globality, Sayyid argues that the West, as a global centre of power, has diminished following decolonization. For Sayyid, this process of decentring has intensified in recent years, because the 'identity and coherence' of the West as a singular source of power and ideas has been undermined by a growing schism between Europe and the United States (Sayyid, 2003: xvi). This schism was evidenced by the sharp ideological differences between George Bush and his European counterparts over a range of political issues that are symptomatic of an increasing ideological gap between Europe and America. The West as a coherent centre of global power has been further fractured during the past 30 years because naturalized narratives of Western universalism have been challenged from within the West through various discourses of postmodernism, as well as from outside it through discourses of global Islam (xvii). Second, Sayyid argues that in the absence of a great Islamic power, 'Muslims remain unrepresented at a global level' (xiv). According to Sayyid, this absence of political representation is significant because it marginalizes large numbers of Muslims from the global political system. Paradoxically, this lack of political power is precisely why Islam has become so highly politicized in recent years as Muslims seek a way to 'represent the Muslim Ummah at a global level' (xix). Third, Sayyid argues that the project of global political Islam is facilitated by globalization because globalization enables Muslims around the world to identify with a unified Muslim community – the Ummah – to an unprecedented extent. In this respect, globalization promotes a transnational sense of Muslim identity that represents an alternative 'paradigm to what lies beyond the nation state' (xx).

Sayyid's conception of global Islam has significant implications for reading *Beyond Belief* because it challenges the assumptions of Western universalism that are implicit to Naipaul's stylistic choices. More specifically, Naipaul's claim that he can act as an objective witness to the 'Muslim world' and represent the stories of the people and places he visits underpins *Beyond Belief's* narrative approach outlined in the preface to the book. Such an approach is predicated upon Naipaul equating the 'West' with the 'universal civilization' and using both as interchangeable terms. As has been seen, this enables Naipaul to represent the rejection of Western values as the rejection of modernity in order to show Islam (and political Islam in particular) as regressive and 'parasitic' upon the West. Contrary to this view however, Sayyid argues that political Islam is not antithetical to modernity but simply a rejection of Eurocentrism. Political Islam, therefore, is a project that offers an alternative passage of global modernity to the West rather than one that rejects modernity outright. Put simply, for Sayyid the discourse of political Islam is both modern and Islamic and, therefore, to reject westernization is not necessarily to reject modernity. Framed in this way, the conflict between Islamic and Western world-views evident in both *Among the Believers* and *Beyond Belief* is not the intrinsic conflict that Naipaul represents it as. Rather, it is a genealogical struggle to define the future trajectory of the world. Sayyid describes this struggle in the following way:

> The denial of the possibility of rejecting the West is itself a gesture of the West which is intended to recuperate any possible dislocation. Thus, it re-describes its own genealogy. Now the emergence of Islamism – which points to the erosion of Western supremacist discourses – opens up the struggle for the articulation of genealogies. The contest between these attempts is part of the hegemonic struggle to construct the narrative of origins. The conflict between the logic

of Islamism and the logic of eurocentrism is the contest about how to write the history of the future. (159)

The articulation of a global political Islam, therefore, represents a refusal of the sorts of universalizing beliefs in Western identity that Naipaul perpetuates. The effect of political Islam's rejection of westernization is, according to Sayyid, that it is not only disruptive to the Western-led geopolitical order, but also to 'an episteme which has been dominant for perhaps the last three hundred years' (160). From this perspective, global Islam represents a world-view that refuses representation within Naipaul's narrative and, in so doing, disrupts the assumptions of universality that are foundational to it. Hence, it is not simply that travelling to the 'Muslim' world offers Naipaul a chance to herald the 'triumph of the West,' or 'universal civilization' – to reinforce a neo-imperial narrative of globalization – but also that his encounters with Islam challenge his own assumptions about the world. It is precisely this foundational challenge to Western universalism that global political Islam represents that renders it threatening to Western discourse, and why at times it proves so disturbing to Naipaul's narrative style in *Beyond Belief*. During such moments of disturbance, Naipaul's subjectivity and stylistic skill as a novelist disrupt the sense of objectivity that he seeks to achieve in the book and, rather than let the stories of these Muslims 'come to the front,' his persona as a travel writer intrudes to shape these stories into the broader narrative of Islam that he outlines in the preface to the book.

Consider for example Naipaul's experience at the Jamaat commune in Pakistan. The chapter begins with Naipaul characterizing the commune as the centre of an Islamic 'fundamentalist' movement. It then goes on to describe the story of Mohammed Ranjha and his son Saleem who drives Naipaul to the commune to meet his father. Once at the commune, Naipaul writes:

And now father and son spoke together in a kind of duet, exchanging ideas about that golden Islamic age. After the talk in the car about the modernity of Jamaat in matters of dress and organization, after the tweed jacket and the tie and *The Economist* and the talk of cricket, it was strange to see Saleem, the customs officer, matching his feudal father phrase for phrase. (297)

What is so disconcerting and 'strange' for Naipaul is that Saleem and his father appear quite comfortable with discourses of modernity and Islam – discourses that in Naipaul's world-view are diametrically opposed. As the scene progresses, further evidence of such ambivalence emerges as both Saleem and his father respond to questions about freedom and democracy in ways that challenge Naipaul's narrative of Islam. Naipaul presses these issues further by asking:

> how the state would define what was Islamic. That had given General Zia a lot of trouble, in spite of his Islamic Ideology Council. There would be debate, Saleem said. He added, surprisingly, that everybody didn't have to agree. He, for example, didn't always agree with his father. His father, again surprisingly said, 'There is freedom in Islam.' What they wanted, the father said was a state where everyone accepted Islam voluntarily, with all his heart. And I began to understand how freedom and submission run together. (Naipaul, 1999, 298–9)

'Strange', 'surprised' – this is not how Saleem and his father seem to feel about their embrace of modernity and political Islam, but is rather Naipaul's response to their thinking. But why should we be surprised about a father and son disagreeing over a theoretical issue? Why should Naipaul use the word 'surprisingly' when his style throughout the book is to keep the use of modifiers to a minimum?

For Naipaul, surprise at Saleem's welcome of debate stems from the aspects of his and his father's thinking that unsettle the book's broader narrative of Islam and its characterization of the Jamaat commune as exemplary of 'the fundamentalist way of thinking' (Naipaul, 1999: 291). In order to reassert this fundamentalist narrative in the face of the seemingly ambivalent evidence that Saleem and his father represent, Naipaul's presence as a narrator begins to encroach upon the scene: at first through his reaction of surprise, and later by his comments that 'I began to understand how freedom and submission run together.' For Naipaul, to 'understand' in this instance is a way of drawing conclusions for the reader, despite his claim in the introduction that 'there are complexities enough in these stories' and therefore that 'the reader should not look for "conclusions."' In other words, a noticeable shift has taken place in the sorts of formal decisions that Naipaul makes in reconciling his 'random experience of the observed culture with the desire to give a representative sense of that culture' (Nixon, 1992: 72–3). Consequently, in order to shape his experience with Saleem and his father to fit *Beyond Belief*'s broader narrative of Islam, Naipaul's authorial presence increasingly encroaches upon the scene. And, in contrast to the stripped-down prose that is used to reveal the contradictions in Islamic thought, Naipaul's language takes on an increasingly poetic tone. For instance, at one point he interrupts Mohammed's explanation of Islamic freedom by commenting that his 'eyes became uncertain, as liquid and melting as his son's' (Naipaul, 1999: 290). In such instances, it is not enough for the story to speak for itself because it might contradict or at the very least offer ambivalent evidence for Naipaul's general claims about Islam. Rather, Naipaul uses his skill as a novelist to shape these encounters into the general narrative of Islam he wants to tell without resorting to the sort of polemics that characterize *Among the Believers*.

Yet the intrusion of Naipaul's subjectivity in this chapter goes further still. When the young son of Saleem is brought in and Naipaul is informed that the six-year-old is learning to recite the Koran by heart, Naipaul interrupts the scene and comments that 'I couldn't stay. My breathing had become very bad' and abruptly ends the interview. The reason for this interruption is ostensibly Naipaul's sudden sickness from Karachi's air pollution, but its effect upon the narrative is that Naipaul's subjectivity comes to dominate the scene. Naipaul the travel writer is no longer in the background of the narrative letting the voices of the people he meets unfold, but its focal point. So destabilizing is the conjunction of Islamic belief and modern discourse that the three generations of Ranjha males represent to Naipaul's world-view that the sorts of subtle stylistic changes previously outlined are no longer able to shape the account of his personal experiences at Jamaat into the book's broader narrative of Islam.

In other words, Jamaat signifies the extent to which Naipaul's conception of 'the West', or 'universal civilization' is forced to confront its own limits to which the only textual response Naipaul can imagine is abruptly ending the narrative. Thus, Jamaat's simultaneous embrace of the 'modernity' and 'ideas about that golden Islamic age' signify its refusal to accept the Western narrative of global modernity that Naipaul advances in *Among the Believers* and *Beyond Belief*, while evidence of the 'satellite dish' and '*The Economist*' indicates that globalization does not inevitably result in the westernization of identity (Naipaul, 1999: 300). Rather, the commune's interaction with the outside world through global communication networks only appears to strengthen the politicization of Islam by situating it within the context of global modernity, and connecting life at the commune to other Islamic societies such as Iran. In short, the commune does not indicate 'modernity' to be the 'foreboding' threat to Islam that Naipaul conceives it as in the beginning of the chapter, but rather represents a space that offers a different genealogy of global modernity and appears quite comfortable in disarticulating globalization from westernization: a space that challenges the foundations of Naipaul's narrative style and its assumption of the 'universal civilization' upon which it depends.

Coda and Beyond

Writing in 1992, Nixon argued that Naipaul's 'orientalist' opposition between a 'generous' civilization and a parasitic 'barbarism' in *Among the Believers* resurfaced in Western discourse to legitimate the first Gulf War in 'a depressingly unadjusted mode' (Nixon: 152). To read *Beyond Belief* as a narrative of neo-imperialism however, is to acknowledge only the dominant narrative of Islam that Naipaul wants to tell. Such a reading does not account for the moments in the book when his encounters with the 'Muslim world' challenge the narrative style he outlines in the preface to the book and the assumptions of Western universalization that are foundational to it. Recognition of this disturbance that political Islam represents to Naipaul's conception of the 'universal civilization' is important because it offers a different way of reading the sorts of public discourses about Islam that Nixon identifies.

Consider, for example, Paul Wolfowitz's comments about 'Bridging the Dangerous Gap between the West and the Muslim World' following 9/11. Wolfowitz writes:

> To win the war against terrorism and ... help share a more peaceful world, we must speak to the hundreds of millions of moderate and tolerant people in the Muslim world, regardless of where they live, who aspire to enjoy the blessings of freedom and democracy and free enterprise. These values are sometimes described as 'Western values', but, in fact, we see them in Asia and elsewhere because they are universal values borne of a common human aspiration. (2002)

The parallel between Wolfowitz's comments here and Naipaul's conception of the 'universal civilization' in *Among the Believers* is obvious. But if, as I have argued, *Beyond Belief* is a narrative that at once endorses the West as the 'universal civilization' and, at the same time, exposes the limits of this narrative, then it offers a very different reading of Wolfowitz's comments than the relationship of neo-imperialism that Nixon posits during the first Gulf War. What this essay's reading of *Beyond Belief* exposes in Wolfowitz's comments is why the idea of 'moderate Muslims' has become so important to Anglo-American discourses of the 'War on Terror'; and why Western politicians like Wolfowitz are so keen to define this category of Muslims and target their rhetoric towards them. In *Beyond Belief*, the disturbance that political Islam represents to Naipaul's narrative style comes at the moments when the Muslims he meets embrace modernity while rejecting westernization – Muslims that represent a different genealogy of global modernity to westernization. Naipaul's inability to respond to this challenge stems from his rigid binary division between Western modernity and fundamentalist Islam. Consequently, when Naipaul encounters Muslims in his travels that disrupt this opposition, as he does at Jamaat, his world-view and ability to narrate them is challenged. The category of 'moderate Muslims' might be seen as a response to this crisis of narrative that Naipaul experiences when he confronts the limits of westernization. It represents a tacit way of reclaiming modernity within a Western rather than an Islamic genealogy. 'Moderate Muslims', therefore, becomes a new coda for those Muslims who accept the definition of modernity that Wolfowitz outlines without explicitly identifying themselves as Western. This version of westernization is a long way from the neo-imperialism that Nixon identifies in Naipaul's work in 1992: not the triumph of the West, but the response of the West to a world in which its hegemony is no longer naturalized and Naipaul's conflation of it with the 'universal civilization' is now widely contested.

Works Cited and Consulted

Fukuyama, Francis (1989) *The End of History*, http://www.wesjones.com/eoh.htm, accessed 29th September 2009.

Green, Keith and Bihan, Jill (1996) *Critical Theory and Practice*. New York: Routledge.

Hardt, Michael and Negri, Antonio (2000) *Empire*. Cambridge, MA: Harvard University Press.

King, Bruce (2003) *V. S. Naipaul*. London: Palgrave Macmillan.

Naipaul, V. S. (1981) *Among the Believers: An Islamic Journey*. New York: Vintage.

Naipaul, V. S. (1999) *Beyond Belief: Islamic Excursions Amongst Converted People*. New York: Vintage.

Nixon, Rob (1992) *London Calling: V. S. Naipaul, Postcolonial Mandarin*. Oxford: Oxford University Press.

Pratt, Mary Louise (1992) *Imperial Eyes: Travel Writing and Transculturation*. New York: Routledge.

Pratt, Mary Louise (2001) '"Scratches on the Face of the Country"; or What Mr Barrow Saw in the Land of the Bushman' in Susan Roberson (ed.) *Defining Travel: Diverse Visions*. Mississippi: University of Mississippi, 132–53.

Sayyid, Bobby (2003) *A Fundamental Fear: Eurocentrism and the Emergence of Islamism*. London: Zed Books.

Tomlinson, John (1999) *Globalization and Culture*. Cambridge: Polity.

Wolfowitz, Paul (2002) 'Bridging the Dangerous Gap between the West and the Muslim World', *Department of Defence News*. 3 May. http://www.defenselink.mil/speeches/speech.aspx?speechid=210, accessed 22 September 2009.

3
Travelling Home: Global Travel and the Postcolonial in the Travel Writing of Pico Iyer

Rune Graulund

Revathi Krishnaswamy and John C. Hawley's *The Postcolonial and the Global* (2008) and Suman Gupta's *Globalization and Literature* (2009) are two recent examples of an increasing number of studies questioning the validity of 'the postcolonial' in a world recognized as 'global'. If we are rapidly heading towards a state in which everywhere and everyone are the same, a world in which the power structures of old are close to being, or already have been, dismantled, where does this leave the concepts of 'travel' and 'the postcolonial'? Even more pressingly, where does this leave the *combination* of these two supposedly outdated terms? If travel and the postcolonial are outmoded terms in isolation, then surely 'postcolonial travel' must be doubly obsolete.

In the following, I do not intend a comprehensive and thorough survey of the relationship between literature, the postcolonial and the global as offered by volumes like *The Postcolonial and the Global* or *Globalization and Literature*. What I will be offering here, though, is an investigation of some of the key themes haunting travel in an age that claims to be past difference, a world that has purportedly shed the shadow of colonialism so effectively that it is no longer relevant to discuss anything, least of all travel, in terms of the postcolonial. Specifically, I will be examining these claims in relation to Pico Iyer's *Video Night in Kathmandu: And Other Reports from the Not-So-Far East* (1988) and *The Global Soul: Jetlag, Shopping Malls and the Search for Home* (2000), exposing the ways in which globalization has tested the notions of the postcolonial and of travel.

Video Night in Kathmandu: The Spread of Monoculturalism

More of a traditional travel writing book than the later and far more polemic *The Global Soul*, the premise of *Video Night in Kathmandu*

54

is nevertheless from the beginning characterized by a constant and characteristically postmodern questioning of its own premise. Attempting 'to find out how America's pop-cultural imperialism spread through the world's most ancient civilizations', Iyer (1988: 5) decides to travel the 'not-so-far East' not so much because of any inherent qualities of the countries in question but more for their exemplary *relation* to the assumptions that he intends to test. As Iyer himself points out, any location outside America could, in theory, have served as a test subject in his investigation, yet Asia is envisioned as a space particularly well suited to his project. Its recent rise as an economic force, its colonial history, the fact that it contains three-quarters of the world's population, all of these factors impact his decision to travel the 'not-so-far East' rather than any other part of the world. Most important of all, however, is the fact that 'it was unmatched in its heterogeneity' (Iyer, 1988: 7–8), making it the perfect testing ground for Iyer's hypothesis that 'home has nothing to do with hearth, and everything to do with a state of mind; that one man's home may be his compatriot's exile; that home is, finally, not the physical place, but the role and the self we choose to occupy' (9).

In querying the nature of his subject, Iyer simultaneously puts his own position as a travel writer centre stage, careful always to explain and locate himself in relation to his field of enquiry. Unlike the earlier form of the colonial exploration narrative, where the travelling narrator was more often than not oblivious to 'his' role as observer, or that of late Eurocentric 19th/early-20th-century travel writing, with the travel writer eager to establish credentials as a 'proper' traveller in a world where tourism made 'real travel' ever harder to locate, Iyer exhibits a suspicion towards both world and self typical for an age apprehensive about essentialist positions. Constantly questioning his own motives and the very possibility of travel in a world where the boundaries between home and away have become harder to sustain, Iyer is cautious from the outset: he does not phrase his goals in terms of authenticity. Thus there is none of the explicit goals of Laurens van der Post's *Lost World of the Kalahari* (1958) or Peter Matthiessen's *The Snow Leopard* (1978), and there is no possibility of failure either.[1] As the postmodern subject, Iyer is out to observe the *relations* of his subjects rather than identifying any of their core attributes.

In terms of travel and the postcolonial, then, Iyer's approach is less confrontational than, say, Caryl Phillips's *The Atlantic Sound* (2000). Iyer expresses little concern for history, effectively diffusing the question of agency by focusing on the system rather than those who might have been responsible for constructing it in the first place. First of all, 'pop-cultural imperialism' is not to be compared to the violence of hundreds of years of coercion and enslavement caused by European colonialism. Secondly, Iyer seems to be far more interested in the effects of 'pop-cultural imperialism' than its causes. Nevertheless, mild as Iyer might be, the stated goal of *Video Night in Kathmandu* is an examination of 'the encounters between East and West' (Iyer, 1988: 22), encounters that are physically non-violent but still aggressive. The 'encounters between East and West' may no longer be as spectacularly immoral as we now perceive the colonialism of old to have been. Yet that does not mean that the present relationship between 'East' and 'West' cannot still be traced to their colonial prerequisites, nor that contemporary relations have somehow been cleansed of colonial implications. As Ramón Grosfoguel has pointed out, even if 'it might seem anachronistic to talk about colonies and colonialism today', we need to realize that a 'colonial situation of exploitation and domination, formed by centuries of European colonialism can and does persist in the present' (Grosfoguel, 2008: 95). The more benevolent visions of globalization often present the global as challenging and repositioning former Eurocentric divisions in a 'globalization from below' (Appadurai, 2001: 3), but as a range of critics like Doreen Massey, Michael Hardt and Antonio Negri have proved, globalization has as often reaffirmed and fortified traditional power structures by legitimizing them through a simple yet deceptive dressing up in global clothing.[2]

In contrast to the multi-centred view of globalization as presented in *The Global Soul*, *Video Night in Kathmandu* is concerned with globalization almost exclusively as an American phenomenon. 'Globalization', in other words, is in *Video Night in Kathmandu* more or less equivalent to 'Americanization', hence the world-view presented by Iyer is, initially anyway, that of a hegemony (America) rapidly spreading its influence over a host of weaker cultures. Rather than any deep-rooted interest in the respective countries visited, 'I went to Asia, then, not only to see Asia, but also to see America' (Iyer, 1988: 9), 'to see how America was regarded and reconstituted abroad, to measure the country by the shadow it casts' (11). Iyer's quest is thus curiously similar to a postmodern classic published two years prior to *Video Night in Kathmandu* – Jean Baudrillard's theory-cum-travel-writing book *America* (1986). Baudrillard, an eminent European, allegedly 'went in search of ... the America of the empty' (Baudrillard: 5), yet as Caren Kaplan has pointed out, even if Europe is rarely mentioned in *America*, this does not change the fact that Baudrillard in fact 'defines the [American] West as a mystified reflection of Europe' (Kaplan, 1996: 74). *America*, nominally concerned about the country of its title, is as much a book about Europe. Likewise, *Video Night in Kathmandu* is as much a book about America as it is about Asia.

Different though they may be in tone and approach, Baudrillard's main concern in *America* is at heart not that different from the concerns expressed by Iyer in *Video Night in Kathmandu*. Baudrillard, after all, is both fascinated and frightened by the cultural powerhouse of a country 'neither dream nor reality [but] hyperreality' (Baudrillard: 28), a presence that, from the position of a French intellectual in the mid-1980s, it seemed impossible to offer any sort of resistance to. Similarly, Iyer cannot help but wonder in *Video Night in Kathmandu* if the invasion of American culture is inevitable, an invasion that will eventually overrun and pervade every last corner and nook of the world with American goods and customs. As opposed to the later *Global Soul* that presents globalization as a polycentric trend that promises to influence American culture as much as Americanization has influenced other cultures, *Video Night in Kathmandu* is symptomatic of an era that had trouble envisioning a future inescapably swamped by American brands, movies and values. Significantly, as Iyer's experiences in the Philippines make clear, American culture is however to be equated with American *popular* culture. During his stay in what he describes as 'the world's largest slice of the American Empire, in its purest form' (1988: 181), Iyer remarks how, 'I found no sign of Lincoln or Thoreau or Sojourney Truth; just Dick Clark, Ronald McDonald and Madonna' (183). Like Baudrillard, who went in search of America 'in the speed of the screenplay, in the indifferent reflex of television, in the film of days and nights projected across an empty space' (Baudrillard: 5), so Iyer goes in search of the 'shadow' of America cast by the flickering screens of popular culture. It is, after all, 'video nights' that he experiences in Kathmandu.

These similarities apart, *America* and *Video Nights in Kathmandu* are of course quite different, with the most immediate distinctions being the territories travelled. Baudrillard and Iyer may both have an analysis of American popular culture as the overall goal, yet the fact that one travels *to* America while the other leaves it *behind* inevitably makes for some difference in terms of focus. As much a question of setting, though, the difference between the two is also one of humility.[3] There is a remarkable difference between Baudrillard and Iyer in terms of the way in which they conceive the role of the traveller. Baudrillard commits the typical fallacy of entering the country he intends to travel with a complete set of expectations of what he anticipates finding ('I knew all about this ... when I was still in Paris, of course' [Baudrillard: 5]). Iyer sets out with a clear agenda of what he intends to look for, but he is far more aware of his own duplicitous position as traveller and observer. The most significant difference between *America* and *Video Night in Kathmandu* is not the actual landscapes travelled and analysed, but the fact that Iyer, unlike Baudrillard, acknowledges that *he does not truly understand what he observes*. Accordingly, Iyer may occasionally object to the impact of American culture on the cultures he visits, yet he remains cautious about condemning what he admits is in fact perplexing, eventually confessing that although he set out with the presumption that he would be mapping the inequalities between 'West' and 'East', the more he travels, the more 'my tidy paradigm of West exploiting East began to crumble' (Iyer, 1988: 321).

Admittedly, this can be read as resignation, as a typical postmodern move not to take a stand. Indeed, anyone out to prove Iyer's reluctance to apportion blame need look no further than the introductory chapter of *Video Night in Kathmandu*. By claiming that the relationship 'between East and West ... closely resembled a mating dance' rather than a conflict, hence that 'it made any talk of winners and losers irrelevant' (22), Iyer sidesteps what is often a highly uneven relationship a little too easily. As Patrick Holland and Graham Huggan have pointed out, Iyer may be well-intentioned, but he falls into an 'off-the-shelf postmodernist response' (Holland and Huggan, 1998: 164) far too often:

> Iyer's project is to demonstrate Asia's counterthrust to American cultural imperialism, to show its capacity to absorb, adapt, and reinvent Western cultural products while providing a mirror that reflects the West back on itself at new angles and in new forms. But this project is undermined by Iyer's reluctance to come to terms with his own technologies of representation, and to admit their investment in the ideology of consumerism he sets out to critique. (Holland and Huggan: 63).

Though Holland and Huggan's argument undoubtedly has some traction, not least in their assertion that *Video Night in Kathmandu* tends to overlook the grimmer aspect of globalization in favour of 'a celebration, rather than a critique, of the interconnectedness of consumer culture' (Holland and Huggan: 64), the central tenet of the book is in fact revealed when Iyer is *least* celebrant of 'interconnectedness'. For even if Iyer is by and large hesitant to engage in any sort of normative evaluation of his experiences, he does on occasion slip into the rhetoric of authenticity. Nepal, for instance, is one out of ten locations visited by Iyer; he tellingly chooses the capital for his title, and muses how he 'came closest to the *real* Nepal when I least sought it' (Iyer, 1988: 100, emphasis added). In fact, Iyer feels he has discovered the 'real' Nepal only on the occasions he is left perplexed. As dusk falls, Iyer experiences mixed emotions as he wanders the streets of Kathmandu, reminded of home by the domesticity of the setting yet at the same time realizing he has not at any time in his travels felt more excluded. '[A]ll these rituals were shut off from me, and that, in its way, made me happier than anything. For the first time since I came to Kathmandu, I felt that the city had turned its back on foreigners and was going instead about its age-old ways' (101).

While it is reasonable to accuse Iyer of being a little too naive when it comes to his belief in the relationship between 'East' and 'West' as taking place on a level playing field, his approach to the notion of 'real travel' offers refreshing perspectives on travel for the supposedly globalized, difference-starved world at large, for the postcolonial subject as well as for travel writing as a genre. Employing the genre of travel writing as an analytical tool that identifies the status of travel in a global world, Iyer turns Eurocentric travel writing's stock tropes of acquisition and conquest on their heads and consequently undermines conceptions of the travel writing genre itself. Unlike traditional Eurocentric travel narratives, where travellers desired to break the codes, to reach Mecca or Shangri-La, to infiltrate and imitate foreign ways of life, to find the last bit of the planet uncontaminated by tourists, to *discover* something new that could be logged, described and explained, Iyer never feels closer to what *he* experiences as real travel than when he is least understanding of his surroundings. To Iyer, 'real travel' is not an exercise that includes discovery and the advancement of information of an Other. Rather, real travel only takes place once we become aware of our own position in relation to an exterior world that does not, in fact, have very much (if indeed anything) to do with the foreign, the different and the Other. According to Iyer, then, real travel is an activity tied up exclusively with our personal definitions of what makes up self and home, meaning that the notions of 'authentic' travel, of territory 'genuinely' suited for travel, are effectively dismantled.

As William Langewiesche admonished us in *Sahara Unveiled: A Journey Across the Desert* (1996), we will do well to remember that there 'is no such construct as an inauthentic culture' (225), nor for that matter that of an inauthentic territory. The spectre of belatedness haunting modern travel writing can effectively be laid to rest only when it is acknowledged that travel has never been early or late in any way but in that of the perspective of a given traveller, irrespective of his or her geographical, cultural or ethnic origins. Instead of reading Iyer as subscribing to 'a perceptual legacy of exoticism: a mode of vision in which travel writing, fuelling European fantasy, has acted as a primary vehicle for the production and consumption of cultural "otherness"' (Holland and Huggan: 65), perhaps we might start to read him in a celebration of the very fact that cultural 'otherness' always has and always will exist; yet that such otherness is exactly *not* about a 'European fantasy' but the fantasy of any given individual.

Video Night in Kathmandu may thus be postmodern in its insistence on shying away from fixed points of view, yet it successfully employs the fluidity of the postmodern position to construct a compelling argument about the status of travel in a world supposedly starved of cultural difference. As a consequence of this approach, the notion of 'real travel' ultimately resides with our own position in relation to the territory travelled, not the territory itself. That does not mean that it is pointless to embark upon a physical journey, nor that the activity of travelling cannot be graded into degrees of more or less successful experiences of travel. It simply means that what may seem authentic travel *to me* may very well, is actually most certainly, the worst kind of travel to someone else. Or even more poignantly, that this particular territory is not better or worse in terms of travel, but in fact the place that someone else calls home.

A realization like this should perhaps be common sense, but is far too often forgotten either in the hectic rush to seek out the last untainted space offering 'real' travel (the sense of belatedness haunting modern Eurocentric travel writing), or the ennui generated by the onslaught of the monocultural (the postmodern experience of never going anywhere no matter how much one moves). *Video Night in Kathmandu* offers a valuable contribution to the dismantling of a Eurocentric, or indeed any-centric, point of view of travel. Unlike the *refocusing* of the travel writing genre as exemplified by Amitav Ghosh's *In an Antique Land* (1992), a text that 'created a world in which the West was either nonexistent or irrelevant and where the focus was the relationship between two "non-Western" regions' (Grewal, 2008: 184), Iyer's goal is at length a *diffusion* of focus. As Iyer remarks in his afterword to the 2001 edition of *Video Night in Kathmandu*, 'the core of this book (which is, I think, the core of our travels) has little to do with East and West, or official forms of designation, and more to do with something universal, which never changes: our encounters with the alien' (401). The central lesson of *Video Night in Kathmandu*, then, is that travel is a means of understanding our own notion of home and identity regardless of our point of departure.

The Global Soul: Polycentric Cosmopolitans

At the time *Video Night in Kathmandu* was published in 1988, 'pop culture ruled the world, and America ruled pop culture', with American culture seemingly in the midst of a 'takeover [that] had radically intensified and rapidly accelerated' (Iyer, 1988: 5) over a very short period. This conviction was only affirmed with the fall of the Berlin Wall just one year later. With soft power prevailing over hard power and the Soviet Union rapidly collapsing under cries of free-market reforms and demands for American standards of living, nothing seemed able to stop the onslaught of the American cultural behemoth.

Twelve years after *Video Night in Kathmandu*, as *The Global Soul* was published at the closing not just of the decade but an entire millennium, Iyer could thus proclaim that it seemed as if the global had finally reached a state in which 'the world is one', a world in which we 'were all joined ... for richer and poorer, in sickness and in health' (Iyer, 2000: 14). *The Global Soul* could thus confirm what *Video Night in Kathmandu* had prophesied, albeit with a twist. It is not the American hegemony that the Iyer of *Video Night in Kathmandu* initially set out to investigate, for the world described by Iyer in *The Global Soul* is a space in which everything, everyone and everywhere seem made up by bits and pieces imported from afar. Consequently, the experience of travel Iyer was in pursuit of in *Video Night in Kathmandu* – the incomprehension and exclusion he experienced late at night as he walked the streets of the Nepalese capital – has become increasingly difficult to track down simply because each and every spot on the planet is as much a clutter as the next one.

> Everywhere is so made up of somewhere else – a polycentric anagram – that I hardly notice I'm sitting in a Parisian café just outside Chinatown (in San Francisco), talking to a Mexican-American friend about biculturalism while a Haitian woman stops off to congratulate him on a piece he's just delivered on TV on St. Patrick's Day. (Iyer, 2000: 11)

The Global Soul is thus as indicative of the global condition around the turn of the millennium as was *Video Night in Kathmandu* of the global in the late 1980s. Gone is the idea that globalization necessarily implies Americanization, as is the idea 'that globalization is a Western imperialist plot' (Sklair, 2008: 219). Even if American capitalism, corporate business and consumer culture have laid down the financial law that the rest of the world now follows, cultural exchange is, in *The Global Soul*, no longer envisioned as the one-way street of *Video Night in Kathmandu*. 'Everywhere', after all, is constructed not just of bits of 'America', but of 'somewhere else'. With his metaphor of the 'mating dance' between 'West' and 'East' rather than a conflict, Iyer of course exhibits some recognition of this in *Video Night in Kathmandu*. In comparison, however, *The Global Soul* expresses a much keener awareness of globalization as a truly global phenomenon rather than the consequence of one country (America) asserting its powers over the rest. The earlier book's metaphor of selfish lovers each exploiting the other for their own private needs has in the later book resulted in a mutant offspring, 'a new kind of being ... made up of fusions (and confusions) we had not seen before: a "Global Soul"' (Iyer, 2000: 18), belonging to no state or nation but occupying that of 'the metaphorical equivalent of international airspace' (19), existing everywhere and, consequently, also nowhere.

No passage illustrates this better than Iyer's choice of destination for his first travels of *The Global Soul*. Deciding not to go very far at all, Iyer starts out in the place where 'no one knows where anyone else is coming from ... and no one knows where anyone is at' (Iyer, 2000: 51). In the airport, 'vertiginous places [where] we have nothing to hold our identities in place' (62), Iyer finds a prism of the global condition at large, a space where Indians, Frenchmen, Brazilians, Taiwanese, Japanese, Iranians and Danes congregate around gift shops, 'the closest thing we have, an airport suggests, to a One-World currency' (50), yet also a space where no one seems to be quite at home. Everyone is equal in the airport, Iyer suggests, but at the cost that no one seems to know their place.

The concerns voiced by Iyer here are hardly unique. What Iyer describes is the coming of age of the famous 'global village' as prophesied by Marshall McLuhan's *The Gutenberg Galaxy* (1962), a state of affairs where 'local happenings are shaped by events occurring many miles away and vice versa' (Giddens, 1990: 63) resulting in a 'shrinking of the planet' (Augé, 1992: 31) that threatens to eliminate any kind of cultural difference. From a theoretical perspective, Iyer's decision to take the airport as the initial 'destination' for his travels in *The Global Soul* is not all that original. For Iyer's conclusion that airports remain 'an anthology of generic places' (Iyer, 2000: 43) was spelled out by Marc Augé's short but influential *Non-Places: Introduction to an Anthropology of Supermodernity* (1992) almost a decade prior to *The Global Soul*.

Replacing the myriad of countries of the 'not-so-far East' (*Video Night in Kathmandu*) with the very transit posts that brought the East closer in the first place is all very well, yet the observation that airports offer a particularly useful view of globalization since they are constructed around 'the assumption that everyone's from everywhere else' (Iyer, 2000: 43) is perhaps a little too easy, a little dated and, at close to 40 pages, a little too long. Furthermore, if *Video Night in Kathmandu* is prone to promote and romanticize postmodern ideas of the liberated nomad subject, *The Global Soul* is doubly so. Cherishing the almost superhuman ability of the 'Global Soul' to adapt to any situation it may find itself in, Iyer obviously believes in his term, investing so heavily in it that he deems it fit not just as the title and lead motif of his book, but as the celebrated core of his personality. 'I exult in the fact that I can see everywhere with a flexible eye; the very notion of home is foreign to me, as the state of foreignness is the closest thing I know to home' (Iyer, 2000: 24). Clearly, this comes dangerously close to repeating the myth of the modern artist's view of exile as liberating, which, as Edward Said among many others has pointed out, potentially risks ignoring the very real pain of existing in a constant state of homelessness: 'To think of exile as beneficial, as a spur to humanism or creativity, is to belittle its mutilations' (Said, 2006: 440). Iyer's is of course an updated version, one toned down from the modern idea of the solitary artist fighting a heroic fight for his or her art. The 'Global Souls' described by Iyer are not heroic artists with grandiose aesthetic visions. They are ordinary people whose lives simply happen to be defined by motion and travel rather than dwelling and stasis.

Even so, however monotonous and everyday Iyer's portrayal of countless hours spent in airports, planes and hotel bars may be, however unromantic and unappealing the lives of people 'thrown this way and that way by the global marketplace' (Iyer, 2000: 107), this is still a privileged vision. As the geographer Doreen Massey has pointed out, the problem with the globalization debate is often that, all-encompassing as it pretends to be, it turns out not to be very inclusive at all when scrutinized in detail. Globalization has undoubtedly had an impact on the lives of most people on the planet in some way or other, but to the majority of the world's population, it is questionable just how radical this impact has been. There is no shortage of descriptions of the drastic changes brought about by globalization yet 'much, if not all, of what has been written has seen this new world from the point of view of a (relative) elite. Those who today worry about a sense of disorientation and a loss of control must once have felt they knew exactly where they were, and that they *had* control' (Massey, 1994: 165). As Massey reminds us, we need to recall that 'amid the Ridley Scott images of world cities, the writing about skyscraper fortresses, the Baudrillard visions of hyper-space ... most people actually still live in places like Harlesden or West Brom. Much of life for many people, even in the first world, still consists of waiting in a bus-shelter with your shopping for a bus that never comes' (Massey, 1994: 163).

As pointed out in *World City* (2007), Massey's investigation of London as an illustration of the phenomenon known as world/global cities, the growth of these world cities 'comes at the expense of other regions [as well as] the planet as a whole' (18). On the surface promoting themselves as global utopias, as spaces in which all that is best about the global is focused in a central melting pot that all cities should eventually aspire to, Massey convincingly argues that not only is a world city like London 'the most unequal place in the country' (Massey, 2007: 19), but that world cities deepen inequality globally. Seen in this light, it is therefore of no little consequence that the spaces travelled by Iyer in *The Global Soul* are all set in cities that are in some way or another remarkable for their positions of privilege; for just as the free-roaming globalized subject is in fact representative more of 'a (relative) elite' (Massey, 1994) than the globe's population as a whole, so world/global cities are obviously not representative of the world at large either. Time–space compression as first conceived in the heyday of the postmodern was eventually supposed to level out all spatial differences, but it should by now be obvious that, as Massey points out, the cities (and the rest) of the world have in fact *not* become united in one global village.[4] The positioning of large cities the world over may have undergone radical changes over the past couple of decades, with former backwaters finding themselves unexpectedly influential in global affairs. Cities like Dubai and Seoul, Mumbai and Istanbul, Beijing and Jakarta, all these may now find themselves further up the ladder. Yet the hierarchy itself remains, as do the top players, with New York, London and Tokyo as much at the top of the list of 'global cities' as they were two decades ago when Saskia Sassen first coined the term in her influential study *The Global City: New York, London, Tokyo* (1991).

As a consequence of this focus on cities, it is only natural that the characters Iyer marks out as outstanding exemplars of the 'Global Soul', writers like Kazuo Ishiguro who – though supposedly as 'fit to travel' as is Iyer, as likely 'to blend in and navigate through a variety of geographical and cultural environments' (Molz, 2006: 6) – feels 'increasingly at home in big cities' (Iyer, 2000: 106). For the 'Global Soul' as defined by Iyer is nothing if not a cosmopolite, a refined city dweller of infinite cultures who may in theory be able to fit in anywhere but in practice feels most comfortable in the metropolis. Iyer, too, of course, self-professed 'Global Soul' that he is, is a cosmopolite and, as the son of middle-class parents and a graduate of Eton, Oxford and Harvard, the product of privilege. This privilege may once again be one only of 'a (relative) elite', certainly different from the days when long-distance travel was open only to a select few of the likes of a Gustave Flaubert or even a relatively recent example like Robert Byron, yet a privilege it remains. It is arguably a privilege available to a greater percentage of the world's population than in the days of Flaubert or Byron, but it is still the privilege of only a small minority of the world's population.

Travelling Home

Iyer makes a valid point, however, when he argues for the uniqueness of the 'Global Soul', especially as exemplified by his own position. Whether it is in comparison to that of the dispossessed, the refugees and the immigrants, or that of the travellers of privilege that formerly dominated earlier ages of travel, Iyer's situation is different *exactly* in the terms of home, of rooting and of origins. 'The biggest difference between me and those of my parent's generation, I felt, was that I'd never had a strong sense of departures (or arrivals); I'd grown up without a sense of a place to come to or from which to leave' (Iyer, 2000: 259). In fact, Iyer believes himself so pure a version of the 'Global Soul' that he outclasses even his contemporary colleagues. Unlike a Salman Rushdie, for instance, Iyer's 'imaginary homeland' is thus generated not by a 'sense of loss, some urge to reclaim, to look back' (Rushdie, 2006: 428), for what should he look back to, what should he reclaim? Iyer's story, after all, in *Video Night in Kathmandu* as in *The Global Soul*, is that of 'a British subject, an American resident and an Indian citizen' (Iyer, 1988: 25), 'a person with an American alien card and an Indian face and an English accent' (Iyer, 2000: 10). Iyer may have 'an Indian face' but allegedly feels little affinity with India as 'a homeland', imagined or otherwise. Unlike, say, the case of Edward Said, a writer whose life in personal as in critical terms was constructed around the events leading up to and following the creation of the state of Israel, meaning that 'by the early spring of 1948 my entire extended family had been swept out of the place, and has remained in exile ever since' (Said, 1999: xiv), Iyer has no such trauma to which to anchor his constant state of foreignness. Whereas Said and Iyer can thus both be said to be defined by the 'overriding sensation ... of always being out of place' (Said, 1999: 3), their respective approaches to the 'problem' of being 'out of place' could hardly be more different. Said sees this 'overriding sensation' as the symptom of a malaise that needs to be cured if he is ever to be a healthy human being. For Iyer, on the other hand, to be 'out of place' is a state of normalcy rather than a state of exception; the very essence of his identity, the one fixed quality of his character he knows he can rely on rather than a split he wants to heal.

Careful to point out that he does not intend to chart the lives of immigrant workers or refugees but that of his own position as a particular kind of global citizen, accusations of privilege are somewhat mitigated by Iyer's repeated admission that he is very much aware that his position is not representative of the planet as a whole. 'A person like me can't really call himself an exile (who traditionally looked back to a home now lost), or an expatriate (who's generally posted abroad for a living); I'm not really a nomad (whose patterns are guided by the seasons and tradition); and I've never been subject to the refugee's violent disruptions: the Global Soul is best characterized by the fact of falling between categories' (Iyer, 2000: 23). Iyer is fully conscious of the fact that, 'I worry about the effects of E-Mail and transprovincialism, while two-thirds of the people in the world have never used a telephone' (Iyer, 2000: 26). We might castigate Iyer for not consistently attending to the plight of those who do not possess his privileges, but since *The Global Soul* expressly and candidly sets out to examine the status of the privileged global traveller, a sustained discussion of this kind would not be useful. Furthermore, even if *The Global Soul* is, quantitatively speaking, devoted to exploring the notion of the liberating powers of the 'Global Soul', Iyer is in the end critical of the idea of a complete lack of rooting. Suggesting that the notion of the 'Global Soul' is perhaps not so much a question of being at home everywhere as much as a question of never fitting in, Iyer lays out a parallel, and far more hesitant, track to that of the otherwise so jubilant praise of the power of 'discerning Edens where the locals see only Purgatory' (Iyer, 2000: 159). Comparatively weak to begin with, the questioning of rootlessness becomes progressively stronger as the book nears its completion, eventually returning to the place that, even for a 'Global Soul' like Iyer, we will all return to: home.

***

As is the case with *Video Night in Kathmandu*, *The Global Soul* concludes with Japan, the place Iyer finds 'most alien' (Iyer, 1988: 361) of all, a country 'more alien than anywhere I know' yet paradoxically also a place that 'speaks the language I was trained to hear' (Iyer, 2000: 275). Not the Japanese language, which Iyer speaks only haltingly, but the language of foreignness: the fact that, to the Japanese, Iyer will always be *'gaijin*, or outsider person' (Iyer, 2000: 272). That Iyer knows with utmost certainty that this is a place that 'will never be entirely my home' (2000: 273), this is effectively, if paradoxically, what makes it the most homely place of all, the only place in which Iyer feels he can, for once, relax. Stressing that 'a sense of home or neighborhood can emerge only from within' (Iyer, 2000: 282), *The Global Soul* repeats the lesson learned from *Video Night in Kathmandu*: 'I recognise that Japan can appear as soulless, to a native, as sad with loneliness or loss, as London or LA can to me' (294). The final lesson taught by Iyer is that home, as well as travel, is what we make of it.

Granted, the ending of *The Global Soul* reverts to a pastoral, even monastic, move in Iyer's decision to move 'far from anywhere' and discarding all but the most rudimentary of technologies in an attempt at 'living more slowly, and trying to clear some space, away from a world ever more revved up' (Iyer, 2000: 287, 288). Once again, however, Iyer's ability to consider the views of others makes his occasional (and they are rare) lapses into romanticism far more palatable. Iyer is fully aware of the fact that while *he* finds himself most comfortable in a small Japanese town some distance from any major city, this does not mean that we should all do the same. Iyer does not want us to follow his specific example of retreating to the countryside, but to widen our horizons generally to the possibility that *new* homes – homes that are the results of change – are equivalent to the ones handed down to us through generations. 'The homes we choose, in short, deserve a tolerance we might not extend to the homes we inherit, and in a world where we have to work hard to gain a sense of home, we have to exert ourselves just as much to sustain a sense of Other' (Iyer, 2000: 285).

What I would suggest here is that Iyer may offer a way of circumventing the problem identified by Michael Hardt and Antonio Negri in *Empire* (2000) of 'pushing against an open door', of attending to problems that are no longer relevant in a world of global capital that has long since embraced the very 'politics of difference, fluidity, and hybridity' that the postcolonial is supposed to employ 'in order to challenge the binaries and essentialism of modern sovereignty' (Hardt and Negri: 138). For as is the case with *Video Nights in Kathmandu*, so it is with *The Global Soul*; Iyer's approach is not one of writing 'back', nor is it one of 'countering' as suggested by Holland and Huggan; nor is it even that of a 'refocusing' as exemplified by Ghosh's *In an Antique Land*. Rather, it is one of writing *with*, a sort of inversed notion of Hardt and Negri's 'will to be-against' (Hardt and Negri: 218).

Iyer may have an 'investment' in the global, but we all do, at least if Hardt and Negri's model of the contemporary, global world is to be believed. Accordingly, Iyer has little choice *but* to work from the inside of this all-pervasive system. As Revathi Krishnaswamy points out in the introductory chapter to *The Postcolonial and the Global* (2008): 'To globalize or not – that is no longer the question. What kind of globalization – that is the question both postcolonial and globalization studies must grapple with' (15). In a world in which the presence of the global is an irrefutable fact, writing 'back', 'countering' or 'refocusing' risk obsolescence if the impact of the global is played down or, even worse, ignored. It does not mean, however, that the postcolonial is therefore 'insufficient for theorizing contemporary global power' (Hardt and Negri: 138). The globalization debate, whether it is of the damning or the exuberant variant, is prone to depict the (post)colonial as a thing of the past, forgetting that the 'logic of coloniality (or the colonial matrix of power) is constitutive of modern Western and capitalist empires' (Mignolo and Tlostanova, 2008: 119). Global capitalism may, for good and for worse, have inundated the entire planet, yet the former colonial matrix is still in place. It may have been tweaked here and there, dressed up in the latest fashion of contemporary global clothing; it may even have let in a handful of new players, yet the system itself remains largely unchanged as does the bulk of its (postcolonial) legacy. Thus it is not a question of the postcolonial *or* of the global, but of the postcolonial *and* the global.

That Iyer writes from a position within the global capitalist system does not mean that he is automatically blind to the colonial aspects of globalization. At the very least, he successfully manages to dismantle the stereotype of the travel narrative as exclusively Eurocentric, as a challenge to, as the Introduction to this book puts it, the notion of travel as 'a predominantly European activity, an imagined trope connoting modernity, technological advancement and power'. For Iyer, travel is not bound up with a particular mode of seeing and constructing the Other. Unlike the colonial Eurocentric travel narrative that reinforced preconceived notions of the Other, travel is to Iyer a means of getting us to realize that the place we leave behind is not superior to the destination we are headed towards. Here, travel is a fundamental tool for increasing our awareness that while we all need a sense of rooting, this rooting must consistently be renegotiated.

This does not mean that we are all beyond difference, that we should all bond in a heady celebration of unity and sameness that somehow transcends Empire and the colonial. On the contrary, Iyer's admonition for us to continually re-evaluate our notions of home is but one step down a very long and winding road. His is the first step in a journey that may one day take us beyond Empire and the colonial, for Iyer's notion of home is never stable and fixed. This is, however, a good place to start. In the end, *Video Night in Kathmandu* and *The Global Soul* offer us valuable insights for the future, rather than the past, of both postcolonial *and* travel.

Works Cited and Consulted

Appadurai, Arjun (2001) 'Grassroots Globalization and the Research Imagination' in Arjun Appadurai (ed.) *Globalization*. Durham, NC: Duke University Press, 1–21.

Augé, Marc (1992) *Non-places: Introduction to an Anthropology of Supermodernity*. London: Verso.

Baudrillard, Jean (1986) *America*. London: Verso.

Ghosh, Amitav (1992) *In an Antique Land*. London: Granta.

Giddens, Anthony (1990) *The Consequences of Modernity*. Cambridge: Polity Press.

Grewal, Inderpal (2008) 'Amitav Ghosh: Cosmopolitanisms, Literature, Transnationalisms' in Revathi Krishnaswamy and John C. Hawley (eds) *The Post-Colonial and the Global*. Minneapolis: University of Minnesota Press, 178–90.

Grosfoguel, Ramón (2008) 'World-System Analysis and Postcolonial Studies: A Call for a Dialogue from the "Coloniality of Power" Approach' in Revathi Krishnaswamy and John C. Hawley (eds) *The Post-Colonial and the Global*. Minneapolis: University of Minnesota Press, 94–104.

Gupta, Suman (2009) *Globalization and Literature*. Cambridge: Polity Press.

Hardt, Michael and Antonio Negri (2000) *Empire*. Cambridge, MA: Harvard University Press.

Harvey, David (1990) *The Condition of Postmodernity: An Enquiry into the Origins of Cultural Change*. Oxford: Blackwell.

Holland, Patrick and Graham Huggan (1998) *Tourists with Typewriters: Contemporary Reflections on Contemporary Travel Writing*. Ann Arbor: University of Michigan Press.

Iyer, Pico (1988) *Video Night in Kathmandu: And Other Reports from the Not-So-Far East*. London: Bloomsbury, 2001.

Iyer, Pico (2000) *The Global Soul: Jetlag, Shopping Malls and the Search for Home*. London: Bloomsbury.

Kaplan, Caren (1996) *Questions of Travel: Postmodern Discourses of Displacement*. Durham: Duke University Press.

Krishnaswamy, Revathi (2008) 'Connections, Conflicts, Complicities' in Revathi Krishnaswamy and John C. Hawley (eds) *The Post-Colonial and the Global*. Minneapolis: University of Minnesota Press, 2–21.

Langewiesche, William (1996) *Sahara Unveiled: A Journey Across the Desert*. New York: Vintage.

Massey, Doreen (1994) *Space, Place and Gender*. Oxford: Polity Press.

Massey, Doreen (2007) *World City*. Cambridge: Polity Press.

Matthiessen, Peter (1978) *The Snow Leopard*. New York: Penguin.

McLuhan, Marshall (1962) *The Gutenberg Galaxy: The Making of Typographic Man*. University of Toronto Press.

Mignolo, Walter D. and Madina Tlostanova (2008) 'The Logic of Coloniality and the Limits of Postcoloniality' in Revathi Krishnaswamy and John C. Hawley (eds) *The Post-Colonial and the Global*. Minneapolis: University of Minnesota Press, 109–23.

Molz, Jennie Germann (2006) 'Cosmopolitan Bodies: Fit to Travel and Travelling to Fit', *Body & Society* **12**(3): 1–21.

Phillips, Caryl (2000) *The Atlantic Sound*. New York: Alfred A. Knopf.

Rushdie, Salman (2006) 'Imaginary Homelands' in Bill Ashcroft, Gareth Griffiths and Helen Tiffin (eds) *The Post-Colonial Studies Reader*. New York: Routledge, 428–34.

Said, Edward (1999) *Out of Place*. London: Granta.

Said, Edward (2006) 'The Mind of Winter' in Bill Ashcroft, Gareth Griffiths and Helen Tiffin (eds) *The Post-Colonial Studies Reader*. New York: Routledge, 439–42.

Sassen, Saskia (1991) *The Global City: New York, London, Tokyo*. Princeton University Press.

Sklair, Leslie (2008) 'Discourses of Globalization: A Transnational Capitalist Class Analysis' in Revathi Krishnaswamy and John C. Hawley (eds) *The Post-Colonial and the Global*. Minneapolis: University of Minnesota Press, 215–27.

van der Post, Laurens (1958) *The Lost World of the Kalahari*. London: Harcourt Brace.

Notes

1. In van der Post's case 'a search for some pure remnant of the unique and almost vanished First People of my native land, the Bushmen of Africa' (van der Post, 1958: 3); for Matthiessen 'the last enclave of pure Tibetan culture left on earth' (Matthiessen, 1978: 4) as well as, of course, the continually elusive snow leopard.

2. By retaining terms like 'West' and 'East', Iyer initially sustains an Orientalist East–West binary. As the reading of *The Global Soul* in particular will illustrate, Iyer is eventually able to transcend such binarisms. Still, it is important to realize that while globalization may *seem* to have rendered the binarism between 'East' and 'West' obsolete, the dichotomy continues to operate on many, albeit often hidden, levels. When referring to 'East' and 'West' in the following, I do not therefore presume that any such entities exist anywhere else but in discourse, nor that such binarisms are sustainable, only that they are still very much in play.

3. As one of the most famous (and self-aggrandizing) patriarchs of postmodernity, Baudrillard's bombastic descriptions of 'primitive' American culture certainly are not humble. 'We in Europe possess the art of thinking, of analyzing things

and reflecting on them' (Baudrillard, 1986: 23), he remarks, clearly viewing himself as a master analyst, a brilliant specimen of an already gifted, but ailing, civilization. With the power relation safely secured with, what to Baudrillard, seemed an unassailable American hegemony, the former European master turned underdog can be allowed a little ridicule to soften the blow of his defeat, making it a little easier to swallow facetious comments like 'Americans may have no identity, but they do have wonderful teeth' (34) that we probably would not have tolerated had he been the one, and not Iyer, who was describing video nights in Kathmandu.

4. As David Harvey pointed out two decades ago, the revolution in transport and communication that was supposed to level out differences has in fact done the exact opposite, for 'the less important the spatial barriers, the greater the sensitivity of capital to the variations of place within space, and the greater the incentive for places to be differentiated in ways attractive to capital' (Harvey, 1990: 295–6).

4
Travel Writing and Postcoloniality: Caryl Phillips's *The Atlantic Sound*

María Lourdes López Ropero

I

This chapter approaches Caryl Phillips's travel book, *The Atlantic Sound* (2000), as a postcolonial travelogue. My contention is that the postcolonial travelogue foregrounds new developments that have taken place within travel writing, distinguishing it from its 18th- and 19th-century colonial roots. No longer an instrument of imperial expansion, travel writing has become a powerful vehicle of cultural critique, particularly for postcolonial writers such as Caryl Phillips. Moreover, I suggest that contemporary travel writers are more subject-oriented, and their need to travel and record their experiences often stems from a personal urge to solve inner conflicts about home and belonging.

In *The Atlantic Sound*, Caryl Phillips – a prolific novelist, essayist and playwright – visits three cities involved in the Atlantic slave trade. The venture depicted in the travel text is, however, not only a revisionist excavation of Europe's investment in the trade; but, more importantly, it is an exploration of the elusive notions of home and cultural identity that are troubled by the complex background of a Caribbean-born author, who is raised in England and resides in the United States. Section II of this chapter charts the genre's adaptability to the changed socio-historical conditions of the late 20th century, which elaborates on the notion of the postcolonial travelogue. Section III offers a close reading of *The Atlantic Sound* and explores the contributions of cultural critics to the ongoing debate over cultural identity.

II

Subject-orientation and social awareness may well seem an improbable combination. However, this partnership becomes more cohesive if we bear in mind that the personal urge to travel may respond, as we will see, to an attempt to solve some inner conflict whose examination entails delving into broader socio-historical issues. The foregrounding of the traveller's subjectivity, together with the awakening of social consciousness, are therefore the two most prominent features of contemporary travel writing.

The resilience of travel writing in the late 20th century is partly due to its specialization in the hands of postcolonial, women and gay authors. Lured by the genre's potential for cultural critique, these countertravellers have broken the stereotype of the travel writer as white, male, middle class and heterosexual (Holland and Huggan, 1998). It may be argued that these specialized kinds of travellers have intensified the features that characterize contemporary manifestations of the genre. Far from wishing to delight the reader with the exotic or to boost national identity, *countertravel writing* aims at shaking the reader's complacency through the 'unmapping' of 'mapped' world-views, to borrow Richard Phillips's words (1997: 143). In so doing, it dismantles the Eurocentric views that gave rise to the genre.

Korte (2000) maintains that postcolonial authors have infused their travelogues with the preoccupation with identity and belonging that permeates postcolonial literature. Furthermore, she believes that this inner drive may well be the main reason for them to travel: 'To many postcolonial travelers ... the question of defining one's home still seems to be more urgent than for other travelers, and the search for a home may even be their primary motive for travel' (170). With its twofold investment in the personal and the social, the postcolonial travelogue is arguably an epitome of the changes that have shaped contemporary travel writing. Although Korte surveys a number of authors from the postcolonial world in her study – Salman Rushdie, India; Margaret Lawrence, Canada; Laurens van der Post, South Africa, to cite a few – she highlights the prolific contribution to the postcolonial travelogue of writers of Caribbean descent such as V. S. Naipaul, Ferdinand Dennis and Caryl Phillips (155).

The European Tribe (1987), an account of Caryl Phillips's one-year trip across Europe, sprang from the author's dilemma of 'feeling both of and not of' Europe (xv). Conceived as an instrument to increase the author's self-awareness as a black European, *The European Tribe* turned out to be a scathing study of the widespread racialism of an increasingly multicultural 1980s Europe. Similarly, in his next travelogue, *The Atlantic Sound* – which is outside the chronological scope of Korte's study – Phillips's revision of Europe's historical involvement in the slave trade through his trips across the Atlantic provides him with an opportunity to take up his perennial preoccupation with notions of home, belonging and cultural identity. My analysis of *The Atlantic Sound* revolves around this dual focus.

III

In *The Atlantic Sound*, Phillips explores what Paul Gilroy has heuristically defined as the Black Atlantic world, 'one single, complex unit' drawing together the cultures of people of African descent (Gilroy, 1999: 15). In his journeys across the Atlantic, Phillips revisits the cities historically engaged in the slave trade, an economy whereby English goods were exchanged on the African west coast for human captives, who were then sold into slavery for work on North American and Caribbean plantations in return for cash or exotic products that would be sold back in England. The body of this work consists of three chapters dealing with the three juncture points of the slave triangle – Liverpool, England; Elmina, Ghana; and Charleston, South Carolina – the Prologue and Epilogue depicting two side trips to the Caribbean and Israel respectively.[1]

In terms of form, *The Atlantic Sound* reflects the hybridity that characterizes the travel writing genre, which has accordingly been described as 'hydra' (Glaser, 1991: 48), or *'omnium gatherum'* (Korte, 2000: 5). Some scholars attribute the critical neglect suffered by travel writing to its generic elusiveness (Kowalewski, 1992: 8), which has caused *The Atlantic Sound* to be reviewed not only as a travelogue (Adebayo, 2000; Neel, 2000), but, less compromisingly, as a non-fiction book (Alibhai-Brown, 2000; Childers, 2002) or a book-length essay (Ledent, 2000). In effect, the travel narrative occupies a space of 'discursive conflict' (Holland and Huggan: 10), borrowing freely from a wide array of disciplines such as history, social science, journalism, autobiography and fiction. If, as I have argued elsewhere, Phillips's fiction idiosyncratically straddles several genres, in his new piece the author exploits the formal flexibility that is characteristic of the travelogue. Accordingly, Phillips unleashes the encyclopaedic drive of the travel writer, unashamedly displaying his great erudition. As a result, *The Atlantic Sound* is a melange of intriguing historical passages, geographical descriptions, fictionalized narratives, interviews, newspaper articles, letters, poems, extracts from courtroom proceedings, speeches, an endless string of epigraphs and so on. Besides, Phillips is able to adjust the Western moulds of the genre to the contours of a different episteme; thus, in one of the sections the narrative is interwoven with an anonymous African choral voice – 'The African dispatches the money to the white man ... African voices begin to whisper' (17, 30) – that gives the text an oral quality.

The fact that Phillips chooses to start his Atlantic tour with a trip from the Caribbean to England is symptomatic of the marked personal investment of his travel writing. In the Introduction to *The European Tribe* Phillips explained that the identity 'conundrum' (8) triggering his European tour was rooted in his growing up in culturally exclusive 1970s Britain. Significantly, the Prologue to his new travelogue strikes an equally personal note. It features Phillips's trip on a banana boat from the Caribbean island of Guadalupe to the English city of Dover in the attempt to reopen 'a chapter of [his] own personal narrative' (16). The author refers to the migration of his parents' generation – the *Windward Generation* – to England in the 1950s, which he had fictionalized in his first novel, *The Final Passage* (1985). Though unconsciously, Phillips himself had crossed the Atlantic in his mother's arms as a four-month-old baby.

Through this Atlantic crossing as an adult, Phillips explores the extent to which he can relate to his parents' generation, to soon find out that he is a very different kind of traveller. Unlike his parents, he is not a colonial going to the mother country with a sense of 'hope and expectation', but a well-to-do black British citizen of Caribbean descent travelling towards Britain 'with a sense of knowledge and propriety' (16). Although his choice of a banana boat may stem from the need to invest his experience with a certain degree of authenticity, Phillips insistently complains about the inconveniences of the vessel. He is glad that his cabin has two windows instead of a porthole, and describes sleeping in the boat as 'being on top of a washing machine that is stuck on the spin cycle' (6). As a reviewer has put it: 'You feel his [Phillips's] depressions, the tedium, his forbearance as he lives through each day' (Alibhai-Brown, 2000: 12). Moreover, just before the boat's departure, Phillips acknowledges that he is already longing to take the black taxi cab that will 'whisk' (4) him to his West London home.

In fact, the travelling persona that Phillips projects in this section often seems aloof and elitist, slipping into gestures that we may associate with what David Spurr identifies as tropes of colonial discourse. At times, Phillips perceives the sight from the ship as what Spurr would call a 'negative space' characterized 'by emptiness and absence' (Spurr, 1993: 92–3). Thus, he describes the Atlantic very unromantically as a 'vast unresponsive expanse of sea and sky' (2000: 11). His description of the Costa Rican town of Limon seems indebted to Froud:

> After an hour wandering about the town center, I decide that Limon is little more than a dismal, down-at-heel Caribbean coastal port ... The population is a mixture of black, Hispanic and Indian, most of

whom seem to be idling the day away assiduously not looking for work ... but despite its shabby exterior, Limon does, however, boast telephone booths. (2000: 6–7)

Yet the view of Phillips as a mere Victorian seeing-man – to borrow a term from Pratt (1992: 7) – trying to legitimize his civilizing mission, fails to recognize his sensitivity to neocolonial tendencies in the 'postcolonial' world. Rather, the occurrence of this discourse in postcolonial texts may reveal, as Jesus Varela has said speaking of Bertram Francis's bleak perception of St. Kitts in *A State of Independence* (1986), 'disappointment at seeing the chaos and underdevelopment of the Third World' (Varela, 1999: 401). From the vantage point that his long stay in England as a student has granted him, Bertram fears the ineptitude of the native ruling class and the looming spectrum of American imperialism in the newly independent Caribbean nation. Similarly, in *The Atlantic Sound*, Phillips criticizes the exploitation of the Burmese crew of the boat by the Germans and openly condemns the treatment given by Britain to her helpless colonial offspring back in the 1950s. The following passage emphasizes the colonials' subsequent shattering of expectations in the famed metropolis:

West Indian immigrants, such as my parents ... travelled in the hope that the mother country would remain true to her promise, that she would protect the children of her empire. However, shortly after disembarkation the West Indian immigrants of the fifties and sixties discovered that the realities of this new world were likely to be more challenging than they had anticipated. In fact, much to their dismay, they discovered that the mother country had little, if any, desire to embrace her colonial offspring. (15)

More accurately, in his Atlantic crossing Phillips shuttles between the roles of insider and outsider, between the sensitized son of Caribbean immigrants and the educated British scholar.

Such role-shifting amounts to Phillips's grappling with his inability to pin down his cultural allegiances. Though able to sympathize with the plight of his parents' generation, Phillips is aware that he holds a very different subject position; in spite of his 'being in' British society, the writer has repeatedly complained about not being perceived as 'of' the society (1997: 17). In fact, Phillips himself has shown uneasiness about the critics' penchant for labelling him as a 'British writer, a black writer, a black British writer, a West Indian writer, a Caribbean writer, a black

Caribbean writer, and so on and so on' (1992: 25). Not surprisingly, the author has been regarded as a paradigmatic diasporic intellectual, 'in a state of perpetual wandering' (Williams, n.d.: 1). In this light, neither his transatlantic crossing nor his arrival in England are emotionally loaded experiences. This trend towards undercutting all notions of original identity pervades the whole travelogue.

Once a personal note has been struck, Phillips undertakes the account of his Atlantic journeys. His visit to Liverpool reopens a world the reader may have perceived as closed, for it unearths the city's heavy entanglement in the slave trade. Touring Liverpool's most remarkable buildings – the Town Hall, St George's Hall, Nelson's Fountain – trademarks of the city's past imperial splendour, Phillips puzzles over the fact that 'history is so physically present, yet so glaringly absent from people's consciousness in the Northern city' (2000: 93). In highlighting Liverpool's 'historical amnesia' (79), Phillips restates the claim he put forward in his first travelogue, that Europe 'does not understand the high price of her churches, art galleries and architecture' (1987: 128). Another living proof of Liverpool's history of racial abuse is the segregation of its black population, confined to the Toxteth area, which reminds Phillips of 'scores of other British inner-city areas that have entered a stage of terminal decline' (2000: 88). Toxteth is not very different either from the segregated areas he had visited on his European tour, such as Kreutzburg, Berlin's Turkish ghetto, or the Parisian black ghetto of Belleville; Phillips found that even a 'sanctuary of liberalism' such as Scandinavia 'crumpled to pieces at the first brushes with multi-cultural experience', as Socorro Suàrez (1998) has incisively remarked in her analysis of *The European Tribe* (160). Significantly, Phillips introduces us to the hidden history of Liverpool through the story of Ghanaian John Emmanuel Ocansey, the son of a wealthy palm oil merchant who had travelled to that same city in 1881 in order to sue the English dealer who had cheated his father. Ocansey's trip happened at a time when the British slave trade had been outlawed, but West African–British commercial relations still followed an exploitative pattern.

In spite of this, Phillips's indictment of European imperialism is less harsh in *The Atlantic Sound* than in his previous travelogue. Certainly, the tone of his protest is much less strident. Whereas in *The European Tribe* he exhorted Europe 'to purge herself' and 'perform a historical strip-tease' (127), now Phillips does not see any purpose in arousing a sense of guilt among Liverpudlians. In turn, he concedes, though tentatively, that a certain obliviousness about the past of the city is not unnatural: 'Maybe this is the modern condition and Liverpool is merely acting out this reality with an honest vigour' (2000: 93). The same applies to

Charleston, the next city on his itinerary. It is Sullivan Island, a sandbar where slaves were seasoned after their arrival on the American coast, which has become a summer resort for the wealthy. Phillips rejoices in the undisturbed ease with which black and white Charlestonians enjoy the city's *Festival of African and Caribbean Art* (211–13). As Ernest Renan argued, and Benedict Anderson and Homi Bhabha after him, 'Forgetting ... is a crucial factor in the creation of a nation' (1995: 11). Obliviousness concerning certain deeds of violence, such as the trade with human beings that concerns us here, is at the core of all nations as political formations.

Thus, Phillips casts a sceptical eye over Stephen, the reproachful young guide who takes him around Liverpool, and whom Phillips describes as a 'tightly wound metal coil' (79). Unlike Phillips, who understands that the city's involvement in the slave trade should not necessarily have a bearing on the way modern Liverpudlians perceive themselves, Stephen is obsessed with their refusal to acknowledge the city's African history. The point that Phillips is trying to make through his portrayal of Stephen is that in his outspoken anti-Semitism, pan-Africanism and in his striking disregard of foreign blacks, the guide reveals a highly arguable notion of cultural identity. Stuart Hall's reflections on identity may be useful to understand Phillips's stance: 'Cultural identities come from somewhere, have histories. But like everything that is historical, they undergo constant transformation. Far from being eternally fixed in some essentialized past, they are subject to the continuous play of history, culture and power' (Hall, 1994: 394). The guide's militancy reflects a longing for the recovery of a lost past, impervious to transformation. Phillips's fluid notion of identity is further illustrated by the change undergone by the female protagonist in his novel *Cambridge* (1991). Emily Cartwright's three-month sojourn in her father's West Indian plantation has altered her perception of England as 'a home'. Asked about a return she endlessly postpones, she answers:

> England. Emily smiled to herself ... as though this England was a dependable garment that one simply slipped into or out of according to one's whim. Did he [the plantation's doctor] not understand that people grow and change? Did he not understand that one day a discovery might be made that this country-garb is no longer of a correct measure? (177)

Emily's detachment from her father and her unwanted English suitor has caused her to become aware of and to outgrow the constraints of

Victorian cultural codes. She consequently does not feel a bonding with her former home anymore. Identity is not 'dependable' but unstable, emerging out of the subject's constant positioning in response to specific conditions.

In the African section of the travelogue, ironically titled 'Homeward Bound', Phillips elaborates his anti-essentialist views on cultural identity. At the same time, however, we get a glimpse of the author's own yearning for a sense of wholeness. Asked about his nationality by a flight partner on his way to Ghana, Phillips complains about the complexity of 'the question', which he can only 'attempt to answer' in the 'familiar flustered' way (2000: 98). We in fact sense his hankering after the rootedness that this man can lay claim to as 'an African. A Ghanaian. A whole man. A man of one place' (100). Yet, as the title of the section anticipates, irony will pervade Phillips's pronouncements during his African sojourn.

Phillips visits Elmina, a city on the coast of Ghana famous for its magnificent slave fort, during the celebration of *Panafest*, which, he says mockingly, 'according to the publicity material ... is to be a time when the diasporan family returns to Mother Africa to celebrate the arts, creativity and intellectual achievements of the Pan African world' (133). Elmina is, in fact, one of the fortified sites of slave-trading activity that have recently become places of pilgrimage and cultural tourism for the most affluent members of the African diaspora. Phillips helplessly watches the 'diasporan excesses' of the festival, such as the slaughter of a ram and the wreath-laying to commemorate the victims of the 'African holocaust' (38); or the tee shirts displaying a human cargo in a slave ship with the logo 'Never forgive, never forget', paradigmatic of the 'continual rush to overstatement' (148) that characterizes the festival. The notion of cultural identity underlying festivals like *Panafest* is the target of Gilroy's criticism in his study of race and black nationalism, for identity 'ceases to be an ongoing process of self-making and social interaction. It becomes instead a thing to be possessed and displayed' (2001: 103). Moreover, he daringly links such spectacular manifestations of identity to the encroachment of fascism into contemporary black nationalism (7).

Unlike most of the *Panafest* revellers, Phillips does not perceive Africa as his home, but rather feels that a contrived brotherhood based on the restrictive axis of phenotype is constantly being pressed upon him. Whereas the spirit of *Panafest* aims at a recovery of a lost past in an ancestral homeland, Phillips argues that 'Africa cannot make anybody feel whole' (173), implying that identity is not about a return to roots, but rather about 'coming to terms with our routes' (Hall, 1992: 4). As he has acknowledged in *The European Tribe*, Phillips cannot write in Yoruba or Kikuyu, 'anymore than a black youth born in Peckham or Middlesbrough can hope to feel at home in Addis Ababa or Kingston, Jamaica' (1987: 126). Oscillating between different cultural affiliations throughout his Atlantic journeys, Phillips once more refuses to tilt the balance towards a specific set of identity claims.

The scepticism pervading *The Atlantic Sound* regarding notions of home and identity reaches its climax in the Epilogue. In this brief section entitled 'Exodus', Phillips narrates his stay with a community of African-Americans exiled in a small town in the Negev desert of Israel. These exiles believe themselves to be descendants of the Hebrews dispersed throughout the world, and have thus undertaken an exodus to their 'true homeland'. Again, the stance of this community is based on a territorialized and exclusive notion of identity, one that, to quote Gilroy, 'closes down the possibility of communication across the gulf between one heavily defended island of particularity and its equally well fortified neighbours, between one national encampment and others' (Gilroy, 2001: 103). Not surprisingly, cynicism pervades Phillips's remarks on these black Zionists encamped in the Negev desert. Watching them move around their village performing their chores, Phillips perceives them as 'circus clowns', 'groups of costumed African-Americans wandering the compound together' (215). His utter bewilderment at their self-inflicted isolation finds its reflection in the fractured syntax that the author deploys throughout: 'African-American people. African-American children. In costumes. Who have come to the desert. The lost tribes of Israel. Found in Chicago, Washington, New York' (216). For these black Hebrews, their exclusive identity is a sanctuary against the 'evils' – homosexuality, welfare, obscene music, to cite just a few – of the Western Babylons they have left behind (169).

There is very little room for wonder in *The Atlantic Sound*. Not surprisingly, a critic has charged Phillips with being 'always too controlled' (Alibhai-Brown, 2000: 12). One in fact senses that in Phillips's travel writing the travelled world is secondary to the traveller's preconceived notions of it. His sojourns in Liverpool, Ghana or the Negev desert hold very few surprises but rather seem to confirm the author's views prior to the journey. This is even more conspicuous in *The European Tribe*, where setting is often a mere backcloth to Phillips's musings on certain topics. His visit to Venice, for instance, furnishes the author with the opportunity to render his own reading of *Othello* and *The Merchant of Venice*, two plays featuring cultural Others – the black and the Jew respectively – stigmatized by 16th-century Italian society. Accordingly, all the black communities that Phillips encounters on his Atlantic journeys fail to challenge restricted views of cultural identity.

IV

Phillips's final words in his travelogue insist that 'it is futile to walk into the face of History' (221), summarizing the message he has been trying to convey throughout his Atlantic sojourn. Identity is not in the past to be found, but in the future to be made.

Therefore, though roots are important insofar as they are part of our sense of identity, it is the routes that we take that should eventually determine the way we perceive ourselves. Ancestral homelands are places of no return; though liable to be placed under scrutiny, the violence of history cannot be redressed and should not be used to stir hatred, thus widening the gulf that already severs different racial groups. In this realization lies Phillips's detachment from the places and the black communities that he meets. While *The Atlantic Sound* has been praised for its vivid portraiture and reportage in the manner of Jonathan Raban's or V. S. Naipaul's travelogues, it has also been criticized for the author's detachment, scepticism and excessive intellectual engagement. Diran Adebayo, for instance, asserts that Phillips does not 'bare his soul': 'This book is billed as a personal quest, but I wanted to know more about this Caribbean-born and England-bred author's own deep feelings for home and how they were affected, or not, by his journey' (2000: 26). More insightfully, Bénédicte Ledent has attributed Phillips's unsentimental stance to the 'mature, undogmatic and fluid vision' of identity he has achieved after repeatedly probing into these issues throughout his prolific writing career (2000: 199). Phillips's detachment is an eloquent statement in itself. Though a good companion to *The Atlantic Sound*, *The European Tribe* develops a much harsher critique of European imperialism and conducts a more desperate search for answers to the author's identity conundrum. The same tone pervades Phillips's first novel, *The Final Passage* (1985), where 1950s England is portrayed as a most unwelcoming mother country reminding her colonial offspring of their undesirability with graffiti like 'If you want a nigger neighbour vote Labour' (122). The 13-year gap spanning the publication of the two travelogues accounts for the tempered tone pervading the most recent one.

The shift away from the rhetoric of victimization found in earlier works such as *The Final Passage*, through which Phillips's writing has gained in complexity and appeal, began to manifest itself in the novels written after the publication of *The European Tribe*. In the 'Heartland' section of *Higher Ground* (1989), set in an African slave fort in the heyday of the trade, both enslavers and slaves are portrayed as victims of historical economic contingencies. The Governor of the fort meditates on this idea on his death bed: 'I fear the wheel of history has spun us all into a difficult situation, and no amount of acclimatizing by you [a native interpreter] or by me is going to heal the wound that this economic necessity has inflicted upon our human souls' (51). Avoiding demonizing whites, Phillips brings African complicity under scrutiny by choosing a black collaborationist as a the narrator of the section and by enlisting the cooperation of African leaders, who allow their villages to be raided in exchange for profit. Similarly, the Prologue to *Crossing the River* (1993) features the remorseful voice of an African father who sold his three children to the captain of a slave ship after a bad crop. The whimsical spin of history blurs the distinction between torturers and victims.

British men and women have been writing about travel to colonies and other territories for a much longer time than people from formerly colonized countries have been writing back in this genre. Therefore, there is not yet a large body of travel literature by, for example, Anglo-Caribbean authors such as Caryl Phillips. However, postcolonial authors, alongside other *countertravellers*, are partly responsible for the steady growth of a traditionally Western genre in modern times. Travel writing's inherent concern with spatial displacement and its potential for cultural critique have proved a most adequate ground for authors to stage the issues central to the 'postcolonial condition'. Phillips's wanderings within and also beyond the spectral triangle drawn in *The Atlantic Sound* have allowed him to deal with a wide array of issues such as the complex cultural affiliations of people of African descent, their dispersal in the Atlantic world or their revision of Western history. Furthermore, the subjective drive underlying *The Atlantic Sound*, Phillips's grappling with his complex identity as both black and British, is emblematic of a highly personal inflection in contemporary manifestations of the genre.

Works Cited and Consulted

Adams, Percy (1983) *Travel Literature and the Evolution of the Novel*. Kentucky: University Press of Kentucky.
Adebayo, Diran (2000) 'Africa and Home'. *The Times* 11 May: 26.

Alibhai-Brown, Yasmin (2000) 'Three Sides to the Story'. *The Observer* 21 May: 12.

Anderson, Benedict (1991) *Imagined Communities*. London: Verso.

Bell, Ian (1995) 'To See Ourselves: Travel Narratives and National Identity in Contemporary Britain' in Ian Bell (ed.) *Peripheral Visions: Images of Nationhood in Contemporary British Fiction*. Cardiff: University of Wales Press.

Bhabha, Homi (1995) 'DissemiNation: Time, Narrative and the Margins of the Modern Nation' in Homi Bhabha (ed.) *Nation and Narration*. London: Routledge, 291–321.

Childers, Doug (2002) 'Leaving Home: Caryl Phillips's *The Atlantic Sound*', *WAG Book Review*. http://thewag.net/00philli.htm/, accessed 24 January 2002.

Gilroy, Paul (1999) *The Black Atlantic*. London: Verso.

Gilroy, Paul (2001) *Between Camps: Nations, Cultures and the Allure of Race*. London: Penguin.

Glaser, Elton (1991) 'Hydra and Hybrid: Travel Writing as a Genre'. *North Dakota Quarterly* 59(3): 48–53.

Hall, Stuart (1992) 'Introduction: Who Needs Identity?' in Stuart Hall and Paul de Guy (eds) *Questions of Cultural Identity*. London: Sage, 1–17.

Hall, Stuart (1994) 'Cultural Identity and Diaspora' in Patrick Williams and Laura Chrisman (eds) *Colonial Discourse and Post-Colonial Theory: A Reader*. New York: Columbia University Press, 392–403.

Holland, Patrick and Graham Huggan (1998) *Tourists with Typewriters: Critical Reflections on Contemporary Travel Writing*. Ann Arbor: University of Michigan Press.

Inderpal, Grewal (1996) *Home and Harem: Nation, Gender, Empire, and the Cultures of Travel*. Durham, NC: Duke University Press.

Korte, Barbara (2000) *English Travel Writing from Pilgrimages to Postcolonial Explorations*. Basingstoke: Palgrave Macmillan.

Kowalewski, Michael (1992) 'Introduction: The Modern Literature of Travel' in Michael Kowalewski (ed.) *Temperamental Journeys: Essays on the Modern Literature of Travel*. Athens: University of Georgia Press, 1–16.

Ledent, Bénédicte (2000) 'Ambiguous Visions of Home: The Paradoxes of Diasporic Belonging in Caryl Phillips's *The Atlantic Sound*', *EnterText* 1(1): 198–211. http://brunel.ac.uk/faculty/arts/EnterText/Ledent.pdf/, accessed 24 January 2002.

López Ropero, María Lourdes (2002) 'Irony's Political Edge: Genre Pastiche in Caryl Phillips's *Cambridge*' in Ramon Plo-Alastrue and Maria Martínez-Alfro (eds) *Beyond Borders: Re-Defining Generic and Ontological Boundaries*. Heidelberg: Carl Winter Universitatsverlag, 131–37.

Matos, Jacinta (1992) 'Old Journeys Revisited: Aspects of Postwar English Travel Writing' in Michael Kowalewski (ed.) *Temperamental Journeys: Essays on the Modern Literature of Travel*. Athens: University of Georgia Press, 215–29.

Neel, Eric (2000) 'Sound Travels: *The Atlantic Sound* by Caryl Phillips', *Newcity Chicago*: http://newcitychicago.com/chicago/words-2000-11-16-791.html/, accessed 24 January 2002.

Phillips, Caryl (1985) *The Final Passage*. London: Vintage.

Phillips, Caryl (1986) *A State of Independence*. London: Faber and Faber.

Phillips, Caryl (1987) *The European Tribe*. London: Faber and Faber.

Phillips, Caryl (1989) *Higher Ground*. New York: Vintage.

Phillips, Caryl (1991) *Cambridge*. New York: Vintage.

Phillips, Caryl (1992) 'West Indian Writing Abroad: Naipaul and the New Generation', *Caribbean Review of Books* 3: 16, 19, 24, 25, 27.

Phillips, Caryl (1993) *Crossing the River*. London: Bloomsbury.

Phillips, Caryl (1997) 'George Lamming Talks to Caryl Phillips', *Wasafiri* 26: 10–17.

Phillips, Caryl (2000) *The Atlantic Sound*. London: Faber & Faber.

Phillips, Richard (1997) *Mapping Men and Empire: A Geography of Adventure*. London: Routledge.

Pratt, Mary Louise (1992) *Imperial Eyes: Travel Writing and Transculturation*. London: Routledge.

Renan, Ernest (1995) 'What Is a Nation?' in Homi Bhabha (ed.) *Nation and Narration*. London: Routledge, 8–22.

Said, Edward (1978) *Orientalism*. London: Penguin.

Spurr, David (1993) *The Rhetoric of Empire*. Durham: Duke University Press.

Suàrez Lafuente, Socorro (1988) 'The Slippery Boundaries of Somewhere Else: Caryl Phillips's *The European Tribe*' in Doireann McDermott and Susan Ballyn (eds) *A Passage to Somewhere Else*. Barcelona: PPU, 157–60.

Thubron, Colin (1984) 'Travel Writing Today: Its Rise and Its Dilemma' in A. N. Wilson (ed.) *Essays by Diverse Hands: Being the Transactions of the Royal Society of Literature*. London: Boydell, 167–81.

Varela Zapata, J. (1999) 'Translating One's Own Culture: Coming Back from the Metropolis in Caryl Phillips's *A State of Independence*' in Isabel Carrera Suarez, Aurora Garcia Fernandez and M. S. Suarez Lafuete (eds) *Translating Cultures*. Sydney: Dangaroo Press, 397–406.

Williams, Bronwyn (n.d.) 'A State of Perpetual Wandering: Diaspora and Black British Writers'. *Jouvert: A Journal of Postcolonial Studies* 3(3), http://www.social. chas.ncsu.edu/jouvert/v3i3/willia.htm/, accessed 11 April 2000.

Note

1. The motif of travelling is not confined to the author's travelogues, but also reverberates throughout much of his fiction. It is only in his first two novels, *The Final Passage* (1985) and *A State of Independence* (1986) that Phillips maintains a narrow spatial focus concentrating on England and the Caribbean. In keeping with his preoccupation with fragmentation and dispersion within the Black Diaspora, there is a tendency in Phillips's fiction towards shuttling between continents and times. *Crossing the River* (1993), an emblematic example of this tendency, takes the reader on a journey from Liberia in the 1830s, to the American Wild West, ending up in a Yorkshire village during the Second World War.

5
Decolonizing Travel: James/ Jan Morris's Geographies

Richard Phillips

Travel writing, as Justin D. Edwards and Rune Graulund point out in the Introduction to this book, has been 'demonized', dismissed as a form of colonial discourse. 'Though studies in travel writing remain a lively critical field,' they argue, 'existing investigations of the genre tend to criticize it for perpetuating rather than dismantling colonial paradigms'. Similar claims could be made about related literary forms including adventure fiction and exploration narratives, and of the experiences and narratives they describe, all of which are routinely dismissed as colonial discourse, ideological constructions that speak mainly of power. Travel and travel writing have been vehicles for imperialism, certainly, but also for anti-imperialism and for counter-hegemonic projects that intersect with anti-imperialism such as progressive gender, race and class politics (Phillips, 1997: 12–20), though this has arguably received limited recognition in the critical literature. For the most part, travel writing is labelled an imperial medium, which chronicled and sometimes furthered colonization, doing so particularly vigorously in the Victorian period (see Said 1978; Pratt, 1992; Blunt, 1994). Meanwhile, relationships between travel writing and decolonization, particularly in the second half of the 20th century, remain relatively unexplored. In this chapter, I argue against labelling travel writing in any simple way, and work towards a more nuanced reading of the medium's colonial and postcolonial politics and possibilities. I do so through the figure and oeuvre of a contemporary British travel writer, who is equally impossible to pigeonhole: James/Jan Morris.

Morris's career has spanned the second half of the 20th century and beyond, a period in which Britain lost her empire but in which many of the patterns of imperialism have remained – in other words, a period in which there is still a place and a need for anti-imperialism. Much of

Morris's writing comes across as bubbly, light, and resistant to serious readings. Perhaps this is why the book identified by its publisher as 'the first major study of Jan Morris' should be so slim (110 pages) and uncritical. This contribution to the University of Wales Press *Writers of Wales Series,* written with Morris's cooperation, consists mostly of glossy, celebratory blurb. The author gushes, for example, that 'the irrepressible spirit that is Jan Morris shines like a sparkling beacon' (Clements, 1988: 62). Yet, to gloss Morris in this way is to miss important opportunities for understanding the relationships between travel writing, colonialism and decolonization, which run through her work. Alison Blunt argues that the light, self-deprecating and in some respects self-effacing tone of women travel writers such as Mary Kingsley was in fact a product of conventions, imposed on such writers, to write in a manner befitting their gender. These women should not take themselves too seriously, and should not surprise their readers too much. Beneath their bubbly prose, we can sometimes find a significant writer, with more to say than is generally apparent.

Since the publication of Clements's study of Morris, two full-length books about this author have appeared in print, which begin to explore and chart her work in more detail. Clements's second book about this author, *Around the World in Eighty Years* (2006), presents essays on the subject by 21 writers, while Gillian Fenwick's *Traveling Genius: The Writing Life of Jan Morris* (2008) provides an overview of Morris's work and its immediate reception. Fenwick implicitly underlines the lack of scholarly debate about Morris – the select bibliography of secondary sources she includes is composed almost entirely of brief reviews in newspapers and magazines, while Fenwick herself is consumed largely with reviewing Morris's work rather than developing an argument about its content or significance. Her monograph is a welcome addition to an otherwise thin critical field, though, and it helps to establish the case for reading Morris in the context of other more obviously serious and literary travel writers, such as those examined elsewhere in this book.

Jan Morris has advised would-be travellers to find a purpose, however trivial it may be: she suggests food, architecture, threads of history, almost anything will do. As a writer and a traveller, Morris has pursued all these things herself; but I will suggest that her journey has not been as casual or eclectic as it might first appear, and that her travel writing has a more serious and significant purpose, or series of purposes. Frantz Fanon once reflected that 'In the world through which I travel, I am endlessly creating myself' (1986: 229). Writing in French, he chose his words carefully: 's'acheminer' means to travel with purpose: 'to make one's way towards, head for' (1952: 220; see also Duval and Marr, 1995). Of course, Morris and Fanon are radically different figures, but Fanon's words give some insight into how we might read Morris: as a travel writer who chronicled decolonization, not only in the world around her but in her own body and identity/subjectivity.

James/Jan Morris's career as a traveller and travel writer describes a heady and unsettling journey: from conventionally masculine and thoroughly establishment, imperial adventures to a series of quieter and more complex stories and spaces, in which imperial values and the imperial traveller are progressively and reciprocally destabilized and reinvented. These transformations track Morris's own, from the celebrated reporter who accompanied and described the 1953 Everest Expedition, and later found time to write a vivid trilogy on the British Empire which is still one of the most accessible and engaging histories of its subject, continuing through to the groundbreaking, autobiographical account of Morris's sex change, also written as a form of travel narrative, and in many other travel books and articles, all of which foreground themes of imperialism and the identity of the traveller. Charting Morris's travel geographies, this chapter brings forward debates about imperial travel, linking the confidently imperial past with the uncertainties, the changes and the self-examination of the post-war period. This is not a story of decline or loss, but of deep and genuine discovery.

James/Jan Morris

James Morris became a household name in Britain when he reported the success of the British Everest Expedition, on the eve of Elizabeth's coronation. He later embarked upon a change of sexual role, and since 1974 has lived and published under the name Jan Morris. In a writing career spanning more than five decades, Morris has written more than 40 books and hundreds of articles, published and syndicated by the London *Times* and *Guardian* newspapers, the Toronto *Globe & Mail* and *Rolling Stone* magazine, to name but a few. During this time, Morris has moved from England to north Wales, and has associated herself with republican and anti-imperial politics.

Morris is a travel writer in the broadest sense of the term. She has worked within overlapping categories of history, fiction, architectural criticism, biography and autobiography. Travel writing encompasses many of these, as Jonathan Raban once explained: 'The travel book is an open form. It has no house-rules, no unbreakable conventions [and] the most ingenious reader, scanning the Travel shelf in a bookstore, would be hard-pressed to fathom what the term means, if it now means anything at all' (1992: 6). It is not surprising, then, that Morris should oscillate as she does between refusing to describe herself as a travel writer (personal communication, 1997), and describing almost all of her writing as travel literature (RGS lecture, 17 March 1998). Like other travel writers, Morris's writing is saturated with geographical descriptions. 'This is a lesson in geography, as well as a well-told story', wrote one of Morris's earliest reviewers (Campbell, 1957: 148), and the same could be said of much that she has written since. Her popular geographies consist of lively and evocative descriptions of *Places* (1972), *Locations* (1992) and *Cities* (1963). Many of these books can be read as travel narratives. Some, such as *Coronation Everest* (1958) and *O Canada!* (1992), describe actual journeys to real places. In others, including *Hong Kong* (1988) and the *Pax Britannica* trilogy (1968, 1973, 1978), travel is abstracted and the first person is largely confined to footnotes. Though these books draw upon the experience of travel, and material collected in the course of travel, the sense of movement remains only in the form of a lively narrative. The first of the *Pax Britannica* books, for instance, has been called a 'grand tour of empire' (*Times Literary Supplement*, 7 November 1968: 1241). Morris also describes imaginary journeys, sometimes to imaginary places, as for example in *Last Letters from Hav* (1985). Other books, which might be read as metaphorical travel stories, include the autobiographical *Conundrum* (1974) and *Pleasures of a Tangled Life* (1989).

Morris's travel writing foregrounds a preoccupation not only with geography but also with gender and imperialism. She acknowledges that 'a sexual purpose dominated, distracted and tormented my life' (*Conundrum*: 17). Gender (and sexuality) is examined most directly in *Conundrum*, which describes the author's sex change, and to a lesser extent in the light-hearted (and relatively light-weight) sequel, *Pleasures of a Tangled Life*. Morris has written much about empires, in books which include *The Venetian Empire* (1980) and, on the British Empire and its legacies, *Hong Kong: Xianggang* (1988) and *Sydney* (1992).

A transsexual travel writer, Morris might be mistaken as something of an anomaly, although she can be positioned in relation to important traditions of travel and travel writing, which encompass a series of crossings. Travel and travel writing are concerned with mobility and change, in the figure of the traveller and in the spaces of travel. For the traveller, this change may involve some rite of passage, such as from boyhood to manhood, or it may involve some kind of crossing over, such as from one national identity to another. For example, George

Borrow and Richard Burton both crossed over, Borrow from England to Wales (he learned the language and adopted Welsh customs), Burton from England to the Orient (he travelled in disguise, learned Arabic, Indian and Persian languages, and acquired a taste for what he took to be Oriental customs and sexual practices). Crossing over is not a politically neutral act, but one that may re-inscribe or disrupt the imperial order. By examining the manner in which Morris has crossed from England to Wales, from apparent enthusiasm for empire towards active anti-imperialism, and from manhood to womanhood, it will be possible to throw some light on travel writing's potential as an anti-imperial medium.

Decolonizing Geographies of Travel

Reading Morris chronologically, from the 1950s through to the 1990s, it is possible to trace a path that begins with conventionally imperial geography and leads, through a series of disruptions and departures, towards ambivalent and, ultimately, openly anti-imperial positions. There were few hints of this in the articles dispatched to the London *Times* or in the book that retold them. It is difficult to read *Coronation Everest* as anything other than a conventional adventure story – comfortable in its imperial and masculine values.

Morris's adventure story bears all the hallmarks of its genre: nationalism, upper-class heroics, male pleasure, exotic settings, sublime landscapes, mysteries, obstacles and dangers. There are even sketchy maps, code words and boxes of treasure. The male heroes plot their trip in a London club then cheerfully leave wives and 'civilisation' behind (*Coronation*, 1958: 22). They travel to Nepal, a theatrical space of 'strange exotic characters' (22) and a backdrop of sublime glacial scenery. The 'manly simplicity' (79) of the expedition and its all-male cast is a principal theme of the book. This masculinity is linked to the nation (England) and Empire (British), for *Coronation Everest* is a story of English/British conquest, a performance designed to crown the Queen. On the mountain, the adventurers listen in to the British World Service, and hear 'the voice of an Englishman'.

> Everest had been climbed, he said. Queen Elizabeth had been given the news on the eve of her Coronation. The crowds waiting in the wet London streets had cheered and danced to hear of it. After thirty years of endeavour, spanning a generation, the top of the earth had been reached and one of the greatest of all adventures accomplished.

> This news of Coronation Everest (said that good man in London) had
> been first announced in a copyright dispatch in the *Times*. (143)

Apparently, the adventure becomes meaningful and influential when it
is received and relayed in the imperial centre. Central voices, notably
the BBC and *The Times*, re-inscribe a simple, binary world order, and
these loudly authoritative voices reach everywhere, even the peaks of
the Himalayas. There, they are heard not only by the British adventurers,
but also by the Sherpas and locals who play subordinate roles in the
mountain drama: one Sherpa was pictured reading *The Times* in early
editions of Morris's book.

Morris not only enters into the imperial spirit and 'nationalist fervour';
he stirs it up, as the news report makes clear (*Coronation*, 1993: xiv).
The back cover of a 1993 edition describes Morris, with the benefit of
hindsight and new information, as 'a very parfait gentle journalist' and
'a dark-haired Welshman sensitive as an exposed nerve' – no longer the
hero of an adventure story. In the same edition Morris further qualifies
and reframes the story of the 'frontiers of the old Empire' (xi), asking
readers for 'historical sympathy' (xii) as they read this 'work of historical romanticism' (xi) and reassuring them that Morris is a 'lifelong
republican' (xii), who joined the expedition with the detachment of a
professional journalist. But revisionist editions cannot change the way
Coronation Everest appeared and presumably was read in the 1950s. Then
there were no scare marks or qualifications. James, the protagonist and
narrator, was neither parfait nor sensitive; he was silent on matters of
Welshness and republicanism; and his enthusiasm for the expedition
was apparently equal to that of his fellow adventurers. Morris had used
an old formula to stir old passions. In retrospect, Morris explains her
early enthusiasm for things imperial by reminding the reader that he
was a child of imperial times. But Morris's relationship to the imperial
order was never so passive. Years after writers such as George Orwell had
attacked adventure stories for their racism and jingoism, Morris blithely
revisited the genre in his 1958 book as he had first told it in 1953.

Morris has since described a gentle and gradual descent from this high
imperialism. Other, more explicitly anti-imperial writers have roundly
condemned adventure stories of the *Coronation Everest* variety and
explicitly rejected all they stand for. Morris's critical departures have, by
comparison with overtly anti-imperial stories such as William Golding's
Lord of the Flies (1954) or Thomas Keneally's *Victim of the Aurora*
(1978), been understated and equivocal. Her first, most preliminary
critical departure has been the reduction of colonialism to a historical

benchmark, a system of orientation through which to position herself and assess historical and geographical change. Travelling to former colonies, Morris often uses imperialism as a preliminary reference system and point of departure. Introducing *Sydney*, for example, she writes:

> Having commemorated in a series of books the rise and decline of the Victorian Empire, and having written its elegy in a study of the last great colony, Hong Kong, I wanted to conclude my imperial commitment with a book about something grand, famous and preferably glittering left on the shores of history by Europe's receding tide. (5)

Travelling in the wake of empire, in formerly colonial cities, territories and countries such as Sydney, Hong Kong and Canada, Morris has charted a series of departures from British Empire. These departures begin with returns. Morris returns to Sydney, 'primarily as an aficionado of British imperial history' (5). It is sometimes difficult to know what to make of this claim to be an 'aficionado' rather than critic or enemy of imperialism, and of Morris's self-confessed nostalgia for empire. Affection and nostalgia can, of course, be interpreted as the expressions of an uncritical mind; but other interpretations are possible. They might be interpreted as a means of relegating imperialism to the past, reducing it to the stuff of anachronism. When Morris recalls the Himalayan adventure as a happy but 'rather absurd' last chapter in British imperial history, as she does in *Conundrum*, and when she tells anecdotes about the endearingly, comically old-fashioned *Times* offices and the privileged world of the Queen's Royal Lancers, she saves herself the task of openly criticizing any of them (83). Between the lines of nostalgia, their demise is a *fait accompli*. So while Morris has travelled in the wake of Empire, she has put the latter on the shelf, where it may harmlessly gather dust.

Morris has distanced herself from the centre and recovered a decentred perspective by, and as a result of, positioning herself within Wales. Although she continued to spend as much as half her time 'on the road', Morris moved her base from England to Wales in the mid-1970s, around the same time she completed her sex change (relationships between these two processes of repositioning are considered in the next section). Doing so, she moved from an imperial centre to a place that she and many others have regarded as an internal colony. Indeed, the concept of 'internal colonialism' was formulated in a study of Wales (Hechter, 1975: 37), which 'was quickly adopted into the platform of the Welsh nationalist party: *Plaid Cymru* (Hechter, 1983: 332). This kind of politicized Welsh perspective is apparent in much that Morris has written, in the first instance about Wales. Like many other *Plaid* supporters, Morris opposes what she sees as English colonial rule in Wales. This she does in pamphlets such as the *Princeship of Wales* (1995) and in high profile letters to newspapers. On 2 June 1996, for instance, the best-selling Welsh daily, the *Western Mail,* published a letter in which Morris argued that it was 'high time Welsh institutions stopped fawning upon an alien and discredited monarch' (Morris was joining an increasingly vocal protest against a royal visit to Aberystwyth). Morris also writes books about Wales, including travel narratives, histories and geographies, both non-fiction and fiction, in which she portrays Wales as a colonized country. These range from the spirited history, *The Matter of Wales: Epic Views of a Small Country* (1984), to the utopian novel, *A Machynlleth Triad* (1994). The hero in both of these books is the rebel prince who once attempted to establish a parliament in the Mid-Walean market town of Machynlleth, but was defeated by the English. In both books Morris maps the English colonial conquest of Wales but allows herself to look forward to a decolonized, self-governing future (Morris, *Matter*: 202–12; *Machynlleth*: 61–90, 153–80).

This off-centre perspective throws critical light on other political contexts. For instance, Morris describes the United States' former enclave of Panama as a classic colony, 'a specimen of a particular historical genre' (*Destinations*, 1980: 55). Morris's sensitivity to 'internal colonialism' also enriches her 'epilogue to an empire' – *Hong Kong* (1988). Instead of charting the rise *and fall* of colonialism there, Morris shows how the territory has been fought over and passed between British and Chinese empires. Morris is critical of both regimes, and sensitive to the experiences of indigenous and relatively new Hong Kong residents. Similarly, when visiting Canada. Of Yellowknife, Morris writes that 'as a historian of the British Empire I was fascinated by its colonial overtones' (*O Canada*, 1992: 139). Yellowknife strikes Morris as an imperial outpost, passed down from British fur traders to Canadian bureaucrats and primary industrialists. 'The longer I stayed in Yellowknife,' she explains, 'the more it seemed to me like a town in an occupied territory, the Dene and Métis its subject peoples, the whites its overlords (150). Morris attributes this critical sensitivity to her experience as 'a historian of the British Empire' (139), and to her interest in and experience of Wales. She explains that:

After a time society here began to remind me uncannily of life at home in my own North Wales, where for more than 700 years the English have been occupying the territory of the racially, culturally, linguistically, historically, and perhaps spiritually different Welsh. (151)

Despite some liberal intentions and ethnic sensitivities, the resident whites are an awkward presence, 'snarled up' in a world where they do not belong.

Morris's postcolonial perspective is not only critical of existing imperialism, it is also creative in imagining alternative futures. A creative, visionary approach is reflected in her utopian geographical descriptions. Strands of dystopian colonialism and utopian postcolonialism emerge most explicitly in *Last Letters From Hav*. The imaginary setting of this novel is a thoroughly conventional literary utopia: its people are optimistic, have a sense of humour, do not participate in organized religion, and enjoy an unrealistic and complete freedom from insects. Hav resists formal concentrations of political power, and harbours no ambitions towards becoming a centre, nor even a nation state. Similarly, in Wales, Morris presents an idealized vision of a future Welsh society centred culturally, politically and linguistically upon Machynlleth, but – since this is a small market town without any of the trappings normally associated with seats of political power – centred nowhere in particular, or rather dispersed.

Utopian themes also enter Morris's non-fiction travel writing. Sydney, for example, is portrayed as a city that has departed from its dystopian colonial origins, an unhappy mixture of the suffocatingly genteel and the miserably poor, and, partly through the efforts of Irish and Welsh republicans, become a 'buoyant post-imperial prodigy' (*Sydney*: 24), a glittering city in which the 'imperial factor is an irrelevance' (226). Morris's Sydney is perhaps a little too glossy; disregarding colonial hangovers and neocolonial inequalities, Morris appears uncritical. Unless, that is, one reads *Sydney* as a Celtic, republican utopia, a critical (if not entirely realistic) departure from English imperialism and monarchy.

Morris adopts a series of other postcolonial writing strategies, which also serve to disrupt the imperial order. Like many others in north Wales, and like some other postcolonial writers such as Ngugi wa Thiong'o (1986), she is sensitive to politics of language, particularly to the English language in Wales and in English representations of Wales. Although she writes in English, Morris has also published in translation in Welsh. The Penguin edition of *Machynlleth Triad* appears in both languages, the latter translated by Morris's son Twm. Her sensitivity to postcolonial writing strategies, which more generally include disrupting and/or appropriating colonial language and imagery (Ashcroft et al., 1989), extends to her work on other places. In particular, colonial maps disrupted and reworked, have provided writers with points of departure, imaginative space in which to chart postcolonialisms. Morris's work is replete with such 'mapping strategies' – to borrow a phrase from Graham Huggan's *Territorial Disputes* (1994).

Morris's postcolonial imagination is not only geographic, but more specifically cartographic. For her the map is a critical point of departure, an imaginative vehicle for decolonization. She disrupts the Mercator map, a central image and propaganda tool of European imperialism. In the frontispiece to *Architecture of the British Empire* (1986) she decentres Europe by reversing the order of West and Eastern Hemispheres. In *Sydney* she removes Australia from the margins of the British world map, and instead places the continent at the centre of a map of the Southern Hemisphere. In Yellowknife she does the same, and explains the significance of the cartographic reorientation. Staring at a map of the Arctic region, she dreams up her 'own romantic and far-fetched recipe for the future of Yellowknife':

> I fancied the little city of Somba k'é truly returned to its sovereign origins, liberated from all interferences and embarrassments, as one of the capitals of a circumpolar federation ... Its peoples would be bound by a common spirituality, and its envoys would assemble from their fishing settlements, their trappers' hamlets, their icecaps and mining towns around the parameters of the Arctic, at their symbolic apex, the North Pole itself. (*O Canada*: 153)

Remapping the region means liberating it from the centres that marginalize and colonize, envisaging alterative futures.

Decolonizing the Traveller

Morris has not travelled unchanged through a changing world; her geographical perspective has been transformed as she has also remade and repositioned herself. The spaces of Morris's travel are also the spaces of her identity.

As Judith Butler argued in *Bodies that Matter* (1993), and as Morris insists in *Conundrum*, when asserting her need for hormones and surgery, gender cannot necessarily be performed entirely at will, irrespective of a person's body, or of the wider systems of power and space in which the body is produced and situated. Morris's sex change, as described in *Conundrum*, is situated in a broader context of decolonizing geographies.

Conundrum presents graphic images of shaving in preparation for surgery, followed by reawakening as a physically and spiritually 'whole' person and 'unencumbered' woman (131). This was groundbreaking stuff in the early 1970s to many readers of this mainstream writer, although it was not entirely novel from a literary point of view, or in the context of postcolonial literature more specifically. Michael Dash identifies dismemberment as a trope in narratives of colonization and decolonization. In the latter, he argues, mutilation of the body is often followed by physical reanimation and spiritual resurrection. As Dash puts it, 'revolutionary potential is evoked through the resurrected flesh', 'spiritual awakening expressed in images of revitalised physicality' and in the 'fantasy of an unencumbered body' (Dash, 1989: 24). Though not explicitly politicized, the transformation of Morris's body, described and geographically situated in *Conundrum*, stands to be (re)connected to broader political and geographical systems, material and imaginative. One way to make this connection is to consider how the material and imaginative spaces of Morris's travel map on to her changing gender identity.

Morris introduces *Conundrum* as a kind of journey – a 'quest' for 'identity', which leads the protagonist down a 'long, strange path' (15, 54). This leads away from masculinity and the world of men. One of Morris's critics interpreted her journey as an attempt to renounce masculinity, to 'lengthen the distance between himself' and the 'cruelty' of manhood (West, 1974: 5). Morris hints as much when she speculates that the militarism and imperialism that killed her father in the Great War may have made 'the passions and instincts of men repugnant' to James (*Conundrum*: 14). Morris's attitude towards men is mixed; frequently, she expresses admiration for them; and not only for men, but men in military uniforms, men who embody a strong, even caricatured form of masculinity. But whether Morris claims to feel revulsion or desire for men, she distances herself from them, and from the hegemony their gender represents. In *Conundrum* this process of distancing is constructed in and through a series of spaces of travel, comprising both individual journeys and also the overall life journey.

Conundrum begins by situating James Morris in the imperial centre, notably in the metropolitan, homosocial spaces and institutions in which he lived and worked. The culture and offices of *The Times*, where Morris began his career, were 'very grand in those days, very British, and very masculine' (*Conundrum*: 171). The military school in which young

James was educated, and the London clubs in which he later socialized, were also bastions of masculine identity and privilege. Morris's masculinity was also performed in and partly constituted through conventionally gendered travel, notably travel with the British Army – 'a man's world, the world of war and soldiery' (*Conundrum*: 33) – and *The Times*, which sent Morris overseas as a foreign correspondent, notably to the Middle East and on the British Everest Expedition. The setting of that expedition was not strictly colonial. By the time Morris reached the area, the British had already retreated from the vicinity: India had gained its independence in 1947, and 24 years earlier Britain had recognized the complete independence of Nepal. So this adventure was situated at some historical and geographical remove from imperialism, but its setting was nevertheless constructed as marginal, and imaginatively if not literally it was the setting of an imperial adventure. Looking back on this conventionally masculine narrative, Morris reflected that it was all about the 'meanings of maleness' (*Conundrum*: 84).

Revisiting the Everest adventure later on, however, Morris has recast it as a superficial story, in which masculinity is confined to outward action and appearance. Inside, Jan insists, she was always a woman. So James is revealed physically, and exaggerated to heroic proportions. He is a 'constant against the inconstant background', a man whose 'body tingles with strength and energy, as though sparks might fly from his skin in the dark' (*Conundrum*: 80).

> When, in the bright Himalayan morning, he emerges from his tent to make the long trek down the mountain to the Khumbu glacier below, it is as though he could leap down in gigantic strides. (80)

The male heroes of adventure are not always thus. Despite its emphasis on bodies and actions, adventure is not always so superficially physical (many adventurers address moral and spiritual questions, for example). Focusing on physical surfaces, acts rather than desires, Morris presents James as a caricature of masculinity. Or so she claims in *Conundrum*. Revisiting *Coronation Everest* in that book, she seeks to destabilize its narrative and more specifically its masculine protagonist. Telling *and retelling* stories in this way, Morris describes a journey from the heart to the margins of imperialism, from James's embodiment of and enthusiasm for the man's world of empire to Jan's gradual repudiation of that and her search for alternatives.

In order 'to be transformed … man into woman', Morris seeks out another liminal region of the conventionally imperial geographical imagination. He flies to 'foreign parts beyond the law' (*Conundrum*: 129, 121), to spaces of caricatured amoral otherness, in which British moral and legal restrictions (such as pre-operative divorce) do not apply. There, he finds a doctor who imposes 'no conditions, legal or moralistic' (128). Morris's Casablanca, an Orientalist cliché, is conventionally liminal:

> I sometimes heard the limpid Arab music, and smelt the pungent Arab smells, that had for so long pervaded my life, and I could suppose it to be some city of fable, of phoenix and fantasy, in which transubstantiations were regularly effected, when the omens were right and the moon in the proper phase. (129)

Morris explains that by the time of her operation, she has virtually completed her sex change, which was more a matter of drugs and psychological adjustment than surgery, so the operation is not so much a sex change as the consummation of one, a symbolic rite of passage and moment of liberation. Fittingly, the liminal setting is deeply eroticized, a space in which sexualities are said to be more fluid, sexual desires less restricted, and moralities less rigid, than in England. The doctor's surgery is conventionally sexualized and gendered, like an Orientalist's harem (see Kabbani, 1986):

> The atmosphere thickened as we proceeded. The rooms became more heavily curtained, more velvety, more voluptuous. Portrait busts appeared, I think, and there was a hint of heavy perfume. Presently I saw, advancing upon me through the dim alcoves of this retreat, which distinctly suggested to me the allure of a harem, a figure no less recognisable than *odalisque*. (*Conundrum*: 130)

Her presence in this harem-like space – a gendered space of travel that has been conventionally and notoriously open to Western women travellers, not men – affirms Morris's femininity (even before the sex-change operation) and marks the beginning of her career as a (transgendered) woman traveller and travel writer.

Travel provides Morris with different places in which to perform gender roles: places in which he continues to live as a man, and places in which she begins to live as a woman; and, in the course of travel, places in which Morris is able to retain her ambivalence. *Conundrum* is replete with images of crossed and straddled boundaries, images of transgressed identities and categories. Borderlands accommodate her sexual ambivalence and marginality, her 'double possession' (13).

In dust jacket notes, Morris – protagonist and author – identifies herself as a traveller who 'divides her time' between various places, and 'has spent much of her life wandering'. This sense of marginality and movement is most pronounced and even frantic when Morris's gender identity is least stable – in the middle chapters of *Conundrum*. 'The more distracted I was, the more obsessively I travelled' (93), not to places but from them, between them. In motion, Morris finds the cold comfort of 'a no-man's land' – another significantly gendered metaphor (76). In between places, and on the road or in the sky, Morris recovers in-between spaces of identity, while she seeks out a more permanent space in which to live, and a more settled identity to live out.

This search takes Morris from metropolitan England to one of the places marginalized by British imperialism. Increasingly she identifies as Anglo-Welsh and becomes an adopted patriot, learning some of the language and making a home for herself and her family in north Wales. 'The Welsh are a disordered people,' she wrote, 'a people on the edge. And it came naturally to me to live outside the frame of things' (126).

When *Conundrum* was published, some critics said that Morris had missed an opportunity to really challenge conservative norms of masculinity and femininity; she had simply exchanged one for the other. Her 'notion of the female principle was one of gentleness as against force, forgiveness rather than punishment, give more than take, helping more than leading' (18). By contrast, the 'ideals of manhood had been moulded by military patterns' and she 'liked a man to be in charge of things' (68). This could almost be John Ruskin writing, a century earlier, and seemed anything but feminist. Also rather like Ruskin's, this view of gender is idealized, never convincingly grounded in flesh and blood. As one reviewer complained, Morris's 'coquettish romantic' model of womanhood had 'none of the blood, pain, and more vital sense of sex women-by-birth would recognize' (Ahrold, 1974: 1540). Critics such as Janice Raymond (1979) and Rebecca West considered Morris worse than conservative, dismissing her as an impostor, a man who had not become a woman, but had appropriated femininity.

One response to this sort of criticism is to insist that, for all its author's ostensibly conformist intentions, *Conundrum* destabilizes gender, by exposing it as a kind of performance, nothing more and nothing less. Judith Butler argues that, whether or not they intend to, transvestite and transgendered men and women have the effect of 'subverting and displacing those naturalized and reified notions of gender that support masculine hegemony and heterosexist power' (Butler, 1990: 33). In *Coronation Everest* (1958), James Morris appears as the ultimate drag artiste: she is seen to be wearing not only the clothes but also the body of a man, and tells us that no one was or is convinced by the elaborate performance.

Ambivalence: Towards a Conclusion

Morris's gradual departure from high imperialism and imperial masculinity has led through some equivocal territory. On the one hand, it is uneven in its sensitivity to colonial and postcolonial contexts and concerns, and seems beset with contradictions. For example, her perspective on colonialism and postcolonialism, modelled on Wales and Morris's particular views about Wales, is problematic within Wales and often too restrictive when applied to other contexts. Morris's Wales is a country colonized by outsiders, and a country capable of returning to something like its former state through decolonization. Decolonized Wales, in Morris's view, would be a country of Welsh speakers, dispersed in relatively small settlements, and cleansed of English influence. Even as a utopian daydream this is profoundly intolerant and regressive. For decolonization is not necessarily about recovering pre-colonial people and places, but creating new social and political orders in the wake of colonialism, and doing so in the context of new, syncretic and hybrid social and cultural realities (Ashcroft et al., 1989: 23–31). Morris's simplistic model of decolonization is particularly inappropriate outside Wales. For example, she condemns Canadian multiculturalism, admitting 'I am not very multicultural', but she seems to forget that in much of the country the alternative is probably Anglo or French-Canadian cultural supremacy. Morris appears to contradict herself by regretting the inevitable assimilation of an Eastern European woman who she sees arriving at Toronto airport. Regretting both assimilation and the alternative favoured in Canada – multiculturalism – Morris regrets the existence of the (re)settlement society. This is an understandable perspective, but it evades the complexity of colonialism and its legacies. Furthermore, Morris is not very sensitive to some of the more subtle and indirect forms of colonialism, and to the new forms that exist in countries, some of which have been formally, if sometimes nominally, decolonized. Arguably, for example, the Vietnam and Korean wars were not 'post-imperial conflicts', as Morris suggests, but neocolonial conflicts. Many countries that have been formally decolonized continue to struggle with the same issues that dog neocolonies: loss of language, 'cultural cringe', alienation, economic impoverishment and so on. So Morris is both self-contradictory and over-optimistic when she dismisses the legacies of imperialism, and writes of colonists: 'Gone, all gone, their very world disintegrated: only their images remain to haunt us, and make us wonder still' (Morris, *Spectacle*, 1982: 247).

Other forms of ambivalence in Morris's writing may be more generally symptomatic of postcolonial writing and politics. To be in between the imperial centre and the colonized margin is to be positioned always in relation to imperial and colonial, centre and margin. Morris's strategy of continually returning to and departing from relics of empire means that she is never very far from it. Her points of departure and system of orientation are, as I have explained, primarily the British Empire. For all this enables Morris to do, it also constrains her. *Sydney*, for example, clings to European colonization. European convicts and other set-tlers, particularly the relatively few who arrived in the first half of the colony's history, are given disproportionate attention. Morris attempts to honour Aborigines in *Sydney* by placing them at the very centre of the book, but somehow they seem buried there, and Morris cannot think of much to say about them. This preoccupation with the British Empire, even when directed to opposing it and celebrating its demise, seems to keep that empire alive. Morris lives and writes in the shadow of empire, as she does in the shadow of imperial masculinity. Similarly, Morris's identification with an internal colony is only partly a disavowal of the centre; it is also a form of identification with the centre. As an *internal* colony, Wales is positioned between the metropolitan core and the colonial and ex-colonial margins, halfway down the hierarchy of imperial oppression, not entirely disavowing the trappings of power. As Max Dorsinville (1974) put it, internal colonies are both dominated *and dominating*. Morris's writing is replete with both attraction to and repulsion from imperialism and imperial centres. Still, as she embodies and articulates this ambivalence, through her specific experience as a transgendered woman and a migrant, Morris arguably speaks from a specific to a more general postcolonial condition, one that does not simply inherit – but articulates, contests and ultimately seeks to tran-scend – the centres and margins of empire, and the whole imaginative and political apparatus that goes with them.

So, for Morris, geographies and identities born of empire can be refer-ence points for moving forward in positive ways, such as in contesting and proactively negotiating constructions of gender and geography. Morris teaches us how, living with the legacies and among the remains of empires, and with cultural forms such as travel and adventure writing that have been closely bound up with imperialism and colonialism, but which are not intrinsically imperial, we can find clues for how to adapt to the present and shape our postcolonial futures.

Works Cited and Consulted

Ahrold, A. (1974) 'Review of *Conundrum*', *Library Journal* **99**: 1540.

Amin, Samir (1976) *Unequal Development: An Essay on the Social Formations of Peripheral Capitalism*. New York: Monthly Review Press.

Ashcroft, Bill, Gareth Griffiths, Helen Tiffin (1989) *Key Concepts in Postcolonial Studies*. London: Routledge.

Berneri, Marie Louise (1950) *Journey Through Utopia*. London: Freedom Press.

Blunt, Alison (1994) *Travel, Gender and Imperialism: Mary Kingsley and West Africa*. New York: Guilford Press.

Brydon, Diana and Tiffin, Helen (1993) *Decolonising Fictions*. Sydney: Dangaroo.

Butler, Judith (1990) *Gender Trouble: Feminism and the Subversion of Identity*. London: Routledge.

Butler, Judith (1993) *Bodies that Matter: On the Discursive Limits of 'Sex'*. London: Routledge.

Campbell, John C. (1957) 'Review of *Sultan in Oman*', *New Statesman and Nation* **53**: 148.

Clements, Paul (1988) *Jan Morris*. Cardiff: University of Wales Press.

Clements, Paul (2006) *Around the World in Eighty Years*. Bridgend: Seren Books.

Dash, Michael (1989) 'In Search of the Lost Body', *Kunapipi* **11**: 17–26.

Dixon, Robert (1995) *Writing the Colonial Adventure*. Cambridge: Cambridge University Press.

Dorsinville, Max (1974) *Caliban Without Prospero*. Ontario: Porcepic.

Duncan, James and Derek Gregory (1999) *Writes of Passage*. London: Routledge.

Duval, Alain and Vivian Marr (1995) *Collins English Dictionary*. Glasgow: HarperCollins.

Fanon, Frantz (1952) *Peau Noir, Masques Blancs*. Paris: Editions du Seuil.

Fanon, Frantz (1980) *Toward the African Revolution*. Trans. H. Chevalier. New York: Monthly Review Press.

Fanon, Frantz (1986) *Black Skin, White Masks*. London: Pluto.

Fanon, Frantz (1990) *The Wretched of the Earth*. London: Penguin.

Fenwick, Gillian (2008) *Traveling Genius: The Writing Life of Jan Morris*. Columbia, SC: University of South Carolina Press.

Golding, William (1954) *Lord of the Flies*. London: Faber.

Green, Martin (1990) *The Robinson Crusoe Story*. Pennsylvania: Penn State University Press.

Harvey, David (1988) 'The Body as an Accumulation Strategy', *Environment and Planning D: Society and Space* **16**: 401–21.

Hechter, Michael (1975) *Internal Colonialism: The Celtic Fringe in British National Development 1536–1966*. London: Routledge.

Hechter, Michael (1983) 'Internal Colonialism Revisited' in D. Drakakis-Smith and S. W. Williams (eds) *Internal Colonialism: Essays Around a Theme*. Edinburgh: Department of Geography, 28–41.

Huggan, Graham (1994) *Territorial Disputes*. Toronto: University of Toronto Press.

Kabbani, Rana (1986) *Imperial Fictions: Europe's Myths of Orient*. London: Pandora.

Keneally, Thomas (1978) *Victim of the Aurora*. Orlando: Harcourt Brace Jovanovich.

Lewis, Reina (1996) *Gendering Orientalism*. London: Routledge.

Low, Gail Ching-liang (1996) *White Skin, Black Masks.* London: Routledge.

McDonald, I. (1964) 'Review of *Cities*', *Christian Century* **81**: 366.

Melman, Billie (1992) *Women's Orients: English Women and the Middle East 1718–1918,* Basingstoke: Macmillan – now Palgrave Macmillan.

Morin, Karen (1998) 'British Women Travellers and Constructions of Racial Difference Across the Nineteenth-century American West', *Transactions of the Institute of British Geographers* **23**: 311–30.

Morris, James (1957) *Sultan in Oman.* London: Faber.

Morris, James (1958) *Coronation Everest: An Account by the Special Correspondent of the Times of the Everest Expedition, 1953.* London: Faber.

Morris, James (1963) *Cities.* London: Faber.

Morris, James (1965) *Oxford.* London: Faber.

Morris, James (1968) *Pax Britannica: The Climax of an Empire.* London: Faber.

Morris, James (1972) *Places.* London: Faber.

Morris, James (1973) *Heaven's Command: An Imperial Progress.* London: Faber.

Morris, James (1978) *Farewell the Trumpets: An Imperial Retreat.* London: Faber.

Morris, Jan (1974) *Conundrum.* London: Faber.

Morris, Jan (1980) *Destinations. Essays from Rolling Stone.* Oxford: Oxford University Press.

Morris, Jan (1980) *The Venetian Empire: A Sea Voyage.* London: Faber.

Morris, Jan (1982) *The Spectacle of Empire. Style, Effect and the Pax Britannica.* London: Faber.

Morris, Jan (1984) *The Matter of Wales. Epic Views of a Small Country.* Oxford: Oxford University Press.

Morris, Jan (1985) *Among the Cities.* London: Viking.

Morris, Jan (1985) *Last Letters from Hav.* London: Viking.

Morris, Jan (1986) *Architecture of the British Empire.* London: Weidenfeld and Nicolson.

Morris, Jan (1988) *Hong Kong. Xianggang.* London: Viking.

Morris, Jan (1989) *Pleasures of a Tangled Life.* London: Barrie & Jenkins.

Morris, Jan (1992) *Locations.* Oxford: Oxford University Press.

Morris, Jan (1992) *O Canada!* London: Hale.

Morris, Jan (1992) *Sydney.* London: Viking.

Morris, Jan (1993) *Coronation Everest: The First Ascent and the Scoop that Crowned the Queen.* London: Boxtree.

Morris, Jan (1994) *A Machynlleth Triad, Triwad Machynlleth.* London: Viking.

Morris, Jan (1995) *Fisher's Face.* London: Faber.

Morris, Jan (1995) *Princeship of Wales.* Llandysul: Gomer.

Orwell, George (1949) 'Boys' Weeklies', in *Inside the Whale and Other Essays.* London: Victor Gollancz.

Partridge, F. (1989) 'Review of *Pleasures of a Tangled Life'*. *Times Literary Supplement* 8(December): 1370.

Phillips, Richard S. (1997) *Mapping Men and Empire: A Geography of Adventure.* London: Routledge.

Phillips, Richard S. (1999) 'Writing Travel and Mapping Sexuality' in James Duncan and Derek Gregory (eds) *Writes of Passage.* London: Routledge, 70–91.

Phillips, Richard S. (2001) 'Politics of Reading; Decolonising Children's Geographies'. *Cultural Geographies* (formerly *Ecumene: a Journal of Cultural Geographies*) **8**(2): 125–50.

Pratt, Mary Louise (1992) *Imperial Eyes*. London: Routledge.

Probyn, Elsbeth (1993) *Sexing the Self*. London: Routledge.

Raban, Jonathan (1992) *Writers Abroad*. London: British Council.

Raymond, Janice (1979) *The Transsexual Empire*. Boston: Beacon Press.

Said, Edward (1978) *Orientalism*. London: Penguin.

Thiong'o, Ngugi wa. W. (1986) *Decolonising the Mind: The Politics of Language in African Literature*. London: James Currey.

West, Robert (1974) 'Review of *Conundrum*'. *New York Times Book Review* 14 April: 5.

Williams, S. W. (1983) 'The Theory of Internal Colonialism: An Examination' in D. Drakakis-Smith and S. W. Williams (eds) *Internal Colonialism: Essays Around a Theme*. Edinburgh: Department of Geography, 4–27.

6

'Between somewhere and elsewhere': Sugar, Slate and Postcolonial Travel Writing

Justin D. Edwards

> Between Europe and Africa there is this desert ...
> Between the white and black this mulatto divide. You
> cannot cross it, whoever you are, and remain the same.
> You change. You become, in a way yourself mulatto –
> looking both ways. Looking back to the vertical,
> sideways to the horizontal. Backwards to the old mas-
> tery, sideways to the timeless mystery ... I am a man
> hunting and running; neither infra nor supra, not
> Equatorial black, not Mediterranean white. Mulatto,
> you could say, Sudanic mulatto, looking both ways.
> (Denis Williams, 1963: 208, 221)

This passage, written by the Guyanese novelist, painter and scholar Denis Williams, appears at the end of *Other Leopards*, a novel published in the Heinemann 'Caribbean Writers Series' in 1963. In this quote, the double-named, first-person narrator – Lionel/Lobo – articulates a complicated sense of racial multi-consciousness in terms of space, place and travel. For instance, his use of the gerund forms for 'hunting' and 'running' express a state of being through a linguistic movement from verb to noun, inflecting a multi-consciousness that moves from actions to processes to identities. This merger of form and content then expands outward in the phrase 'looking both ways', as he gazes from a distance and sees here *and* there, inside *and* outside, centre *and* margin to the image of being perpetually in between places, spaces and races.

I do not seek to appropriate *Other Leopards* as a work of postcolonial travel writing. However, I want to suggest that it is fruitful to read Denis Williams's text – a novel that meditates on migration, immigration, diaspora, exile, forced movement and displacement – alongside a highly influential work of postcolonial travel writing: *Sugar and Slate* (2002) by Charlotte Williams. Both texts, I argue, share thematic and formal qualities, but they are also linked in a much more intimate way: Denis Williams was Charlotte Williams's father. In the autobiographical context of *Sugar and Slate*, then, this relationship plays a crucial role in the narrative of growth and development. But her father's writing also had a profound influence on the ideas and conceptual paradigms that shape her own postcolonial travel narrative. In fact, in the opening section of *Sugar and Slate*, Charlotte Williams quotes the above passage from *Other Leopards* to suggest that her father's dilemma – the particular form of multi-consciousness he expressed as 'Sudanic mulatto' – was played out in the fact that he was 'never staying' but was always, in a sense, travelling (54).[1]

I am not suggesting that *Sugar and Slate* is derivative of *Other Leopards*. Rather, I seek to analyse how *Sugar and Slate* draws upon travel writing's potential for cultural critique by expressing a politicized voice that articulates postcolonial experiences from Guyana to Sudan to Wales. For Charlotte Williams, the travelling subject engages in various understandings of dwelling and displacement to engender narratives that simultaneously reflect and question a postcolonial politics of global contacts. What I am particularly interested in is how *Sugar and Slate* removes representations of travel from the dichotomous interplay between home and abroad, and how, in so doing, Charlotte Williams pushes the envelope of Denis Williams's theories of cross-cultural creativity and cultural syncretism. For she depicts postcolonial travel not as a 'progress' or an 'arrival' but as a process, a continuous activity of becoming.

Detour: The Otherness of *Other Leopards*

In *Other Leopards*, the classical trope of the journey as transformation is subverted: the symbolic and physical representations of travel do not follow lines of progression that lead to an ending or closure. Rather, travel is a continuous activity that is linked to a particular relationship between movement, place and an articulation of subjectivity. Here, travel lays the material foundations for cross-culturalism, and it is the relationship between travel and writing that provides the theoretical paradigm for Denis Williams's most profound insights. Indeed, Williams's own travels from Guyana to Europe to Sudan offer access routes into reading *Other Leopards*, a novel about a Caribbean man's experience in the Sudanic Savannah. In fact, the autobiographical inflection of the novel is clear: Lionel/Lobo is, like Williams, an artist and scholar, his lover is a Welsh speaker from north-west Wales, and he consistently challenges characters who search for racial origins or argue in favour of racial purity and monoculturalism. More importantly, though, the autobiographical voice combines his subject-orientation with a social awareness, a partnership that becomes cohesive in an urge to travel as a response to an inner conflict about belonging and a relation to broader socio-historical issues. The foregrounding of the traveller's subjectivity, together with an awakening of social awareness, is therefore prominent in *Other Leopards*, as it is throughout postcolonial travel writing.

As an alternative to racial essentialism and monoculturalism, Denis Williams employs the term 'catalysis' to convey the notion of a cross-culturality and cultural syncretism. Challenging the concept of 'universality' as a hegemonic critical tool to designate cultural hierarchies, Denis Williams saw the radically mixed populations of the Caribbean (particularly Guyana) as offering 'unique possibilities for cross-cultural creativity unavailable to monocultural societies, or to those which aspire to monoculturalism' (Ashcroft et al., 1989: 149). The cross-culturality of catalysis, he argued, could lead to an interaction in which 'each racial group qualifies, and diminishes, the self-image of the other' (Williams, 1969: 19). Within this model, there is a psychic erosion and self-questioning within a totality of groups greater than the sum, thus avoiding the filiastic dynamic that ensures a subservient relationship to the imperial power, the so-called 'mother country'. The result is a form of postcolonial catalysis that negates the parent–child relationship and stresses the creative meaning of the present in terms of the individual.

For Denis Williams, the problem of cultural and racial dialectics arises out of the limitations and pressures of a 'pedigree consciousness' that is vital to the essentialist language of racial purity found in white supremacy or Afrocentricism. In his work *Image and Idea in the Arts of Guyana* (1969), Williams condemns the monocultural ideologies that have demonized 'mongrelism' and miscegenation as a 'nightmare' of all so-called 'pure' races (7).[2] The investment in an imagined notion of racial purity, he argues, cultivates a filialistic and idealistic relationship to an illusory racial ancestor. As an alternative, he proposes an appropriation of the 'situation … of miscegenation, of mongrelism' as exemplified in the 'uniqueness and freedom' of Caribbean peoples (7).

Sugar and Slate: Travel Writing and Postcoloniality

Catalysis, cross-culturalism and mongrelism offer points of entry for considering the relationship between travel and postcoloniality in *Sugar and Slate*. However, it would be misleading to suggest that Charlotte Williams simply adopts the theoretical paradigms put forward by her father, for this would deny the cultural contexts of each writer's work. Denis Williams's texts are embedded in (and sometimes react against) the 1960s discourses of postcolonial liberation, nationalism, white supremacy and Afrocentricism, whereas Charlotte Williams is writing in the context of globalization and the emerging genre of postcolonial travel writing. Thus, as I suggest below, she does not romanticize catalysis or cross-culturalism, but instead recognizes that these ideas can be branded and commodified within the global tourist industry.

Sugar and Slate directly opposes the easy pigeon-holing of a trademark through its resistance to generic classification. Autobiographical passages are, for instance, interrupted by novelized descriptions, as well as poems and quotations from newspaper articles and of course *Other Leopards*. Williams writes that she wanted to 'achieve a blend of art and politics' in order to write herself back into Wales and 'inscribe the nation' (2003: 30). In so doing, her unique blend of genres has drawn the attention of several critics and novelists: Leonora Brito, for instance, calls *Sugar and Slate* an 'imaginative expansion of the autobiographical form' and Francesca Rhydderch identifies it as an 'autobiography which pushes against its own generic boundaries,' a *'nofel ddu'* (black novel) that moves far beyond the contemporary *noir* trend in Welsh writing in English (Rhydderch, 2003: 4). By contrast, Glenn Jordan identifies the text as a diasporic narrative in which Williams articulates her everyday interactions and the processes of subjectification (Jordan, 2005: 73).

Whatever the case may be, the genre-bending and the collage-like structure of the text offers a hybrid form that mirrors the thematic exploration of mixed racial identities and cultural diversities. 'I grew up in a small Welsh town,' she writes, 'amongst people with pale faces, feeling that somehow to be half Welsh and half Afro-Caribbean was to always be half of something but never quite anything whole at all. I grew up in a world of mixed messages about belonging, about home and about identity' (2002: viii). In this, Williams represents, among other things, the search for a stable sense of subjectivity within an unstable web of cultural affiliations and ties to conflicting national, racial and gendered relations. It is perhaps not surprising, then, that the critic Francesca Rhydderch argues that the text represents a figurative journey; what she calls Williams's 'journey of self-awareness', her movement towards an 'understanding of her cultural identity as a mixed race Welsh Guyanese writer' (4). Critics, though, have yet to locate Williams's text within the context of postcolonial travel writing.

This *is* surprising if only because the text's tripartite structure maps out a set of geographical coordinates which are specifically located in continents, countries and nations: Africa, Guyana, Wales. Moreover, the first chapter, 'Small Cargo', immediately signals the voyage out, while the final chapter – 186 pages later – provides closure to the journey (and the narrative itself) through the direct, albeit unsubtle, title 'I goin' home'.

Sugar and Slate is, I want to suggest, consistent with other travel narratives in that it occupies a space of discursive conflict: it borrows freely from a wide array of textual forms and practices to exploit the formal flexibility of the travelogue's amalgamation of autobiography, letters, journalism, fiction, poetry and so on. Accordingly, Williams adjusts the Western moulds of the genre to the contours of a different episteme: she moves between a variety of perspectives and subject positions that continually resist binaristic depictions of colonizer and colonized. She is the ostracized black girl in north Wales, the privileged expat in Guyana, the re-memory of a Black Atlantic history, the voice of a diverse and confident Wales. In this, she does not depict travel as a universalized experience or a way of expressing a unified sense of self but she moves between the travelling identities of tourist and expatriate, immigrant and exile, migrant and displaced person.

This fragmented, hybridized travel text, then, begins with Williams's early memories of travelling from north Wales to Sudan. At this early stage in her life and during her first trip to Africa, she does not identify with a diasporic culture that is oriented towards lost origins or homelands. Rather, she remembers 'home' as being in transit: her idea of belonging is not necessarily linked to an ongoing history of migration, transnational flows but more a highly personalized experience of travel with her mother. She writes:

> So Ma and Dad became lovers, eventually married and moved on. That's how we began to learn about movement. It was movement that was home. Home was not a particular place for us in the very early years. Home was Ma. We arrived in exile; into a state of relocation that was both hers and his. And the journeys were more than physical journeys. They were travels across worlds of thinking, across generations of movements. These boat stories and seascapes, I now know, are part of a collective memory lying buried below the immediate moment. (11)

As we see throughout this volume, many postcolonial writers' motive for travel lies in the desire to reconceptualize notions of home and belonging. For Williams, home is not an idealized return to a real or imagined place; home is in the process and movement found in the mixture of 'boat stories', 'seascapes' and 'Ma'. Thus, the retrospective voice of Charlotte does not describe her first voyage to Africa as a return; rather, her journey is a relocation to a place of stories and memories – an exile. Her sense of self is not expressed in her voyage 'back to Africa'; but her identity is conceived as *'in process*, a matter of *becoming* rather than *being'* (Jordan: 74).

Yet Williams also reflects on this trip as being 'more than physical'. Indeed, the ontological part of the journey – as she articulates later in the text – ties her voyage to an imagined (subterranean?) collective of African diasporic consciousness. Once we begin to focus on intercultural processes, Williams suggests, the notion of separate discrete cultures evaporates; we become aware that all cultures have long histories of border crossings, diasporas and migrations. Here, we see the influence of Denis Williams's theory of cross-culturalism on *Sugar and Slate*, for transcontinental movement engenders a relationship between subject-orientation and social awareness, a partnership that becomes cohesive in an urge to travel as a response to both an inner conflict about belonging and its relation to broader socio-historical issues. The foregrounding of the traveller's subjectivity, together with an awakening of social awareness, is therefore prominent in *Other Leopards*, as it is throughout *Sugar and Slate*. In fact, Lionel/Lobo's travels throughout Sudan bring him face-to-face with the irrational discourses of essentialism. Race, religion, caste, culture, aesthetics – all of these things are discussed and assessed in terms of 'purity' and 'absolutes'. In the face of such certainties, though, the travelling subject in *Other Leopards* is neither black nor white, Christian nor Muslim, African nor European. Indeed, his cultural critique of absolutism engenders a role-shifting sense of self as he grapples with conflicting cultural allegiances.

And yet throughout *Sugar and Slate* Charlotte Williams is wary about a capitalist co-opting of cross-culturalism. In Section One, for instance, she describes a young Black British man asleep in the Piarco Airport in Trinidad: he sports an oversized woolly Rasta hat in 'the colours' and a crumpled T-shirt with a map of Africa printed on the front (8). 'Africa', then, is a commodified product – a brand that has a niche market within a cross-cultural demographic seeking to reconnect with an imagined set of roots.

In his major work of postcolonial travel writing, *The Atlantic Sound*, Caryl Phillips stresses the importance of travel, while also condemning the hapless African-American tourists on the 'roots trail' – those looking for an imagined African ancestry.[3] Phillips's critique of these travellers is shared by Charlotte Williams, who refers to this conception of an African 'elsewhere' as an 'imaginary hinterland' (2003: 30). For her, the person who chooses to 'go back' is more than a tourist but much less than a returnee. Such travellers, she explains, subscribe to and re-inscribe a Western construction of Africa: the packaging of the continent as a product. 'I found myself', she writes, 'thinking about all those African-Americans straight off the Pan-Am in their shades and khaki shorts treading the trail to the slave forts on the beaches of Ghana. And then I thought about all those who couldn't afford it' (3).[4] Here, Williams calls attention to the complex 'roots' and 'routes' that make up the relations between cultures: travel in the present can forge an imagined connection to the past. But Williams's understanding of these routes is also resistant to the framework of a postmodern celebration of inter-cultural connections through the economy of travel. For her, representations of border crossings demonstrate an awareness that certain forms of travel run the risk of decontextualizing specific local instances. The African-Americans in their sunglasses and khaki shorts are not simply caught up in a seemingly universal postmodern condition that is innocent of specific economic determinants. Not at all. Williams, in fact, understands that the routes of international travel are determined by the forces of economic trade: the route to one's roots is open only to those who can purchase the packaged tour.

This is further explored in Section Two of *Sugar and Slate*. Here, the at-homeness in movement, which is central to Section One of *Sugar and Slate*, is problematized in the second part – 'Guyana' – when Williams moves from north Wales to her father's homeland in the Caribbean. Here, she does not so much focus on the process of travel itself as on a failed attempt to fix herself to a location through dwelling. In Guyana, her desire to root herself in a specific place leads to a profound sense of ambivalence: she is 'from here' in terms of family and heritage and yet she shares complex forms of social allegiance to other places, pasts and cultures. She therefore searches for an adequate symbolic language to account for this sense of fractured and pluralistic identity. She writes:

> I wanted to go native, to make the place [Guyana] my own. But belonging can't just be plucked off a tree like a juicy mango. History and attachment don't just flow into your body like the deep breaths of warm air ... that part of your identity can't automatically fit you like the 'I love Guyana' tee-shirt you can buy anywhere on Main Street. Still, I tried. (149)

In this passage, Williams's desire for belonging – her longing to go native – is expressed in her attempt to merge body and place. She breathes the air and imagines herself rooted in the soil. But when this merger fails, she turns to the tourist industry, imagining herself draped in the 'I love Guyana' tee shirt – another failed attempt to merge with the land. Williams, then, expresses a keen awareness of the ironies involved in her desire to 'go native'. Belonging cannot be plucked off a tree, as she says, but nor can it be packaged, commodified or sold. Implied in Williams's description is a critique of diasporic narratives that become idealized as convenient myths of origin, authenticity or belonging. In such discourses, the 'mother country' or the 'fatherland' is often erroneously identified as a single and static place that is associated with an imagined sense of belonging. Or as Caryl Phillips writes, the displaced children of the diaspora see the imaginary homeland as the solution to 'whatever psychological problem they might possess' (*Atlantic Sound*, 2000: 172).

Williams comes to recognize that she cannot find belonging in Guyana. In this, she shrinks from romanticized views of diasporas. After all, diasporic sentimentalism erases the complexities of people and places – the very complexities which make it impossible for Williams to give satisfying answers to the questions, 'Where are you from?' and 'So yuh's a mix, rite?' (135). In this, she returns to herself as an isolated individual and, as such, the solitary representation of self becomes a rampart against dehumanizing systems. But this does not preclude a belief in a community of experience, for she recognizes that the realities of uprootedness, displacement and unbelonging binds many people of African descent. There are, for instance, passages throughout *Sugar and Slate* in which the writing takes as its subject the intersection between travel, community and identity. 'Going away. Going back. Return. Going home', Williams says, 'Both sides of the same coin' (98). Indeed, it is at this crossroads – this intersection – that the travelling subject becomes overwhelmed by the genealogy of travel. Movement in her past, for instance, includes the remnants of the transatlantic slave trade (the 'sugar and slate' of the title), the migrations that followed the dismantling of the colonial system (her father in London and Sudan), and the shift to new forms of Empire as represented in the global tourist industry.

For Williams, then, belonging is not located in a particular place: travelling itself offers a sense of at-homeness. Repeated throughout *Sugar and Slate* is the story of the man who lived in 'the in-transit no-man's land of Schiphol airport for years' as no country would accept him (7, 187). From Williams's perspective, his situation does not necessarily lead to an existential crisis but gives him an unambiguous connection between his sense of self and a specific place. *'Who am I?'* he asks. To which he answers, 'I am that man at Schiphol Airport' (7).[5] Locating home within the airport transit lounge celebrates the conjunctures produced by ongoing histories of migration and transnational flows. According to the anthropologist James Clifford, it is hard to imagine a better figure for postmodernity than the transit lounge, a 'brave new world order of disorder, of rootless histories and selves' (1991: 7–8). And yet the transit lounge is far from universally accessible, a fact that Williams calls attention to throughout her text. We must be suspicious of the ease with which the airport imagines an interlocking of in-betweenness and at-homeness in the context of cultural flows crossing the globe. For this space, with its potential valorization of the cross-cultural connections, is the privileged site of those who benefit from the unimpeded flow of global capital.

But the figure of the transit lounge is a sign of the deadening of the imagination to local differences produced by a privileged cosmopolitanism. In this, Williams does not seek to transcend differences, but to find bridges and work across gaps that separate cultures. She writes:

> I had been chasing the idea of a Guyanese-ness ... [But] until I changed my perception of what it was to be Welsh or what it was to be Guyanese, or both, I would never feel the satisfaction of belonging ... I would have to accept my role as the spectre at the feast and stay in my limbo, in transit at Piarco airport, somewhere and nowhere at all. (184)

The text, then, tries to evade essences – however strategic they might be – while also navigating around the pitfalls of an in-between spectrality or a state of limbo. The universalizing cosmopolitanism whose consciousness would be the product of a worldwide string of departure lounges is not an answer, for it would simply buy into the historical imagination of the Enlightenment and its universalizing ambitions.

By contrast, the flight itself – the journey from Trinidad to London – is described as a bridge that moves beyond universalizing imaginations. Here, diversity is not conflated with difference or alienation. Williams writes:

> The plane takes off ... I don't need to look around the plane to know the whole spectrum of the Caribbean/British link will be represented; the tourist, the trader, the student, the expatriate kid going

back to school, the consultant, the aid worker, the missionary ...
the guy looking for his roots or reeling with discovery of his rootlessness ... I feel at home. (187–8)

The flight, then, is a space of convergence. It allows for complex forms
of social and cultural allegiance in the context of the fractured and
plural identities of those who are committed to the (postcolonial)
Caribbean and yet participate in several cultures. In this context,
Williams bears witness to a cohabitation that goes beyond the limited
concepts of open-mindedness or tolerance. For she articulates the experience of living on the inside *and* the outside, a heightened sensitivity
to sensitivities and being captured by other manners of being and
desires for becoming other. If there is belonging for her, then this is it.
And it arises out of the process whereby the articulation of different,
distinct elements can be rearticulated in new ways because they have
no necessary belongingness.[6]

What I want to suggest here is that the plane not only bridges the
physical gap between the Caribbean and Wales; it also becomes a place
of belonging where Williams becomes 'reconciled to a life of toing and
froing' (187). In this, the narrative comes full circle. For the conclusion
of Williams's physical and textual journey returns to the figure of her
mother. Her mother, who was earlier identified as the site of home, is
now reinvoked, as Williams's sense of belonging on the flight recon-
nects with her early description of her mother's experience of belonging
on her voyages from north Wales to Sudan. 'She like[d] these voyages
[to Sudan]', Williams writes, the 'passage was part of her inner drive'.
She was 'suited to the ... space of the voyage', for the 'place between
somewhere and elsewhere was so right for her' (7).

The in-betweeness of this spatial experience of travel allows Williams
to conjugate difference into a sense of being and belonging. This is
significant not only because it offers a way of articulating a sense of
'outside belonging' – a longing to be – but also because it represents
a way of straddling parallel lives that does not lead to alienation or
estrangement. In this, her writing extends the theoretical paradigm of
catalysis and cross-culturalism by confounding location and embracing
movement, while also bearing witness to transculturality within the
power dynamics of Empire. Williams leads us away from the nostalgic
dream of 'going home' to a mythic, metaphysical location and towards
a recognition that we will always cling to myths and stories about where
we come from. But these stories are not composed in isolation; they arise
alongside other stories, other fragments of memory and traces of time.

Works Cited and Consulted

Abu-Lughod, Janet (1989) *Before European Hegemony: The World System AD 1250–1350*. Oxford: Oxford University Press.

Ashcroft, Bill, Gareth Griffiths and Helen Tiffin (1989) *The Empire Writes Back*. London: Routledge.

Brah, Avtar (1996) *Cartographies of Desire: Contesting Identities*. London: Routledge.

Chambers, Iain (1994) *Migrancy, Culture, Identity*. New York: Routledge.

Clark, Steve (ed.) (1999) *Travel Writing and Empire: Postcolonial Theory In Transit*. London: Zed Books.

Clifford, James (1991) 'The Transit Lounge of Culture.' *Times Literary Supplement*, 3 May, 7–8.

Grewal, Inderpal (1996) *Home and Harem: Nation, Gender, Empire, and the Cultures of Travel*. Durham: Duke University Press.

Holland, Patrick and Graham Huggan (1998) *Tourists and Typewriters: Contemporary Reflections on Contemporary Travel Writing*. Ann Arbor: University of Michigan Press.

Iyer, Pico (2000) *The Global Soul: Jet-Lag, Shopping Malls and the Search for Home*. London: Bloomsbury.

Jordan, Glenn (2005) '"We Never Really Noticed You Were Coloured": Postcolonial Reflections on Immigrants and Minorities in Wales' in Jane Aaron and Chris Williams (eds) *Postcolonial Wales*. Cardiff: University of Wales Press, 55–81.

Korte, Barbara (2000) *English Travel Writing from Pilgrimages to Postcolonial Explorations*. Basingstoke: Macmillan – now Palgrave Macmillan.

Phillips, Caryl (1987) *The European Tribe*. London: Picador.

Phillips, Caryl (2000) *A New World Order*. London: Vintage.

Phillips, Caryl (2000) *Atlantic Sound*. London: Picador.

Rhydderch, Francesca (2003) 'How Black is *Noir*?' *New Welsh Review* **61** (autumn): 2–5.

Williams, Charlotte (2002) *Sugar and Slate*. Aberystwyth: Planet.

Williams, Charlotte (2003) 'From Llandudno to Llanrumney: Inscribing the Nation, Charlotte Williams in conversation with Leonora Brito'. *New Welsh Review* **62**(winter): 27–34.

Williams, Denis (1963) *Other Leopards*. London: Heinemann.

Williams, Denis (1969) *Image and Idea in the Arts of Guyana*. Georgetown, Guyana: The National History and Arts Council, Ministry of Information.

Williams, Denis (1974) *Icon and Image: A Study of Sacred and Secular Forms of African Classical Art*. London: Allen Lane.

Notes

1. In the paratextual Acknowledgments page that begins *Sugar and Slate*, Charlotte Williams states that two of her father's books – *Other Leopards* (1963) and *Icon and Image* (1974) – provided a 'deep foundation' for her life and writing (v).

2. In *Image and Idea*, Denis Williams writes: 'Miscegenation is the nightmare of those "pure" races who have invested the words half-caste, half-breed,

crossbreed, with scorn, contempt, and as we all know, even with hatred. All "pure" races have done this, African or Asian just as much as European.' (7).
3. Phillips's *Atlantic Sound* (2000) suggests that a simplified conception of diaspora has led to a tourist industry that helps the mostly American returnees not only 'to liberate their spirits' but also to 'view history through the narrow prism of their own pigmentation' (138). Such limitations, he writes, lead to a 'roots trail' which fails to make tourists aware of the very system of oppression it is supposed to denounce or at least oppose.
4. Charlotte Williams's poem, 'Icon and Image', puts this even more cynically, when she writes, 'I've seen Africa / I've seen it / in the Africa shop at the Liverpool dock ...' (2002: 92).
5. Pico Iyer presents similar descriptions of people living in international airports. In the 'Airport' chapter of *Global Soul* (2000), for instance, he writes that 'a dozen people or more often live, around the clock, in Kennedy Airport, making the most of the ubiquitous snack bars, the climate control, the strangers rendered openhearted by jet lag or culture shock' (43). Caryl Phillips in the *European Tribe* (1987) also describes visiting London while studying at Oxford and, unable afford a hotel, he would go to Heathrow airport and spend the night there.
6. Iain Chambers describes 'impossible homecomings' in contemporary texts about travel that reappropriate the 'return home' topos in order to deconstruct it: 'Always in transit, the promise of homecoming – completing the story, domesticating the detour – becomes an impossibility' (1994: 5).

7
Where the Other Half Lives: Touring the Sites of Caribbean Spirit Possession in Jamaica Kincaid's *A Small Place*

Anne Schroder

> we Antiguans thought that the people at the Mill Reef Club had such bad manners, like pigs; they were behaving in a bad way, like pigs. There they were, strangers in someone else's home ... And what were these people from North America, these people from England, these people from Europe, with their bad behaviour, doing on this little island?
>
> (The narrating 'I' in Kincaid, *A Small Place*, 1988: 27–8)

> In accounts of their corrupt government, Antiguans neglect to say that in twenty years of one form of self-government or another, they have, with one five-year exception, placed in power the present government ... And might not knowing why they are the way they are, why they do the things they do, why they live the way they live and in the place they live, why the things that happened to them happened, lead these people to a different relationship with the world, a more demanding relationship, a relationship in which they are not victims all the time of every bad idea that flits across the mind of the world?
>
> (The narrating 'I' in Kincaid, *A Small Place*, 1988: 55–7)

> what is Kincaid's point of view, Antiguan or tourist?
> (Jane King, 'A Small Place Writes Back', 2002: 894)

Contemporary postcolonial travel writing presents a multiplicity of avenues for exploring the dialectics of place and self. Travel writing is generically structured around the itinerary of the travelling subject, but narratives which focalize their material through the prism of postcolonialism are as much concerned with mapping the traveller's own subject positions and sites of enunciation. If, as Bill Ashcroft asserts, travel writing is about 'another place in the mind' rather than about travel itself, then the topological features delineated within the text must necessarily include the traveller's imaginary landscape (Ashcroft, 2009: 229). In constructing an account of the journey, the traveller/writer navigates a set of epistemic coordinates in addition to the range of specific geographical locations visited, and these dual and mutually constitutive planes intersect in producing the traveller's experience of place. The heterogeneity and global (as distinct from universal) context of the postcolonial highlights the need for careful interrogation of the complexities and implications of any traveller's geographical and epistemological location. By situating the voice and agency of the traveller/writer in relation to a cartography of specific, local and particular vis-à-vis representative, global and general sites of enunciation it becomes possible to articulate travel within the domain of the postcolonial. As such, postcolonial travel writing approaches its subject material with and through the realization that the act of writing a place is a simultaneous production of the self and its range of identifiable speaking positions.

This chapter examines Jamaica Kincaid's *A Small Place* (1988) as an example of postcolonial travel writing. *A Small Place* is a travelogue, an essayistic piece of writing, containing four short sections. Situated between outburst and poetics, the text is stylistically remarkable in its fusing of an uncompromising political explosiveness with a carefully crafted prose style.[1] According to Patrick Holland and Graham Huggan, Kincaid's text is an instance of *counter*travel writing which illustrates the point that postcolonial travel writers have to contend with 'a genre that manufactures "otherness" even as it claims to demystify it' (Holland and Huggan, 1998: 50, 65). Kincaid's appropriation of the genre does indeed follow the postcolonial injunction to disrupt and redirect the currents of imperialist discourse by problematizing the construction of Otherness through travel. And Holland and Huggan's reading of *A Small Place* as countertravel writing highlights the text's oppositional relation to the specific discourse and practice of leisure tourism which is ridiculed and castigated in the piece. The narrative's overtly oppositional stance, however, coincides with its use of a narrator whose subject position seems to elude any attempt at defining it within the binary produced by the text itself. What is not addressed by the concept of countertravel writing, then, is the difficulty of placing the voice which is speaking to us in *A Small Place* in either of the univocal categories indicated by the distinction between travel writing and countertravel writing. The argument presented in this chapter interrogates the sites and speaking positions of the traveller/narrator of *A Small Place* by locating Kincaid's text on a continuum of vocalization which spans and transcends the categories of autobiography, performance and ventriloquism. Breaking with the stylistics and format of traditional travel writing, Kincaid's text reads like a spoken performance which radically reconfigures the binary of travelling/narrating Self and native/local Other while probing how the traveller negotiates the structures of knowledge which pertain to different forms of travel. The fraught question of how knowledge is produced is central to travel writing's nexus of movement, place and subjectivity, and what qualifies as knowledge in this paradigm depends on the twin issues of who is doing the travelling and who is able to speak on behalf of whom. In *A Small Place*, Kincaid uses the genre of travel writing to investigate how the location of knowledge about place is intimately connected to the identity of the speaker and the mode of travel undertaken.

Jamaica Kincaid's *A Small Place* is a travel text that offers a portrait of postcolonial Antigua. In her 80-page polemic, the author presents the contemporary realities of this small Caribbean island by constructing a powerful narrating voice which guides the reader through the complexities and paradoxes of this postcolonial space. The narrator/traveller who refers to herself as 'I' throughout is evidently charged with the task of vocalizing Kincaid's own views, but the narrator-tour-guide's supreme ability to ventriloquize mutually exclusive speaking positions along with the curiously 'hovering' quality of the prose style opens up the possibility of positioning Kincaid's text within the scope of postcolonial travel writing and theorizing *A Small Place* as a travel narrative which deploys the dynamics of Caribbean spirit possession. As a Caribbean writer, Kincaid is concerned with the ways in which the genealogies and structures of domination which define present-day Antigua can be explored linguistically, stylistically and discursively. The eponymous 'small place' which designates her representation of postcolonial Antigua also refers to the precarious site of enunciation and possibilities for subaltern speech which any Antiguan would have to negotiate in order to create a voice as strong as the one which controls *A Small Place*.

A Small Place is based on a very simple premise. The narrating 'I' grew up in Antigua, left many years ago but has now returned to the island to give the reader a tour of the most important sites. The tour, however, is not a conventional and straightforward experience. Cataloguing the differences and similarities between Antigua as a colony of the British Empire and the new post-independence Antigua, the narrator's guided tour is as much concerned with showing the overlapping, incompatible and contradictory temporalities which define this nation-state as with pointing out its spatial configurations. This travel text, then, records the observations of a native Antiguan describing the characteristics of a place already known to her and whose travel constitutes a homecoming rather than a journey into the domain of the foreign and the unknown. But *A Small Place* departs further from the conventions of the genre of travel writing by having not only one but two travelling subjects: the narrator who is constructing the narrative and the figure of the archetypal (that is, North Atlantic) tourist who is on holiday in Antigua. Both travellers' viewpoints and speaking positions are inscribed in the text, but it is the narrating 'I' who remains in supreme control of the text.

Kincaid's choice of a first-person voice invites an autobiographical reading. Indeed, the ease with which the 'I' can be construed as articulating Jamaica Kincaid's own personal views has led many scholars to conflate the fictional character of the narrator/traveller with the real-life person of the author.[2] *A Small Place* does not always conform to the autobiographical mode, however, and the structure of the text positions it between fact and fiction. Most significantly, the traveller's use of the second-person pronoun to delineate and incorporate the North Atlantic tourist's perspective into her account serves to implicate the reader's own sphere of existence as a necessary part of the description and understanding of contemporary Antigua. By employing the personal pronouns 'I' and 'you', Kincaid inscribes both a narrating position and a reading position in her text, and this dualism transposes the respective discursive positions of Antiguan and tourist outside the exclusive domain of the text, as the categories of reader and tourist are collapsed into one single entity through the personal pronoun 'you'.

The pronouns lock the narrator/traveller and the reader/tourist into a personal yet formalized relationship. At once reduced and elevated to the general principles of distinct grammatical categories, 'I' and 'you' are juxtaposed under the sign of grammatical difference as constituent parts of a shared linguistic and conceptual framework in which each is made to represent a wider discursive formation of Antiguan native and North Atlantic tourist respectively. The pronouns clearly distribute the speaking parts within the text, for although the structural 'you' is the grammatical subject of many an utterance in *A Small Place*, the narrating/travelling 'I' remains the overall subject of the text by enunciating her subject position through the first-person perspective and thus speaking in her own voice while merely representing the perspective of the reader/tourist through the second person. The ambiguous presence of an addressee both inside and outside the narrative reconfigures the formulaic Self/ Other hierarchies of traditional travel writing as the archetypal Other is moved from a third-person to a second-person position. As such, the narrative as a whole constitutes a performance which disrupts travel writing's pretence of discursive objectivity in favour of a direct and confrontational mode of address which makes no attempt at obfuscating the power relations pertaining to any description of Others.

The grammatical classification of Antiguan 'I' and North Atlantic 'you' creates an asymmetrical binary of singular and plural categories. While 'I' is always singular, 'you' denotes a plural as well as a singular form. The singularity of the travelling/narrating 'I', then, implies a stable and univocal site of enunciation when contrasted with the more indeterminate proliferation of speaking positions for the touristing/reading 'you' which refers equally to the individual tourist described in the text and to a faceless mass of North Atlantic colonizers past and present. In opting for a first-person account, Kincaid would seem to retain and endorse the much fetishized liberal humanist notion of the individual as the site of knowledge which informs normative colonial travel writing. While the narrating 'I' remains in control of the knowledge conveyed within the textual domain of her narrative, however, she is all too aware of her own powerlessness in influencing the socio-economic realities of Antigua which continue to be dominated by the power brokers of the North Atlantic. The boundary drawn between 'I' and 'you' in *A Small Place*, then, separates the locus of knowledge from the locus of power, as the struggle between the two archetypal protagonists of yet another (post)colonial encounter plays itself out in Kincaid's text. In this travel narrative, there is no correspondence between the subject of knowledge and the subject of power.

The split between power and knowledge is connected to the historical trajectories of movement which have brought each traveller to Antigua. The Antiguan 'I' and the North Atlantic 'you' evidently represent two very different types of travel. But leisure tourism and homecomings are not the only forms of movement that Kincaid integrates into *A Small Place*. The experience of displacement and forced migration is central to Afro-diasporic communities scattered and scarred by the experience of slavery. Paul Gilroy's articulations of The Black Atlantic as a way of 'figur[ing] a deterritorialised, multiplex and anti-national basis for the affinity ... between diverse black populations' (Gilroy, 1996: 18) parallels Jamaican sociologist/novelist Erna Brodber's explorations of what she terms 'The Continent of Black Consciousness' (Brodber, 2003). Kincaid's Antiguan 'I' has a claim to this deterritorialized continent produced through 'the transatlantic imagination [which] sees the Middle Passage as a transformative process that bridges the geographical space from East to West and from West to East, fills the space between memory and history, reconstructs the space left by historiographical omission, and negotiates the space between colonizer and colonized' (Pedersen, 2001: 265). In the Caribbean, the idea of travel and displacement is repeatedly conjured up in the religious rituals surrounding the phenomenon of spirit possession.[3] Voodoo, obeah and myalism are all examples of Afro-Caribbean syncretic belief systems which incorporate a re-enactment of the Middle Passage in their elaborate dance rituals as a way of re-articulating their historical experience of uprooting and enslavement. During these ceremonies, ancestral spirits known as *loa* are summoned from their abode in the original homeland beyond the great sea, and the *loa* respond to the invocations of the living by repeating the movement of the Middle Passage, as they voluntarily cross the ocean in order to arrive in the midst of the congregation of their living descendants.

The communication and movement across the Atlantic suspends the spatial and temporal differences between pre-slavery Africa and present-day Caribbean. As Wilson Harris puts it: 'the journey from the Old World to the new ... needs to be re-activated in the imagination as a limbo perspective when one dwells on the Middle Passage: a *limbo* gateway between Africa and the Caribbean' (Harris, 1995: 379). For the duration of the ritual, the separate planes of the living and the dead overlap and intersect on the bodies of all those who participate in the ritual. Having negotiated this vast spatial distance, the *loa* emerge to take possession of the body and, crucially, the voice of each proselyte who now serves as a vessel for the *loa*. Through this living body, the benevolent ancestors then communicate through actions and words, giving advice intended to benefit their living descendants.[4] In the Afro-Caribbean belief systems, the *loa* return to influence the present and the future by transmitting knowledge based on their own lifetimes of accumulated experience. The ancestral spirits need the living to provide bodies through which they can manifest themselves and materialize in the present, while the living depend on their ability to invoke the deities and receive their communications in order to prosper in the future. When a spirit of the dead takes possession of the body of a living person, this person becomes a medium which merely voices the views and opinions of the deity that has taken possession of it. In the pantheon of deities, each *loa* embodies an archetypal principle as well as the individual characteristics of specific ancestors, and, through this fusion of the general and the particular, the spirits function as the repository of a community's collective knowledge (Deren, 1975: 35–40; Davis, 1987: 220–1).

The *loa* travels in order to be able to speak in the appropriated voice of an Other. In Afro-Caribbean forms of ancestor veneration, then, the act of reclaiming the Black Atlantic and reconnecting the peoples on either side of its spatial and temporal divide is (quite literally) articulated through the medium of the human voice in a ritual characterized by ventriloquism. Addressing the issue of displacement on several levels, the ritual involves a discrepancy between the voice that produces the *loa*'s speech (the proselyte) and the agency behind it (the *loa*). As such, it is not only the notion of location, but the very idea of identity which is subverted in a ritual where the speaker can by no means be viewed as a unified subject.

The narrating 'I' of Kincaid's travel text has returned from an indeterminate elsewhere to voice her dismay at the state Antigua is in. Although we never learn where she has been for so long, she does give a specific example of what her existence outside Antigua has been like. Briefly recounting a conversation she has had with an Englishman, the narrator prefaces the exchange by remarking that 'this happened in my present life' (30). Her interlocutor is described as one of those Englishmen who, 'since the demise of the empire, [has had] nothing to do ... [and is now] sitting on the rubbish heap of history' (30–1). The exact location in which this meeting takes place is not mentioned, but the Englishman is described as an obsolete life form and a relic from colonial days. Conforming to the archetypal idea of the post-imperial English subject, the Englishman functions to counterbalance the narrator who self-reflexively voices the opinions and enacts the part of an archetypal postcolonial subject: 'I was reciting my usual litany of things I hold against England and the English' (31). The clash of the archetypal principles of colonizer and colonized can be positioned within the Afro-Caribbean pantheon of ancestral deities who are still influencing the present. The two individuals who are here fighting each other for control of their shared history and for the power to produce their own version of it are representative of their respective genealogies. Within this framework, the narrator's distinction between her 'present life' and her past life in Antigua frames her return to the domain of her former life in order to give advice to the people living there now.

The narrator of Kincaid's text radically departs from the conventions of the travelling I/eye by employing a discursive strategy characterized by the multivalent positionalities of the observer. Despite a very precise delineation of where the voice of the narrating agency is coming from, Suzanne Gauch rightly points out that the narrator-tour-guide is located 'neither here nor there' (Gauch, 2002: 917). Early on in the narrative, she explicitly positions herself within the discursive formation of the local Antiguan population by asserting her individual identity in relation to the identity politics of nationality: 'we Antiguans, for I am one' (8). She then proceeds, however, to distance herself from the Antiguans to whom she refers throughout as 'them'. The narrator, then, both is and is not one of the local Antiguans whose lack of autonomy and self-determination causes her to describe them as 'children, eternal innocents ... or lunatics who have made their own lunatic asylum' (57). This rather cruel and dismissive treatment of her fellow islanders inscribes the mode of the conventional travel text: the narrating 'I' is removed from the space of the disenfranchised Others and positioned outside the 'lunatic asylum' which has subsumed the small island of Antigua. Yet this traditional position does by no means remain stable, for while the returning narrator fails to wholly identify with her countrymen, she nevertheless identifies more with their point of view than with that of the North Atlantic tourist who visits and treats Antigua as nothing more than a holiday resort.

In her article 'A Small Place Writes Back', Jane King takes issue with Kincaid's representation of Antiguans and, by extension, of the peoples who inhabit the Caribbean islands.[5] Still living and writing in her native St. Lucia, King's triple heritage of African, Carib and British ancestry combined with her first-hand experience of what it is like to live in this small place puts her in a powerful position to castigate Kincaid for disseminating inaccurate descriptions of Caribbean life. King rightly points out that *A Small Place* 'doesn't pretend to be a novel' and that '[Kincaid's] fiction is ... so close to autobiography that it is hard to imagine that readers will take it to be imaginary' (King, 2002: 889, 899). While this might seem obvious, it nevertheless addresses the complex issue of how to classify and read *A Small Place*.[6] King's most enlightening contribution to these debates is arguably her insight into the discursive fabric of the Caribbean which, she argues, informs Kincaid's text to a greater extent than do any facts of material reality. In her scathing critique of *A Small Place*, King implicitly addresses one of the central issues of travel writing, as she accuses Kincaid of allowing the well-established colonial discourse about Caribbean peoples and places to supersede the more complex actualities which the author could (and should) be conveying to her readers.

The dynamic first section of Kincaid's piece describes the tourist's arrival in Antigua. Doggedly tracing every step of his journey from airport to hotel, this initial part of the narrative introduces the narrating 'I' and the touristing 'you' in terms of their speaking positions, different modes of travel and the manner in which each relates to the category of knowledge. A close examination of these opening pages will demonstrate the pertinence of reading this travel text through the framework of Caribbean spirit possession.

The text (and tour) of *A Small Place* begins by positioning the reader in relation to the place about to be explored: 'If you go to Antigua as a tourist, this is what you will see' (3). This opening sentence provides 'visitor information' on a number of different levels. As it subtly suggests that the experience of Antigua is contingent on the manner in which one approaches it, this initial remark merely hints at a potential conflict between the tourist and the actualities of Antigua. Signposting the Antigua which can be seen, the narrator-tour-guide simultaneously indicates the existence of other aspects of the island which remain invisible to the tourist. *A Small Place* nevertheless provides a comfortable starting point for the reader. The offer of a tour of Antigua promises to stay within the limits of the conventional tourist experience and not reveal any facts about this Caribbean nation-state which the tourist/ reader might not wish to know. At the same time, however, the tour guide's promise of a careful and sensitive negotiation of the categories of ignorance and knowledge raises the slightly disconcerting question of who is in control of the knowledge which will be transmitted. Is it the tourist whose socio-economic privilege entitles him to the luxury of a specifically tailored 'Antiguan experience' or is it the local Antiguan who inhabits the small place that the tourist is about to visit?

The identity of the narrating agency is not immediately clear. On the very first page of the narrative, however, the reader is startled by a passage which reveals the full extent of the significant use of the second person to address the tourist:

> As your plane descends to land, you might say, What a beautiful island Antigua is – more beautiful than any of the other islands you have seen, and they were very beautiful, in their way, but they were much too green, much too lush with vegetation, which indicated to you, the tourist, that they got quite a bit of rainfall, and rain is the very thing that you, just now, do not want, for you are thinking of the hard and cold and dark and long days you spent working in

North America (or worse, Europe), earning some money so that you could stay in this place (Antigua) ... where the climate is deliciously hot and dry for the four to ten days you are going to be staying there; and since you are on your holiday, since you are a tourist, the thought of what it might be like for someone who had to live day in, day out in a place that suffers constantly from drought ... must never cross your mind. (3–4)

This passage establishes the narrator's speaking position in direct opposition to that of the tourist/reader. Corinna McLeod describes the touristing 'you' as the protagonist/antagonist of *A Small Place*, while Diane Simmons argues that the subject matter of the text quickly becomes the visiting tourist rather than Antigua, the tourist destination. As the section quoted above illustrates, Kincaid's inscription of the North Atlantic tourist's perspective is accomplished by filtering his thoughts and reactions to Antigua through the voice of a hostile narrator. This channelling process demonstrates the narrator's intimate knowledge of the discourses and mindset with which the tourist approaches the site for his holiday, even as the antagonistic tone places the narrating agency at a distance from the thoughts expressed through her voice. Evidently adopting the perspective of the inhabitants of Antigua whose everyday lives are defined by a constant scarcity of fresh water, the narrator's uncanny ability to ventriloquize the views of the approaching tourist suggests a redeployment of the structures of traditional Afro-Caribbean spirit possession. In such a reconfiguration, the narrator becomes the returning ancestor whose transmission of knowledge strengthens the link between past, present and future, while the act of possession here is hostile rather than benevolent. Speaking directly to the tourist whose desires, anxieties and prejudices are all known to the narrator, she addresses him throughout with the confrontational 'you' as a way of emphasizing that he (and we, the readers) is the intended recipient of the knowledge she has to impart. In the new realities where postcolonial independence intersects with neo-colonial domination and exploitation as manifested through the tourist industry, Antigua constitutes a site where the processes and contests involved in spirit possession can be articulated in new ways. The narrator sets up and then straddles the two mutually exclusive positions of 'native' and 'tourist' by moving back and forth between the discourses of each.

A Small Place stages a contest between Antiguan and tourist by exploring the antagonistic relationship between North Atlantic leisure tourism and the forced migration which has created the Afro-diaspora. Focalized through this framework of multiple voices, shifting viewpoints and overlapping sites of enunciation, Kincaid's travel narrative goes far beyond the univocal perspective implicit in Holland and Huggan's notion of countertravel as the postcolonial travel writer's strategic means of discursive resistance to traditional paradigms. Kincaid's narrator-tour-guide exhibits a supreme ability to inhabit the mind of the North Atlantic tourist/neocolonizer and ventriloquize his views, even as her own speaking position is evidently located elsewhere. As the narrative unfolds, the narrator/traveller sets up an insurmountable barrier between the categories of North Atlantic tourist and Antiguan local while simultaneously positioning herself outside of this binary. This displaced quality of the narrative voice comes about as she moves effortlessly between these two sites of enunciation while maintaining them as irreconcilable opposites and making the chasm between them ever wider. While spirit possession is not explicitly present in Kincaid's text, it is part of her cultural framework as an Antiguan, and her references to obeah in such works as *Annie John* (1985) and *The Autobiography of My Mother* (1996) make it pertinent to read *A Small Place* in this context. Moreover, by placing *A Small Place* in the context of Afro-Caribbean spirit possession, it becomes possible to theorize the narrator/traveller as a contemporary avatar of the traditional *loa* and to view the text as a whole as a ventriloquial performance designed to exorcise Antigua of the continuing patterns of exploitation and domination.

The narrator grew up in Antigua during the colonial era. And the decolonized and postcolonial space she finds upon returning is criss-crossed by the neocolonial power structures of a global economy. Most noticeably, the former English colonizer has been replaced by the North Atlantic tourist who views Antigua with the same sense of entitlement in all his interaction with members of the local population. It is this tourist who is taken on a tour of Antigua and to whom the narrator-tour-guide addresses her remarks about the Antigua which is generally unseen and which, for the tourist, belongs to the realm of the unknown. The lack of specific positionality which Suzanne Gauch identifies as a central characteristic of the narrative voice explains the free-floating quality of the prose style which moves effortlessly if forcibly between the perspectives of the native Antiguan and the North Atlantic intruder/tourist without weaving a deceptively seamless web of free indirect discourse. The reader is never in doubt as to whose perspective is being ventriloquized by the narrating agency which continuously demonstrates its supreme mastery of both discursive positions. And not only are all possible arguments and narratives on both sides familiar to the narrator; she is also able to castigate and so distance herself from both sites of enunciation inscribed in her diatribe. Jane King writes: '*A Small Place* begins with

Jamaica Kincaid placing herself in a unique position able to understand the tourist and the Antiguan and despise both while identifying with neither', and she sums up her frustration with the narrative by asking: 'what is Kincaid's point of view, Antiguan or tourist? It becomes increasingly difficult to tell' (King, 2002: 895, 894).

Reading *A Small Place* through the framework of spirit possession does not make the narrative apolitical. On the contrary, it provides a distinctly Caribbean prism for focalizing the identity politics and power dynamics at work in this travel text.[7] The ease with which the voice of *A Small Place* is able to ventriloquize views that are mutually exclusive and which belong to highly different discursive positions and formations indicates that the text is situated on a plane which lies beyond simplistic forms of identity politics. Kincaid's narrative explores gender as well as race relations, but the us/them dichotomy which is repeatedly invoked is consistently transposed on to a more fertile ground of examination where identity politics can be articulated in more complex ways.[8] Here, it is the very category of knowledge which is at stake, as the main conflict of the text is staged between the narrator's attempts to convey knowledge and the tourist's moves to deliberately avoid this knowledge and plead ignorance of the structures of domination which enable his holiday in the Caribbean. The possibility of drawing on the framework that Caribbean spirit possession provides in order to position the narrating/travelling 'I' highlights rather than negates the political in Kincaid's text. Far from operating within a spiritual domain which supposedly transcends the human realm of power relations, the practice of spirit possession is structured around a sophisticated reconfiguration of the master/slave dialectic in which the categories of travel, possession and knowledge are so intertwined as to be inseparable, and where the issue of who can speak for whom is central.

A Small Place is set in Antigua. Providing both the context and the subject material for the narrative, Antigua constitutes the stage on which the contest between the categories of tourist and native is played out. The text pits Antiguan 'I' and North Atlantic 'you' against each other by problematizing the issue of how each traveller comes to be in Antigua. As the structures of leisure tourism sharply contrast with the forced migration which has brought the current Antiguan population into being, the two protagonists/antagonists of the narrative are further differentiated by their respective positions in relation to the category of knowledge. In this, Kincaid's text accomplishes a separation of the traditionally inseparable nexus of power and knowledge central to the genre of travel writing.

Kincaid's text is a diatribe against the archetypal tourist. Writing her anger and contempt for the North Atlantic consumer vacationing in her native Antigua, Kincaid's text is a sustained attack on the specific type of tourist activity which characterizes contemporary socio-economic exploitation of the Caribbean. In Kincaid's exploration, the power dynamics which shape the relationship between North Atlantic neocolonizer and Antiguan neocolonized have multiple interpersonal as well as collective dimensions, but these are all negotiated through the central question of how the travelling 'I' relates to the category of knowledge. The tourist's mode of travel constitutes an act of escapism intended to place him in a fantasized 'elsewhere' where he can suspend all critical thinking for the duration of his holiday. Far from conforming to the role of the conventional colonizer/traveller who seeks to compile knowledge about a place in order to possess and control it, the tourist is conceptualized as a hollow animal-like creature 'whose determination to consume everything in sight renders him bloated and ugly' (Simmons, 1994: 471). Along with his unappealing hyper-corporeality, the tourist is shown throughout to not only lack interest in obtaining any kind of knowledge about this small place but to wilfully negate and erase the knowledge he does possess about his own complicity in the structures of domination which maintain Antigua in its disenfranchised position within the global economy. As the narrator shows him the specific sites on which the tourist's consumption can be clearly seen as intersecting with and sustaining the material reality of Antiguan poverty and corruption, his attempts to surround these areas of potential insight with obfuscation and ignorance are exposed as deliberate attempts to remove himself from an epistemological plane on which the connections between Antiguan native and North Atlantic tourist can be understood and articulated.

Back in the opening section of *A Small Place*, the tourist emerges from the airport and takes a taxi to his hotel. Although he is eager to get to the destination to relax, the narrating agency makes sure that the short ride constitutes a tour of Antigua: 'You are looking out the window (because you want to get your money's worth)' (6). On the way, they pass a number of key locations through which the geographies of power in Antigua are introduced. The school building is so dilapidated that the tourist assumes it is a public latrine, while the hospital is simply ignored until the narrator steps in and warns the tourist not to get sick while on the island, as no Antiguan would willingly consent to being treated there. Next, the taxi drives past the colonial library which was damaged during an earthquake more than a decade ago, while Government

House, the Prime Minister's Office and the Parliament Building move the tourist onwards along a trajectory which reveals sites of increasing influence within the Antiguan nation state, and 'overlooking these, with a splendid view of St. John's Harbour, the American Embassy' (10). After these official manifestations of local as well as global political power, they pass in quick succession the ostentatious mansion of a Middle Eastern business family who 'own a lot of Antigua' (11), the equally impressive home of a drug smuggler, and, finally, that of a woman commonly known as Evita because of her lucrative liaison with a government official. The narrator-tour-guide's careful mapping of the spatially and nominally separate but de facto intertwined and overlapping domains of government, business, crime and interpersonal relationships provides a brief but concise introduction to Antigua. When she drops the tourist at his hotel, she has demonstrated that she possesses intimate knowledge of both the situation in Antigua and the thought patterns of the visiting North Atlantic tourist.

The tour of Antigua simultaneously maps the psychic topographies of the archetypal tourist. As the narrator reveals aspects about this Caribbean island which the visitor either does not know or does not want to know, her comments are accompanied by contemptuous remarks about the tourist's ignorance or unknowing. Transforming the 'objective' I-narration of the conventional travel narrative, each piece of supposedly objective and innocuous information concerning the sites they pass is shown to be inextricably bound up with the tourist's own subject position. The geographies of Antigua's material, historical and political reality have logical counterparts in the tourist's own mental landscape in which the North Atlantic cartographies of knowledge determine which areas of human experience are deemed inaccessible. Indeed, the narrator guides us through the tourist's reactions to Antigua with a familiarity that suggests an ability to inhabit and move around within his personal topologies as well as on the multiple and overdetermined planes of Antiguan ontology. The guided tour involves a voice-over function which constantly displaces the tourist from the category and location of knowledge, repositions him in proximity to it, and then exposes his wilful construction of a fault line between himself and any forms of knowledge that he does not wish to possess. As a result, the tourist emerges as a being who is constantly struggling to remove himself from the realm of thought by erasing what he knows or suspects about his unearned but privileged place in the world and rejecting a potentially flourishing mental activity in favour of the blank spaces of unknowing. Using the device of the tour, the narrator is able to present her facts and information about Antigua as a sequential ordering of specific points of interest, even as these turn out to be the nature of the tourist's triggered responses as much as any aspect of postcolonial Antigua.[9] The catalogue of references to what the tourist carefully avoids thinking about on the car ride serves to delineate his complicity in the idiosyncrasies of extreme wealth and extreme poverty that confront him as he looks out the window: the horror of the difficult daily lives of people who live in a place of perpetual drought 'must never cross your mind' (4); the sight of expensive cars driven by impoverished drivers 'would not really stir up these thoughts in you' (7); the narrator's examples of the discrepancy between the nominal fact of Antigua's independence and the material fact of its inability to emerge into a state in its own right are followed by the terse 'you should not think of the confusion that must lie in all that' (9); the economic inequalities between Antigua and the tourist's home in the North Atlantic part of the world lead the tour guide to remark: 'you needn't let that slightly funny feeling you have from time to time about exploitation, oppression, domination develop into full-fledged unease, discomfort; you could ruin your holiday. They are not responsible for what you have; you owe them nothing' (10). And, finally, as the narrating agency informs the tourist of the extent of the hatred and ridicule which the local population subjects him to behind their closed doors, she anticipates his attempt at incredulity: 'They do not like you. *They do not like me!* That thought never actually occurs to you. Still, you feel a little uneasy ... Still, you feel a little out of place' (17–18). This repeated emphasis on thoughts that do not appear in the tourist's mind indicates a split between the location of the tourist and the location of the realm of thought.

The short journey through Antigua frames the conflicting epistemologies of tour guide and tourist. Her moves to impart knowledge and his endeavours to remain in a state of unknowing are provoked by and intersect with the Antiguan realities they are driving past. Antigua, however, is not merely a stage on which the contest between Antiguan forms of knowledge and North Atlantic forms of deliberate ignorance are played out. In fact, this particular tour serves to position Antigua between the factual and the fictional, as it presents an Antigua which has a metaphorical dimension to it. Every tour is designed to present a certain version of the place under scrutiny by highlighting some features while downplaying or ignoring others. As such, the very concept of a tour constitutes a negotiation of the mechanisms of inclusion and exclusion which determine how a place is experienced. The narrator-tour-guide and the tourist come across a series of discrepancies which they interpret differently. The ubiquitous brand new Japanese cars are built to run on non-leaded gasoline, but as no such gasoline is available (or even known) in Antigua, the cars are actually fuelled by leaded gasoline. Similarly, these signs of affluence are driven around on roads in serious need of repair because, as the narrator informs us, government ministers own the car dealerships in Antigua and so provide financial incentives for people seeking to purchase new cars, while there is no profit to be made from maintaining the infrastructure of the island (5–7). These examples of everyday Antiguan reality as witnessed by the tourist and explained by the tour guide read like carefully crafted metaphors of a postcolonial state's indeterminate status between the planes of a first world and a third world country.

The brief tour of Antigua delineates a place densely layered with ambiguous signs of the postcolonial. Passing the old library that was damaged before Antigua became independent from Britain, the narrator notes that the sign placed in front of the building to inform the public that 'REPAIRS ARE PENDING' is the same original sign that was put up by the colonial administration immediately after the earthquake (9). Meanwhile, the taxi driver's reckless and dangerous driving constitutes a blatant disregard for 'the road sign, a rusting, beat-up thing left over from colonial days' which commands drivers not to exceed the speed limit of 40 mph (6). Scattered around Antigua, then, are various signposts that are left over from colonial times. Rusting, fading and disobeyed, these signs have neither been substituted with post-independence signs nor simply removed, but are still present as part of the Antiguan landscape.

For the narrator-tour-guide, the sign on the library signals an 'unfulfilled promise of repair' (9).[10] The tourist, however, has a different interpretation of the obvious discrepancy between the assurance of imminent action inscribed on the sign and the prolonged neglect of the no longer functional architectural structure behind it. Ascribing it to 'a sort of quaintness on the part of these islanders, these people descended from slaves', the tourist contemplates 'what a strange, unusual perception of time they have ... but perhaps in a world that is twelve miles long and nine miles wide (the size of Antigua) twelve years and twelve minutes and twelve days are all the same' (9). In the tourist's analysis, life in a small place is lived in a perpetual present with no possibility of distinguishing the categories of past, present and future. Furthermore, the tourist explicitly connects this supposed inability to grasp and manage the concept of time as a linearly progressing phenomenon to the fact that the islanders have descended from slaves. This casual invocation of the Antiguans' enslaved ancestors is followed up a few pages later when the narrator describes the tourist's self-congratulatory smugness at his ability to profit from contemporary patterns of domination which were established through exploitation in the past: 'this ugly but joyful thought will swell inside you: their ancestors were not clever in the way yours were and not ruthless in the way yours were, for then would it not be you who would be ... backwards in that charming way?' (17). The tourist acknowledges that his privilege arises from his ancestors' dehumanizing treatment of others and articulates this knowledge as a comparative analysis of the way in which this ancestral power continues to influence the present. As such, the relationship between North Atlantic tourist and Antiguan native is partly articulated as a contest about who possesses the most powerful ancestors.

The tourist reaches his hotel, but the tour is not over. The narrating agency continues her relentless running commentary on his thoughts and emotions as he now anticipates inserting himself into the stunningly picturesque Antiguan scenery of his holiday resort: 'you see yourself lying on the beach ... You see yourself taking a walk on that beach ... You see yourself eating some delicious, locally grown food. You see yourself, you see yourself' (13). While the self-obsessed visitor can now begin his enjoyment of a safely packaged and commodified 'Antiguan' experience, the narrator leaves him with one final observation on the underlying inequalities that underpin his consumption of the supposedly unlimited beauty, freedom and luxury provided by Antigua's material resources: 'it's better that you don't know that most of what you [will be] eating came off a plane from Miami. And before it got on a plane in Miami ... it came from a place like Antigua ... where it was grown dirt-cheap, went to Miami, and came back' (14). Antigua's uneasy postcolonial status is here unambiguously articulated in terms of its marginal and disenfranchised position within the overarching structures of a global economy. Decolonization and political independence notwithstanding, the networks of production, distribution and consumption have subsumed Antigua into a new hierarchical system where commodification has replaced slavery and where trade relations are negotiated and dictated elsewhere.

This image of the tourist eating 'local' food comes immediately before a gap in the text. Contemplating the way in which the tourist's consumption of Antigua points to its enmeshment in a new globalized reality, the narrator abruptly ends the first part of the tour by simply stating that '[t]here is a world of something in this, but I can't go into it right now' (14). Turning away from the overwhelming realities and effects of globalization, the narrating agency instead turns back to the individual tourist and launches a scathing and very personal attack: 'The thing you have always suspected about yourself the minute you become a tourist is true: A tourist is an ugly human being' (14). The ensuing diatribe reveals the narrator's profound insight into the realities of a life lived in the North Atlantic. The lethal combination of hard work and extreme boredom which characterizes any quotidian existence causes the people of any place – small or otherwise – to desperately desire an escape from the dehumanizing grind of everyday life. As such, the tourist experience is construed as a matter of life and death for the tourist:

> you make a leap from being that nice blob just sitting like a boob in your amniotic sac of the modern experience to being a person visiting heaps of death and ruin and feeling alive and inspired at the sight of it; to being a person lying on some faraway beach, your stilled body stinking and glistening in the sand, looking like something first forgotten, then remembered, then not important enough to go back for. (16)

This sophisticated and carefully constructed image is counterbalanced by outbursts such as 'An ugly thing, that is what you are when you become a tourist, an ugly, empty thing, a stupid thing, a piece of rubbish pausing here and there to gaze at this and taste that' (17).

The tourist experience is clearly separate from the field of the ordinary. As the native of one place seeks to escape the boredom and banality of his life in that place by becoming a tourist, however, he merely makes a leap from one site of ordinariness to another, but in the process, loses his human characteristics and becomes an 'ugly thing'. In Kincaid's formulation, the relationship between human and tourist is articulated through the framework of the ordinary vis-à-vis the archetypal: 'ordinarily, you are a nice person, an attractive person ... a person at home in your own skin ... a person at home in your own house (and all its nice house things), with its nice back yard (and its nice back-yard things)' (15). Being ordinary in the realm of an everyday life, then, simply signifies feeling at home in one's body and within the specific location of that body. The need to escape this ordinariness whenever it becomes oppressive, however, is paradoxically connected to the very category of ordinariness: 'one day ... [an] awful feeling of displacedness comes over you, and really, as an ordinary person you are not well equipped to look too far inward and set yourself aright, because being ordinary is already so taxing, and being ordinary takes all you have out of you' (16). Fleeing this sense of not being at home where one is supposed to be at home, the tourist approaches a place like Antigua in order to merge with and experience the category of the extra-ordinary. As the tour guide tells the tourist: 'when the natives see you, the tourist, they envy you, they envy your ability to leave your own banality and boredom, they envy your ability to turn their own banality and boredom into a source of pleasure for yourself' (19).

The transmutation involved in the move from being an ordinary human to becoming an archetypal tourist entails an increased corpo-reality along with a diminished use of mental faculties. The tourist's excessive consumption is accompanied by his wilful cultivation of ignorance which renders him an object of contempt and ridicule for Antiguans. At the same time, however, his ability to invade, consume and reconfigure the material realities of the locale makes him a power-ful force which inspires fear and hatred. The life-and-death struggle between narrator-tour-guide and tourist takes place on an indetermi-nate site where the ontology of Antigua intersects with and is produced through the conflicting epistemologies of tourist and native. As the tour guide attempts to convey her knowledge of Antigua past and present, the local Antiguans are unable to escape from their tiny 'lunatic asylum' and the visitor repeatedly positions himself at a distance from the source of knowledge.

By way of conclusion, it is worth reflecting on Holland and Huggan's statement that *A Small Place* is an oppositional text that is 'invested in the politics of (cross-)cultural representation' (1998: 64). Such a reading, however, reduces the voice of the text to a univocal mode of expression in which the narrating 'I' speaks from a singular subject position that resists the dominant North Atlantic discourses of travel, tourism and Empire. While the text inscribes oppositionality by having the narrator perform mutually exclusive positionings, the work as a whole is not straightforwardly oppositional. For what distinguishes *A Small Place* as a unique postcolonial travel text is precisely its 'hovering' narrative voice and the ways in which the narrator travels between overt political stand-point and discursive understandings of subjectivity. By simultaneously identifying as Antiguan and distancing herself from 'them', the narrator/ traveller moves between conflicting, even contradictory, positions and contests the sites of Self/Other and native/tourist. As such, the political commitment of Kincaid's thematic critique of contemporary tourism is wholly coextensive with a multivocal narrative voice; vocal movements, then, replace the conventional travelling 'I' with a stylistics that draws on the Caribbean ontology of spirit possession.

Works Cited and Consulted

Ashcroft, Bill (2009) 'Afterword: Travel and Power' in Julia Kuehn and Paul Smethurst (eds) *Travel Writing, Form, and Empire*. London: Routledge, 229–41.

Brodber, Erna (2003) *The Continent of Black Consciousness*. London: New Beacon Books.

Byerman, Keith E. (1995) 'Anger in a Small Place: Jamaica Kincaid's Cultural Critique of Antigua'. *College Literature* 22(1): 91–102.

Davis, Wade (1987) *The Serpent and the Rainbow*. New York: Warner Books.

Deren, Maya (1975) *The Voodoo Gods*. Herts: Paladin.

Frederick, Rhonda D. (2003) 'What If You're an "Incredibly Unattractive, Fat, Pastrylike-fleshed Man"?: Teaching Jamaica Kincaid's *A Small Place*'. *College Literature* 30(3): 1–18.

Gauch, Suzanne (2002) '*A Small Place*: Some Perspectives on the Ordinary'. *Callaloo* 25(3): 910–19.

Gilroy, Paul (1996) 'Route Work: The Black Atlantic and the Politics of Exile' in Iain Chambers and Lidia Curti *(eds) The Post-colonial Question*. London: Routledge, 17–29.

Gourdine, Angeletta K. M. (2006) 'Caribbean *Tabula Rasa*: Textual Touristing as Carnival in Contemporary Caribbean Women's Writing'. *Small Axe* 20(June): 80–96.

Harris, Wilson (1995) 'The Limbo Gateway' in Bill Ashcroft, Gareth Griffiths and Helen Tiffin (eds) *The Post-colonial Studies Reader*. London: Routledge, 378–82.

Holland, Patrick and Graham Huggan (1998) *Tourists with Typewriters*. Ann Arbor: University of Michigan Press.

Hurston, Zora Neale (1938) *Tell My Horse*. New York: Harper & Row, 1990.

Kincaid, Jamaica (1985) *Annie John*. New York: Farrar, Straus and Giroux.

Kincaid, Jamaica (1996) *The Autobiography of My Mother*. New York: Farrar, Straus and Giroux.

Kincaid, Jamaica (1988) *A Small Place*. New York: Farrar, Straus and Giroux, 2000.

King, Jane (2002) 'A Small Place Writes Back'. *Callaloo* 25(3): 885–909.

McLeod, Corinna (2008) 'Constructing a Nation: Jamaica Kincaid's *A Small Place*'. *Small Axe* 25(February): 77–92.

Newman, Judie (1995) *The Ballistic Bard*. London: Arnold.

Pedersen, Carl (2001) 'Sea Change: The Middle Passage and the Transatlantic Imagination' in Susan L. Roberson (ed.) *Defining Travel*. Jackson: University Press of Mississippi, 258–66.

Scott, Helen (2002) '"Dem tief, dem a dam tief": Jamaica Kincaid's Literature of Protest'. *Callaloo* 25(3): 977–89.

Simmons, Diane (1994) 'The Rhythm of Reality in the Works of Jamaica Kincaid'. *World Literature Today* 68(3): 466–72.

Notes

1. Employing a very useful approach to Kincaid's text, Helen Scott positions *A Small Place* in relation to postcolonial debates about the relationship between the political and the aesthetic in assigning literary value to any work. Scott commends Kincaid's strong and unambiguous political position

which avoids the pitfalls of a postmodern de-politicizing tendency, even as Kincaid is able to successfully draw on the aesthetic fluidity and indeterminacy of narrative techniques that are often associated with a supposedly 'ideologically neutral' position (Scott, 2002: 979–80).

2. Diane Simmons states that in *A Small Place* 'the author revisits her home, the island of Antigua, after an absence of twenty years' (1994: 466). Keith Byerman briefly notes that 'Kincaid establishes her authority by speaking in the second person to the 'tourist', which allows her to characterize the audience and its voice in the text', but completely ignores the existence of a narrating 'I' which has to be positioned in relation to Kincaid, the author (1995: 92). Jane King (2002) similarly fails to mention the narrator and simply refers to what 'Kincaid' says in *A Small Place*.

3. Writers as diverse as Zora Neale Hurston, Harvard ethnobotanist Wade Davis and US film-maker Maya Deren have recorded their personal experiences with Caribbean spirit possession and the cultural and religious discourses and practices which frame this ritual. See Hurston, *Tell My Horse* (1938); Deren, *The Voodoo Gods* (1975); and Davis, *The Serpent and the Rainbow* (1987).

4. Judie Newman explains the connection between deities and the dead in West African religions as a form of ancestor worship, in which these 'return as spirits ... to revisit their families' (Newman, 1995: 16). With characteristic irreverence, on the other hand, Zora Neale Hurston suspects that many people in the Caribbean use the idea of the dictating *loa* as a subterfuge in order to say things they could not say as themselves (Hurston, 1938: 221).

5. King does not attempt to disguise her own anger at Kincaid who, with *A Small Place*, King argues, 'has established nothing but her profound dislike for her former homeland' (2002: 898). Ironically, the text alienates the Caribbean as well as the North Atlantic reader, as demonstrated by Rhonda Frederick's (2003) article 'What If You're an "Incredibly Unattractive, Fat, Pastrylike-fleshed Man"?: Teaching Jamaica Kincaid's *A Small Place*' which provides tips on how to teach Kincaid's text to North Atlantic students of literature without making them hostile and defensive.

6. Corinna McLeod informs us that 'The Library of Congress has labelled the text as biography, travel, and the ubiquitous 'homes and haunts' ... [while] on the bookshelves in bookstores, the text appears under autobiography, travel literature, fiction, and essay' (McLeod, 2008: 77–8). Suzanne Gauch offers a curious range of non-locations for Kincaid's text by stating that it is '[n]either quite travel narrative nor theory', and that it 'does not claim to be either a manifesto or a song of praise' (Gauch, 2002: 910, 917). Similarly, Angeletta Gourdine simply calls it 'Jamaica Kincaid's nonfiction *A Small Place*' (2006: 80).

7. Diane Simmons (1994) links the style of *A Small Place* to its Antiguan setting. Arguing that Kincaid's characteristic use of rhythm and repetition is much more pronounced in those of her works that are set in Antigua than in novels that take place in the United States, Simmons describes Kincaid's prose style in terms of incantation, magic rhythm and chanting (467). As an example, Simmons cites the increasingly hostile repetition of the phrase 'You are a tourist' in *A Small Place* which, she writes, functions as 'a drumbeat of indictment ... repeated as a sort of refrain after every fresh example of insensitive and dehumanizing behaviour' as the narrating voice catalogues

the many instances of tourist disregard for the material and social realities of the holiday destination (470).

8. Keith Byerman (1995) examines *A Small Place* in the context of the author's repeated exploration of a distinctly female speaking position within Antiguan culture and society (92). Although the idea of gendered voicing is less prominent in *A Small Place* than in her well-known accounts of gender dynamics within family life, Byerman argues that Kincaid, 'by saying in public what other Antiguans can say only in private ... violates the female role of passivity and voicelessness inscribed in the culture' (92). Not only does the narrator of *A Small Place* make the private public by publicizing what is said about the North Atlantic tourist in the private spaces of Antiguans' homes, she also violates traditional gender roles by attacking 'the male world of politics, business, and public life' (91). Byerman's insistence on fixing the narrating agency to a specifically gendered position, however, wholly overlooks the dislocated nature of the voice which speaks to us in *A Small Place*.

9. McLeod argues that Kincaid's narrative strategy of constructing a 'fictional anti-travel narrative' allows her to 'preserve ... the distance between spectator and spectacle' as '[t]he mutually antagonistic voices that Kincaid uses in the text create a space in which the mythical identity of Antigua is both upheld and debunked' (McLeod, 2008: 80).

10. McLeod offers the insightful observation that 'the author relates, chronologically, the destruction of the library to Antiguan independence [which happened not long after the earthquake] ... Unlike the date of the library's destruction, however, Independence Day is not given a date by Kincaid' (2008: 82).

8
Floral Diaspora in Jamaica Kincaid's Travel Writing

Zoran Pećić

In the Introduction to *The Best American Travel Writing 2005* (2005), the editor, Jamaica Kincaid, writes: 'And what of the essays here? Every one of them reminds me of two of the many sentiments attached to the travel narrative: curiosity and displacement' (xviii). The two terms – 'curiosity' and 'displacement' – are indicative of much of Kincaid's writing. In *A Small Place* (1988), for instance, a narrative condemning European imperialism and the neocolonial forces of tourism, Kincaid expresses her feelings of displacement in terms of anger, discontent and loss, as she candidly describes the negative impact of slavery and tourism on Antigua. Usually focusing on the issues of language, (post)colonialism and mother–daughter relationships, Kincaid's writing takes a horticultural turn with the 1999 publication of *My Garden (Book)* and *Among Flowers: A Walk in the Himalaya* (2005). While the latter falls into the category of travel writing, documenting Kincaid's journey from the US to Nepal to gather seeds for her garden in Vermont, the former is a series of essays concerning gardens and plants and their place in the history of colonization and imperialism. The two texts complement each other; they provide both the theory and the practice for Kincaid's exploration of the postcolonial spaces of global travel and the garden. But why this sudden focus on plants, flora and seed collecting in Kincaid's writing? And what do 'curiosity' and 'displacement' have to do with the seemingly innocent practice of collecting seeds? In this essay, I explore how the author of Caribbean postcolonial novels such as *Annie John* (1985) *Lucy* (1990) and *The Autobiography of My Mother* (1996) utilizes the genre of the travel narrative to expose – through the language of travel writing and horticulture – the effects of colonial transplantation and the failure of the colonial imagination to generate pleasure. Thus, I argue that Kincaid's travel writing interrogates the desire to see and to understand

138

the garden as a site of pleasure, but her text also expresses her sense of frustration and displacement as she reflects on her own position as a travelling subject. For Kincaid's journey in *Among Flowers* documents the ambivalence of travel, cultural difference and language as she critiques the discourses and ideologies of Empire.

Kincaid's exploration of the garden and its connection to the history of colonization lies at the heart of *Among Flowers*. The text is both an act of resistance and a means for appropriating the Western institution of botany to voice untold stories of exploitation. For in various cultures and historical periods, the garden has functioned as a site of self-reflection *and* as a space for expressing economic power and socio-political privilege (Crozier, 1999: 627). But the garden is also a significant trope in the postcolonial context: it is connected to the notion of hybridity, both in the material sense (hybridity of plants and races) and in the political sense (the hybridization of cultures). For Kincaid, then, the garden functions not only as a trope of imperialism, remembrance and mourning, but also as a site of hybridity, liminality and ambivalence. According to Anne Collett, 'Kincaid's *Garden (Book):* is an essay in memory or perhaps, "re-memory" ... in which "the world" is pulled to pieces and put back together – differently. This is a process that seeks to actively engage the reader' (2006: 61). In this, Kincaid realizes that gardening is a pastime that derives from reading, writing and representation: 'I was reading a book and that book (written by the historian William Prescott) happened to be about the conquest of Mexico, or New Spain, as it was then called, and I came upon the flower called marigold and the flower called dahlia and the flower called zinnia, and after that the garden was to me more than the garden as I used to think of it. After that the garden was also something else' (1999: 6). Here, Kincaid shows how the historical narratives of colonization and transplantation interlock with the discourses of gardening to reveal discourses of power and control. In her reading about gardens, therefore, Kincaid becomes aware of her conflicted relationship to gardening: the politically problematic imperial projects of acquisition and transplantation lie in sharp contrast to her passion for collecting plants and building her garden. Typically tied to the pleasures of domesticity, Kincaid's garden is also a space connected to a global (imperial) history that transforms her gardening from a leisurely activity to a philosophical exercise fraught with questions of colonization, hybridization and displacement. More importantly, by reading about the colonial history of gardening, Kincaid recognizes that she has 'joined the conquering class: who else could afford this garden – a garden in which I grow things that it would be much cheaper to buy at the store?' (1999: 123). In this context, her garden is, like so many others, a site of privilege, status and wealth.

Transplantations

In his book *Thirdspace: Journeys to Los Angeles and Other Real-and-Imagined Places* (1996), Edward Soja theorizes the 'trialectics of spatiality', which he defines as the discursive construction of space as real, imagined and perceived.[1] Building on Henri Lefebvre's 'moments' in the production of space as a means of disintegrating the dual mode of thinking about space as Firstspace (concrete materiality of spatial forms) and Secondspace (imagined interpretation of human spatiality), Soja argues that the social production of space is built upon three premises. First, there is the 'spatial practice', that is, the material forms of social spatiality made up of things like houses, streets and cities. Second, there are 'representations of space', which are constituted by 'the conceptualised space, the space of science, planners, urbanists, technocrats, artists' (66). Spatial practice (Firstspace) and representations of space (Secondspace) comprise, he continues, the 'real' material world and the perceptions and perspectives that interpret this reality. But, he adds, there are also 'spaces of representation' which form a symbiosis of the two. This interaction between Firstspace and Secondspace points towards a 'thirding' of the spatial imagination which complicates material and mental spaces, and ultimately pushes towards a Thirdspace, which Soja sees as 'simultaneously real and imagined and more (both and also ...)': 'the exploration of Thirdspace can be described and inscribed in journeys to "real-and-imagined" (or perhaps "realandimagined"?) places' (11).

Soja's concepts of space offer an access route into a reading of Jamaica Kincaid's travel text, *Among Flowers*. For the trialectics of spatiality theorized by Soja provide insights into Kincaid's own use of a 'Thirdspace' as a way of recapturing the past in order to change representations in the present. Moreover, it is important to conceptualize Soja's Thirdspace as directly related to postcolonial theories of liminality and in-between spaces, which Homi Bhabha and others see as vital for understanding hybridity and providing new possibilities for political engagement: 'hybridity to me is the "third space", which enables other positions to emerge' (Rutherford, 1990: 211). In contrast to Soja, who employs Thirdspace to investigate the effects of physical space in the socialization of human interaction, Bhabha's 'third space' comprises a postcolonial critique of modern ideas about the location of culture. In fact, Bhabha utilizes this space discursively, for he argues that a 'third space' is produced in and through language, pointing towards the instability of signs and symbols as a method for resisting cultural purity: 'Third Space ... constitutes the discursive conditions ... that ensure that ... even the same signs can be appropriated, translated, rehistoricized and read anew' (1990: 55).

If space is an effect and a practice rather than a given structure, then *My Garden* is more about the practice of gardening (and garden making) than about the actual garden. More importantly, though, *My Garden* is about the practice of drawing upon past experiences as a way of recapturing the past and, in turn, rewriting history. After all, the articulation of silenced stories is a central motif in 20th-century Caribbean writing, and it is present when Kincaid writes about her perusal of the seed catalogues and the history of botany. For example, in the chapter 'In History', Kincaid reflects on Carolus Linnaeus's career in a deeply ironic tone, but Kincaid also relates her own position as a Caribbean subject to the power dynamics of transplantation and renaming in the history of European colonialism: 'What to call the thing that happened to me and all who look like me? Should I call it history? If so, what should history mean to someone like me?' (153). The practice of drawing upon history, however, is fraught with difficulties, frustration and suffering: 'How agitated I am when I am in the garden', writes Kincaid. By representing the garden as a site of colonial history *and* transplantation (rather than pleasure and beauty), Kincaid challenges the garden as a 'natural' space and suggests that gardening is an act of 'naturalizing' the imperial landscape. In this, her agitation when it comes to gardening arises out of the complex and multilayered histories of colonization and imperialism. But gardening also brings her joy and satisfaction: 'how happy I am to be so agitated. How vexed I often am when I am in the garden, and how happy I am to be vexed. What to do? Nothing works just the way I thought it would ... (I mostly worry in the garden, I am mostly vexed in the garden)' (14, 19).

Therefore, Kincaid's representation of gardening is multilayered. Her experience of worry and vexation symbolizes the merger of her own history with the effects of colonization and transplantation. Yet the enjoyment she experiences is a result of being agitated and vexed – an enjoyment she repeats many times throughout the text – and represents her inability to control the garden or order it to her satisfaction. Indeed, her failed attempts to employ the garden purely as a site of pleasure speak to her failure to recapture or understand the relationship between space, plants and transplantation. For if the 'reality' of the garden (Firstspace) is a place of power and control, then the Secondspace of the garden is an imagined site where the imagination seduces us with idealized versions of what the garden could be – what it might become. Kincaid's gardening, then, is situated within a Thirdspace: it relies on the power and pleasure of the imagination to envision an idealized (failed) space, but it also exposes the material impact of colonial trans-plantation and the 'denaturalized' landscape it engenders. Indeed, for Kincaid, the imagination is part of a desire to see and to understand that which inevitably leads to the Enlightenment ideals of mapping knowledge. Closing the essay 'The Garden in Eden', she admits that 'Eden is ... so rich in comfort, it tempts me to cause discomfort; I am in a state of constant discomfort and I like this state so much I would like to share it' (229). Here, the 'Edenic garden' is queried and Kincaid situ-ates herself in a Thirdspace that separates the Firstspace of anti-colonial discourse from the Secondspace of an Enlightenment ontology that seeks out essences and ideals. This experience of being 'in-between' is emphasized when she asserts that what gives her pleasure is the notion of acting. 'What to do?', she asks. For the pleasure of gardening lies not in the visual beauty of her plants but in the fact that discomfort, although it brings vexation, is productive because it forces her to find groundbreaking spaces and new directions.

The Spaces *Among Flowers*

Opening up new spaces is also significant for understanding Kincaid's travel text *Among Flowers*, which expands on her earlier representa-tions of space, gardens and transplantation. While *My Garden* focuses on the implications of colonialism, uprooting and forced movement, *Among Flowers* represents her journey to a foreign land, document-ing her travels through the Himalayas to gather seeds for her garden in Vermont. Accompanied by her friend Daniel Hinkley – 'the most outstanding American plantsman among his peers' – and his botanist friends, Bleddyn and Sue, Kincaid goes 'hunting in southwestern China for seeds which would eventually become flower-bearing shrubs and trees and herbaceous perennials' in her American garden (1). Readers of Kincaid's earlier work might expect to encounter characters suffer-ing from the after-effects of colonization, but *Among Flowers* departs from her earlier themes and, at times, invokes the conventions of the traditional travel narrative. The text begins:

> We were all set to go in October 2001. Starting in the spring of that year, I began to run almost every day ... And so I ran for miles and

miles, and then I lifted weights in a way designed to strengthen the muscles in my legs … And Dan had said that I needed a new pair of boots and that I should break them in, and so I wore them all the time … I suddenly remembered that my passport … had not come back from my travel agent. I called to tell her that she ought to hurry them up because I applied for my visa in June and here was August. (4–5)

Unlike Kincaid's novels, *Among Flowers* depicts only four people, three of whom receive just a few lines of description. In this, Kincaid depicts Daniel, Bleddyn and Sue as background figures on her private voyage to an unknown land and, as the narrative continues, we realize that her story echoes the cosmopolitan (Western) globetrotter's account of going to China and back. Indeed, Kincaid admits that her journey is one of privilege and comfort; she does not need to struggle to survive or battle with nature. 'Not once', she writes, 'was my life in any danger, not even when I was close by to places where the Yangtze River was in the process of flooding over its banks just at the moment I was driving by its banks in my rather nice, comfortable bus' (2). What do we make of Kincaid's travel text? And how do we read her use of the conventional travel narrative? Perhaps Kincaid's recognition of her own privileged position is part of her refusal to employ the imagination in order to generate pleasure. And maybe this approach forces the reader to view the narrative not in terms of anticipation and suspense but as an account of the inner thoughts and reflections of the author.

Throughout the narrative, Kincaid moves between conflicting positions. On the one hand, she is driven to improve her garden in Vermont (thus continuing to enjoy the domesticity of the gardening process). On the other hand, though, she recognizes that her acts of travel and transplantation are potential re-enactments of the colonial enterprise. These competing positions lead to a fragmented sense of self, and her desire to explore the flora of a foreign land engenders an experience whereby being somewhere else is also being someone else. 'The greatest difficulty I experienced', she writes, 'was that I often could not remember who I was and what I was about in my life when I was not there in southwestern China' (2–3). But this experience does not lead to a crippling sense of alienation. Rather, Kincaid takes pleasure in this feeling of estrangement in the same way as she enjoys the discomfort and vexation when she is in her garden: 'I suppose I felt that thing called alienated, but it was so pleasant, so interesting, so dreamily irritating to be so far away from everything I had known' (*Among*: 3).

Space, then, alters Kincaid's conception of self and, as such, her representations of space function in diverse ways. As she travels through the Himalayas, for instance, her narrative focuses on the Firstspace representation of the 'real' journey: she chronicles her route and describes what she sees. But under the surface of the Firstspace narrative, there is an uneasiness and ambiguity that arises out of her engagement with the travel genre. For *Among Flowers* combines a series of tensions that move fluidly between curiosity and displacement, pleasure and frustration, enjoyment and vexation. This, then, ruptures binary oppositions between the materiality of Firstspace and the imaginary qualities of Secondspace and, as result, her travels foreground a Thirdspace of ambiguity and liminality – a space that combines competing emotions and discourses to exist on a continuum between materiality and imagination. Throughout *Among Flowers*, for instance, the liminality of Thirdspace is captured when Kincaid glimpses the familiar within the unfamiliar, thus complicating the spatial relations of 'here' and 'there':

> This account of a walk I took while gathering seeds of flowering plants in the foothills of the Himalaya can have its origins in my love of the garden, my childhood love of botany and geography, my love of feeling isolated, or imagining myself all alone in the world and everything unfamiliar, or the familiar being strange, my love of being afraid but at the same time not letting my fear stand in the way, my love of things that are far away, but things I have no desire to possess. (7)

This uncanny experience – the familiar within the unfamiliar, the real within the unreal – corresponds to Soja's description of Thirdspace: the 'realandimagined' space of his theoretical paradigm. For Kincaid, Kathmandu displays the curiosity and displacement of the 'realandimagined' experience that she depicts as being vital to the genre of travel writing: 'When I was in ... the Thamel ... I was reminded of the feelings I had when I was a child, of going to something called "the fair", something beyond the every day, something that would end when I was not asleep, when I was not in a dream. I did truly feel as if I was in the unreal, the magical, extraordinary' (17–18).

Among Flowers represents the uncanny experience of a Himalayan journey that moves between the foreign and the familiar, the homely and the unhomely. According to Nicholas Royle, the uncanny 'involves feelings of uncertainty, in particular regarding the reality of who one is and what is being experienced' (2003: 1). And this is highlighted in Kincaid's characterization of the people on the street as having 'no purpose to being themselves as if the only reason to be there was just to be there' (*Among*: 18). Here, Kincaid emphasizes the dreamlike qualities of the town, relying on her imagination to understand the roles of the people and why they are there. 'But the uncanny is not simply an experience of strangeness or alienation', Royle continues. 'More specifically, it is a peculiar commingling of the familiar and unfamiliar' (2003: 1). During her trip to Thamel, Kincaid describes a strong sense of the uncanny – a sudden sensation that becomes transposed onto herself as she realizes that 'because of my own particular history, every person I saw seemed familiar to me. But then again, because of my own particular history, every person I saw in the Thamel was familiar also' (18). Here, the voice of the traveller articulates a complex representation of the (uncanny) spatiality of Kathmandu: Firstspace and Secondspace exist only as markers for locating the in-between site that challenges clear-cut definitions of the real and unreal, home and away. In this, the narrative depicts home and away not as stable or fixed spaces, but as fluid locations that gesture towards the identificatory instability of the travelling subject. I do not want to suggest that Freudian definitions of the uncanny are identical to Soja's Thirdspace, but the in-betweenness and liminality of the uncanny combines with the psychic and spatial conception of the unhomely – the *unheimlich* – to echo Soja's theory. Moreover, Kincaid's descriptions of curiosity and displacement can be read as uncanny experiences that interrogate the instability of identity when one is caught in-between belonging and estrangement.

But the uncanny Thirdspace of *Among Flowers* is not only figurative or rhetorical. For the travelling subject embraces displacement as a means of finding new spaces and directions: Kincaid, for example, transforms the traveller's pleasure of seeing and discovery into a unique set of spatial relations that highlight the symbolic alongside the concrete, and the material consequences of travelling through a new space. The unfamiliar places affect Kincaid's perception of herself, and she comes to see herself as neither a gardener nor a seed collector. Rather, she conceives of herself as experiencing a place in-between the garden in Vermont and the Himalayan sites of a global travel industry, for she describes herself as a traveller who loses her way (and her sense of self) as she walks the line between the seen and the imagined. Thus, instead of stabilizing foreign space through her gaze as a traveller, she looks for displacement and describes discomfort as central to her intervention in the travel genre: 'For the traveler (who will eventually become the Travel Writer) is in a state of displacement, not in the here of the familiar (home), not in the there of destination (a place that has been made familiar by imagining being in it in the first place)' (*Best*: xiv). Preferring displacement to stability, Kincaid's travels are about loss: the loss of stability, comfort, balance – the 'loss of every kind' (xiv).

Being Lost *Among Flowers*

It is not only the experience of the familiar within the unfamiliar that provokes a jarring feeling of displacement for the traveller-narrator. Describing the sharp contrasts between the landscapes of Vermont and Nepal, Kincaid is frequently reminded of her role as a traveller in a foreign land: 'I could see ahead of me, my way forward, a landscape of red-colored boulders arranged as if deliberate and at the same time the result of a geographic catastrophe. I was making this trip with the garden in mind to begin with; so everything I saw, I thought, How would this look in the garden?' (43–4). Beginning the journey with the Vermont garden at the forefront of her mind, Kincaid describes the foreign geography as a Secondspace by projecting the Nepalese landscape onto her own garden. This projection is made explicit when she states that 'the garden itself was a way of accommodating and making acceptable, comfortable, familiar, the wild, the strange' (44). Suddenly, she is made aware that, by collecting exotic plants for her garden at home, she is perpetuating the colonial activity of mapping knowledge. Locating plants such as *Dicentra scandens*, *Agapetes serpens*, *Begonia* and *Strobilanthes*, Kincaid's motivation for travel (collecting seeds) places her in the position of a 'possessor'; she seeks to acquire plants and take control of them through uprooting and transplantation.

In her insightful book *Plants and Empire: Colonial Bioprospecting in the Atlantic World* (2004), Londa Schiebinger notes that in the 'eighteenth-century botanical nomenclature ... a rich diversity of traditional names was funneled ... through the intellectual straits of Linnaean nomenclature to produce standardized naming' (20). Exploring the history of plant names, Schiebinger argues that 'naming practices devised in the eighteenth century assisted in the consolidation of Western hegemony and ... embedded into botanical nomenclature a particular historiography, namely, a history celebrating the deeds of great European men' (198). In addition, the naming of plants 'celebrat[ed] European kings and patrons who had contributed to the cost of oceanic voyages, botanical gardens, extensive libraries. The point again was glory, or immortality. Anyone whose name was "gloriously" immortalized by science had, Linnaeus maintained, "obtained the highest honor that mortal men can desire"' (204). In *Among Flowers*, Kincaid takes on some of the characteristics of the plant collector; she even admits that procuring the seeds from a *Codonopsis* plant brings on a 'godlike' sensation of having 'invented *Codonopsis*' (33). This feeling of divinity is, however, undermined when she approaches a village and sees a vegetable garden, 'carefully trellised and then allowed to run onto the roof of a nearby building' (65). Here, she is reminded that 'the Garden of Eden is our ideal and even our idyll, the place where food and flowers are one. After that, food is agriculture and flowers are horticulture all by themselves. We try to make food beautiful and we try to make flowers useful, but it seems to me that this can never be completely so' (65). For Kincaid, the divine representation of the Edenic garden does not bring joy, for the processes of identification, naming and possession are merely attempts to structure the Firstspace garden through an imaginative Secondspace. In this, Kincaid is self-reflexive about her attempts to recreate a 'Garden of Eden' in her Vermont garden.

Recognizing her multivalent position as both inside and outside the 'conquering class', Kincaid's motive for travel exposes the effects of colonial transplantation and uncovers the failure of the imagination to generate pleasure. The creation of a Thirdspace, for instance, allows Kincaid to 'denaturalize' the relationship between landscape and identity, pointing back to the garden as a site for interrogating colonial spaces. More precisely, Kincaid expands the intellectualization of her journey to encompass the reality of her presence in Nepal as both a wealthy tourist (subject) and a victim of colonial enterprises (object). In fact, the emphasis on the historical transplantation of flora (which *My Garden* links to the transmigration of people under colonialism) is also present in *Among Flowers*; but here, the traveller-narrator acknowledges her own complicity in the continued exploitation of the 'native population' that is reiterated in her horticultural curiosity. By contrast, in *My Garden* Kincaid identifies herself as marked by colonial history and, by extension, someone who is alienated from the Caribbean landscape: '[I]gnorance of the botany of the place I am from (and am of) really only reflects the fact that when I lived there, I was of the conquered class and living in a conquered place'. This condition is emblematic of the condition where 'nothing about you is of any interest unless the conqueror deems it so' (120).

In *Among Flowers*, though, the conqueror–conquered relationship is replicated in Kincaid's interactions with (and descriptions of) the Sherpas, her local porters. Here, Kincaid is the privileged traveller who uses her position as a tourist and seed collector to engage with the local population in order to satisfy her horticultural desires. Unlike *A Small Place* (1988) in which Kincaid challenges (and reverses) the powerful gaze of the Western tourist, her journey to Nepal mimics the position of the tourist by replicating the amazement and wonder of the foreign experience and exoticizing the people, smells and sounds she sees. In an early passage, for example, Kincaid describes her porters as follows:

> I then met my other traveling companions, the people who would make my journey through the Himalaya a pleasure. There was Cook; his real name was so difficult to pronounce, I could not do it then and I cannot do it now. There was his assistant, but we called him "Table," and I remember him now as "Table" because he carried the table and the four chairs on which we sat for breakfast and dinner. (26)

Kincaid's tone when describing the porters is characterized by solemnity and ambivalence: she sees her companions and their efforts as a natural part of the journey, but she also emphasizes the asymmetrical power relations between the traveller and the local citizens. She depersonalizes the Sherpas by renaming them according to the work they do for her. As a result, Kincaid depicts Nepal in the context of a labour-based global economy of travel, focusing on the big business of tourism as a powerful tool in the exploitation of Nepal and its citizens. Commodification and consumption, then, play vital roles in her journey. After listing the hiking equipment she purchased for the trek (underwear, socks, glove liners), she describes her hotel in Nepal: 'My hotel was in that area of Kathmandu called the Thamel District. It is a special area ... filled with shops and restaurants and native European people, who look poor, dirty, and bedraggled'. This is, she continues, 'a look of luxury really, for these people are travelers, at any minute they can get up and go home' (17).

Yet Kincaid's awareness of the disparity between the traveller and the local citizen also incorporates a sense of curiosity and displacement to reveal glaring inequalities. In fact, these inequities actually contribute to the wonder and displacement she feels throughout her journey. Commenting on the travel texts she read before travelling to Nepal, she remarks: 'I had read so much about European travelers in Kathmandu, none of it leaving a good impression' (17). Thus, she realizes that such Western travel narratives do not relate to her own sense of curiosity and displacement in Nepal. But instead of abandoning the project, Kincaid continues travelling ('seeing these people then in that place did not make me think I ought to change my mind') and inserting the unsettling landscapes of liminal and ambivalent spaces into her narrative, destabilizing the division between home and away:

> There were many other people, all attached to our party, and they were so important to my safety and general well-being but I could never remember their proper names ... This is not at all a reflection of the relationship between power and powerless, the waiter and the diner, or anything that would resemble it. This was only a reflection of my own anxiety, my own unease, my own sense of ennui, my own personal fragility. I have never been so unconformable, so out of my skin in my entire life, and yet not once did I wish to leave, not once did I regret being there. (27)

The identity of the conqueror, Kincaid states, is not necessarily stable or fixed. Rather, she exposes the dependence of the conqueror on the conquered – a dynamic that causes the tourist (and subsequently the reader) to feel both anxiety and discomfort. For by exposing herself and the reader as fragile and dependent, Kincaid reverses the typecasting method she uses in *A Small Place*, turning the critical eye on herself as a garden maker, a seed collector and a globetrotter. In this, the narrative forces readers to see their own participation in transnational economic disparities.

Thirdspace and the Postcolonial Travel Text

What does it mean to be 'out of one's skin'? For Kincaid, this feeling – 'I felt out of my skin' – is part of her Nepalese travels and alludes to conceptions of racial difference and personal identity. But it also gestures to the discourses of marginalization within the conventional travel genre, particularly as they exist in the choices of inclusion or exclusion and the traveller–native dynamic. The emphasis on 'being out', though, also situates Kincaid's travel narrative within the larger tradition of travel writing, for 'being out' suggests the travelling body's relationship to spatial configurations (inside and outside). Here, the uncanny movement between the familiar and unfamiliar extends to include the dimensions of centre and margin, displacement and identity. Being at home in her skin, then, is challenged in an uncanny transformation whereby her privileged status as a tourist erases the social construction of her blackness, and marginalized subjectivities are transferred to her local guides and porters. In this, Kincaid begins to associate with white tourists and, as she explores the 'exotic' Nepalese landscape, she experiences an uncanny feeling that 'disturbs any straightforward sense of what is inside and what is outside' (Royle, 2003: 2). Within this disjuncture, the 'real' composition of Firstspace and the mental representations of Secondspace are reworked into (an uncanny) Thirdspace – a space lodged between the familiar and the unfamiliar, the real and the unreal, and forms a liminal conception of identity:

> It may be that the uncanny is a feeling that happens only to oneself, within oneself, but it is never one's 'own': its meaning and significance may have to do, most of all, with what is not oneself, with others, with the world 'itself'. It may thus be construed as a foreign body within oneself, even the experience of oneself *as* a foreign body, the very estrangement of inner silence and solitude. (Royle, 2003: 2)

Kincaid's description of her dependence on the Sherpas is discomforting. In one section, for instance, the guides are ahead of Kincaid and her companions; they are unable to find water on the mountain and without the Sherpas to help set up camp they become irritable. 'We, and by that I mean me in particular and especially, began to whimper and even complain', Kincaid writes. Yet her irritation with the porters is conveyed with irony, for Kincaid is fully aware of her irrational frustration:

> What had the porters been doing all day? someone said – meaning, What had they been doing when we were exploring the landscape, looking for things that would grow in our garden, things that would give us pleasure, not only in their growing, but also with the satisfaction with which we could see them growing and remember seeing them alive in their place of origin, a mountainside, a small village, a not easily accessible place in the large (still) world? (83)

Kincaid's representation of a Thirdspace in the Nepalese landscape is grounded in her attempt to relate the imaginative act of writing to the physical acts of gardening and seed collecting. Her sense of suspension – being 'in-between' – speaks to her ambiguous feelings of pleasure and vexation, thus disrupting the coherence and transparency of conventional travel writing.

This intervention in the genre is foregrounded when Kincaid refers to the writing of Frank Smythe (1900–1949), the British botanist and mountaineer who published *The Kanchenjunga Adventure* in 1930. Indeed, during her trek, Kincaid writes about her conflicted emotions to Smythe's book: 'it was as if a spell had been cast over me; first the book and then the mountain, and all the way on my walk, there was nothing I wanted to see more' (31). This 'spell', though, is not disorienting. For Kincaid juxtaposes her own travel text with Smythe's narrative of possessing and producing knowledge. Her self-reflection, the acknowledgement of her own privilege, and the insertion of a Thirdspace all contribute to a remapping of the genre whereby Kincaid exposes the power relations of travelling and deterritorializes the boundaries separating her garden in Vermont from the Himalayas and the 'Garden of Eden'. Commenting on Smythe's travel writing, for instance, Kincaid highlights his European vision of the 'Garden of Eden' – a vision that motivates his efforts to climb the world's highest mountains:

> I was reading my book by Frank Smythe about his failed attempts to climb Kanchenjunga in 1930. Three weeks ago I would have had no interest or understanding of his account of climbing a mountain. I knew of him through his writing as a plant hunter. I had no idea that the mountaineer and the plant collector were the same person. Much later, I came to see that he became a plant collector because it was a way for him to climb mountains. (96–7)

Here, Kincaid's conflicted reactions to Smythe's account arise, in part, out of her realization that the seed collector and the colonial traveller (the mountaineer) are not mutually exclusive activities or identities. Yet Kincaid's description of Smythe's work also demonstrates how the mapping of landscape is achieved through an imaginative leap that traverses the gaps between a Firstspace 'reality' and a Secondspace ideal of divinity on Earth. In this, Kincaid reads Smythe's work as conflating the Nepalese landscape with an idealized 'Garden of Eden': 'His [Smythe's] most famous book of plant collecting, *The Valley of Flowers*, is full of the many little side trips he took to climb some summit, insignificant by Himalayan standards but major when compared to the rest of the world's geography. It became clear to me that while trying to climb Everest in the twenties, and then Kanchenjunga in the thirties, the spectacular beauty of a Himalayan spring left such an impression that it either made him a gardener or made him see those mountains as an extension of the garden' (97).

Connecting her seed collecting to Smythe's, Kincaid extends her travel text to other accounts of the Himalayan landscape by British explorers – all of whom have contributed to her enthusiasm for Nepalese plants. In this, her trip is influenced by textual travels and travel writing that have sparked her imagination and motivated her journey. For instance, as she travels to Thudam, she admits that despite not having much knowledge of the place she feels it is magical and enchanted, relying on her imagination to provide sufficient information required to 'know' the place. More importantly, though, she recalls reading a description of Thudam written by Roy Lancaster, the British botanist and member of the Royal Horticultural Society. She writes:

> I had known of Thudam through the book *A Plantsman in Nepal* written by the great plantsman Roy Lancaster. That and a similar volume he wrote about plant collecting in China are two of the most important books in the canon of modern plant collecting, and any amateur interested in this area of the garden will only be pleased with the encouragement and pleasure that is to be found in them. (119–20)

Here, Kincaid's textual travels open up an idealized Secondspace that, in turn, informs her vision of Thudam as a mysterious and wondrous locale. At the same time, though, her self-reflection about this process demystifies the literature of plant collecting and, by exposing its imaginative underpinnings, she places her sense of awe in the context of a dream-like conception of the Himalayas.

Reading, then, informs her understandings of the power dynamics involved in travel and seed collecting. Indeed, when she first finds the *Rheum nobile*, a plant 'only [to] be found in books written by plant hunters and only ones who have been to certain areas of the Himalaya' (132), she describes how knowledge of the plant came to her by way of the colonial traveller and botanist Sir Joseph Dalton Hooker (1817–1911). Rather than describing the plant in her own words, Kincaid quotes from Hooker's *Himalayan Journals, Notes of a Naturalist* (1854):

> 'On the black rocks the gigantic rhubarb forms pale pyramidal towers a yard high, of inflated reflexed bracts that conceal the flowers, and overlapping one another like tiles, protect them from wind and rain: a whorl of broad green leaves edged with red spreads on the ground at the base of the plant, contrasting in color with the transparent bracts, which are yellow, margined with pink. This is the handsomest herbaceous plant in Sikkim.' (133)

Here, Kincaid gives voice to a leading figure in 19th-century British colonialism and empire building. After all, while travelling in India and Nepal in the early 1850s to collect plants, Hooker (a close friend of

Charles Darwin) was also director of the Kew Royal Botanic Gardens, the site of the world's largest collection of plants. Kincaid's insertion of Hooker in *Among Flowers* situates her travels in relation to the British colonial enterprise, for seed and plant collection was a significant part of the colonial project and the creation of London as the colonial centre.[2] But where Kincaid's travel text differs from Hooker's is in the recognition of herself as a privileged traveller and the experience of displacement that this engenders. Hooker, by contrast, does not question his privileged status or comment on the asymmetrical power relations that enable his journey. Instead of feeling displaced in India or Nepal, Hooker considers himself 'at home' in the expansive (and expanding) British Empire, and he is steadfast in his belief that flora and vegetation should be transported from the colonial peripheries to the imperial centre of London, thus maintaining Kew Garden's status as the hub of the horticultural world.

Hybridity and Travel Writing

If the writings of Joseph Hooker, Frank Smythe and Roy Lancaster are representative of many colonial travel narratives (depicting the activities of collecting, hunting and knowledge production), then where do we place *Among Flowers* in relation to this tradition? Or, we might ask, how does Kincaid's travel text relate to the discourses of exoticism, control and territorial domination characteristic of so many colonial travel narratives? On the one hand, Kincaid's journey to collect seeds establishes her within a tradition that reiterates Victorian colonial practices: she seeks to possess foreign plants for transplantation and then write about the expedition of their acquisition. On the other hand, though, Kincaid opens up a Thirdspace that exists in-between the 'real' and 'idealized' spaces of the journey and, in so doing, she challenges the exotic pleasure generated within the colonial imagination – a pleasure that can only be sustained in a position of power and privilege. This makes *Among Flowers* much more nuanced and ambiguous than its colonial predecessors. For Kincaid's sense of curiosity is undercut by her feelings of displacement, locating her in an uncanny space between the familiar role of a gardener and the unfamiliar position of the world traveller. Still, Kincaid recognizes that she is not exempt from the exploitation and problematic power structures found in the contemporary (global) tourist industry. Indeed, she comes to understand that her journey perpetuates the domination and marginalization of local citizens and cultures (as her depiction of the Sherpas-as-servants makes clear). And yet her self-reflection on these matters leads to a 'loss of self' – an alienation that even displaces her from the homely site of her skin.

With the intent of 'reflect[ing] on the complexity of space/place relationships that have informed the rise of interest in postcolonial travel writing', Edwards and Graulund, in the Introduction to this book, express their hope that travel might lead to a 'sense of homelessness through a disintegration of nation-based notions of identity', where 'the cessation of one identity ... leads to an experience of being out-of-place' (7). Kincaid's *Among Flowers* is, I suggest, a unique example of how a postcolonial writer can draw on the material conditions and figurative conceptions of hybridity to examine global travel and challenge the limited spatiality of First- and Secondspace. In fact, by engaging in the colonial travel customs of 'hunting' and 'collecting' and simultaneously constructing a Thirdspace from which she can reflect on colonial practices, Kincaid herself becomes a hybrid figure. And by simultaneously invoking and subverting the colonial travel narrative, she makes an important contribution to nuanced representations of space as well as narratives that try to document a quest for knowledge and understanding.

Works Cited and Consulted

Bhabha, Homi (1990) 'The Third Space: Interview with Homi K. Bhabha' in Jonathan Rutherford (ed.) *Identity: Community, Culture, Difference*. London: Lawrence & Wishart, 207–21.

Bhabha, Homi (1994) *The Location of Culture*. London: Routledge, 2004.

Collett, Anne (2006) 'Boots and Bare-Feet in Jamaica Kincaid's *Garden (Book):*' *Wasafiri* 21(2): 58–63.

Crozier, Michael (1999) 'After the Garden?' *The South Atlantic Quarterly* 98(4): 625–31.

Freud, Sigmund (1955) 'The "Uncanny"' in James Strachey (ed.) *The Standard Edition of the Complete Psychological Works of Sigmund Freud*. Vol. 17. London: Hogarth, 218–52.

Holland, Patrick and Graham Huggan (1998) *Tourists with Typewriters: Contemporary Reflections on Contemporary Travel Writing*. Ann Arbor: University of Michigan Press, 2000.

Kincaid, Jamaica (1988) *A Small Place*. New York: Farrar, Straus and Giroux, 2000.

Kincaid, Jamaica (1999) *My Garden (Book):* New York: Farrar Straus and Giroux.

Kincaid, Jamaica (2005) *Among Flowers: A Walk in the Himalaya*. Washington D.C.: National Geographic.

Kincaid, Jamaica (2005) 'Introduction' in Jamaica Kincaid (ed.) *The Best American Travel Writing 2005*. Boston: Houghton Mifflin Company, xii–xix.

Lefebvre, Henri (1991) *The Production of Space*. Trans. Donald Nicholson-Smith. Oxford: Blackwell. Trans. of *La production de l'espace*. Paris: Anthropos, 1974.

Royle, Nicholas (2003) *The Uncanny*. Manchester: Manchester University Press.
Rutherford, Jonathan (ed.) (1990) *Identity: Community, Culture, Difference*. London: Lawrence & Wishart.
Schiebinger, Londa (2004) *Plants and Empire: Colonial Bioprospecting in the Atlantic World*. Cambridge, MA: Harvard University Press.
Soja, Edward W. (1996) *Thirdspace: Journeys to Los Angeles and Other Real-and-Imagined Places*. Oxford: Blackwell.

Notes

1. Soja is influenced by Henri Lefebvre's theory of the politics of space. Lefebvre identifies several 'moments' in the production of space: spatial practice, representations of space and representational spaces. Lefebvre connects these moments in order to emphasize a renewed approach to perceiving space. See Henri Lefebvre, *The Production of Space* (1974).
2. Schiebinger (2004) notes that 'the great Linnaeus ... like most botanists in this period ... taught that national wealth could be aggrandized through the exact study of nature' (6–7). In the case of Britain, Schiebinger notes that 'Sir Hans Sloane at one end of the eighteenth century and Sir Joseph Banks at the other both joined economic ventures to botanical exploration' (7). Importantly, 'botanists at this time were "agents of empire": their inventories, classifications, and transplantations were the vanguard and in some cases the "instruments" of European order' (11).

9
Post-Orientalism and the Past-Colonial in William Dalrymple's Travel Histories

Paul Smethurst

William Dalrymple tends to be dismissive in interviews and articles when considering the influence of postcolonial theory on his work. He reacts against what he sees as the tendency in academic scholarship to disparage historians and travel writers whose subjects include the languages, history and literatures of the East. It is as if they are all, past and present, tarred with the increasingly pejorative brush: 'Orientalist'. In his preface to Michael Fisher's recent anthology of European travel writing on Mughal India, he attacks this kind of blinkered criticism:

> Following the success of Edward Said's groundbreaking 1978 work *Orientalism,* the exploration of the East – its peoples, habits, customs and past – by European travellers has become the target for what has effectively been a major scholarly assault. 'Orientalist' has been transformed from a simple descriptive label into a term of outright academic abuse, and men as diverse as the sophisticated French jeweller and aesthete Jean-Baptiste Tavernier, a Cornish pilchard merchant's son Peter Mundy and the grand British judge and linguist Sir William Jones have all alike come to be seen as complicit in the project of gathering 'colonial knowledge' – and accused of being agents of colonialism, attempting to 'appropriate' Eastern learning and demonstrate the superiority of Western ways by 'imagining' the East as decayed, degenerate and 'picturesque', fit only to be colonised and 'civilised'. (Fisher, 2007: vii–viii)

Dalrymple's complaint simplifies Said's polemic but it captures the thrust, and it is indicative of how the practice of Oriental Studies has become ideologically charged. The time has come to investigate this complaint through Dalrymple's own work, and to reconsider the influence, legacy and efficacy of Said's *Orientalism*. The compass for postcolonial studies was reset by Said, but it has come a long way, if elliptically, in the past 30 years. Indeed, Dalrymple's work (especially *City of Djinns* from 1993 and *White Mughals* from 2002) connects with some strands of postcolonial theory which, as Robert Young has pointed out, are contra Said anyway (Young, 2009: n.p.). For example, in Dalrymple's description of 18th-century India, a certain theoretical terrain is clearly discernible:

> The Kirkpatricks inhabited a world that was far more hybrid, and with far less clearly defined ethnic, national and religious borders, than *we* have been conditioned to expect, either by the conventional Imperial history books written in Britain before 1947, or by the nationalist historiography of post-Independence India, or ... by the post-colonial work coming from new generations of scholars [who] follow the path opened up by Edward Said. (2002: xl–xli, my emphasis)

Themes of hybridization, transculturation and boundary-crossing figure strongly in Dalrymple's work, and they are also typical of postcolonial theory. This suggests he is more attuned to theory than he might realize.

I emphasize 'we' in the above quote to help 'us' locate the implied readership (presumably British first and by extension Westerners). It is important to recognize that Dalrymple is addressing the West. His strategy is to disorientate (or de-occidentalize) Westerners by challenging historicizations through which the West has identified itself relationally against its others. This extends postcolonial theory, because we can see that it is not only the mind of the colonized, but also that of the colonizer, that needs decolonizing: 'It is as if the Victorians succeeded in colonising not only India but also, more permanently, *our* imaginations' (2002: xliii, emphasis added). His response to this colonization of the *Western* mind is to work towards the reconciliation of two worlds, Western and Oriental. For Dalrymple, this necessitates the recovery and accentuation of historical crossings and acculturation, combined with challenges to, and weakening of, historical division and difference. His geographical and historical focus is that 'patch between Constantinople and Calcutta', where relations between the Islamic world and the West have played out over several millennia (Youngs, 2005: 51).

Given that he is not obviously a postcolonial subject himself and one of his major works (*White Mughals*) is not travel writing per se, I should begin by explaining why Dalrymple is included in a book on *postcolonial travel* writing. Like the novel, travel writing was until recently conceived as a specifically Western genre. What characterized this genre historically was a form and style shaped by the assumption of authority by Western travellers to describe the rest of the world vis-à-vis the West. Postcolonial studies subsequently brought non-Western travel writing to light as a counter-discourse, and contemporary postcolonial travel writing continues to disrupt the geographical, ontological and symbolic boundaries of 'the West and the Rest'. Such writers as Salman Rushdie, Amitav Ghosh, Pico Iyer, Caryl Phillips and V. S. Naipaul have increasingly adopted and adapted the genre to respond to the Western discourse of travel. In doing so, they have 'extended the discursive boundaries and the poetic dimensions of the form' (Dissanayake, 2002: n.p.). With Dalrymple, however, we have to ask if this same discursive space and form can, or indeed should, be occupied by white Western writers. Questions of postcoloniality, positionality and form in his work need to be addressed. He might 'disappear' as a travel writer to follow historical routes but, as a Western writer and historian, can he extricate the history of India from colonial discourse, and avoid postcolonial nostalgia?

Although he has revealed himself to be the product of an 'interracial liaison' with 'Indian blood in his veins', Dalrymple is not a postcolonial subject escaping the confines of Western hegemony to seize agency and write back against the Empire (2002: xli). Rather, it seems his own family and that of his wife were directly involved in colonialism, and family memoirs have guided his research.[1] This does not exclude him from writing a postcolonial text, however, particularly as Dalrymple is not the principal subject of his narratives (except in *In Xanadu* [1989]). In fact, he has consciously sought to 'disappear' as a witnessing travel writer, claiming: 'My own style, increasingly I think, is letting a person speak for themselves [sic]' (Youngs, 2005: 52). Superficially, he and his wife are the subjects of a travel narrative in *City of Djinns*, but actually Delhi is the focus, and the form of the travel narrative is extended into historiography. The subjectivities of residents and visitors to Delhi, past and present, are brought to life through travel memoirs, letters and testimonies, and systematically *placed* in this history of Delhi. Dalrymple's first impressions as a traveller are that the city has 'managed to shed its colonial baggage'; he is 'astonished how little evidence remained of British rule' (1993: 70). This is no more than an opening ruse, however, and, as he weaves his way back to the British Raj and beyond, the superficial progress of the travel narrative is arrested by a historical mode which is essentially regressive. The resulting form I call 'travel history' because travel writing is used as a vehicle to bring the narrator to historical sites where he then travels back in time. The sites Dalrymple dwells on, and discourses on, might be called 'time-objects': the physical monuments, buildings and texts which are encountered in the present, but which encapsulate, resonate with, and evoke earlier times. The travel history has a parallel timeline in the present, however, and this *presencing* of the past occurs not only through archives and physical sites, but can also be found in encounters with 'human ruins'. Then, as in Foucault's concept of heterotopia, we find different times occupying the same space: 'the different ages of man were represented in the people of the city. Different millennia coexisted side by side. Minds set in different ages walked the same pavements, drank the same water, returned to the same dust' (1993: 9).

Dalrymple's research for *City of Djinns* and *White Mughals* took place mainly in India, and in these works there is a palpable sense of writing *from*, as well as *about,* India. This reverses the trajectory of those Indian diasporic writers who travel to the West to write about the East. A major theme is the acculturation that occurred in India before and during the colonial period, not just as historical fact, but as evidence of the transmutability of cultures across history. This is *revisionary* in the context of post-Orientalism, because Said always emphasizes Western hegemony, and the asymmetrical power relations between West and East. We hear very little in colonial discourse, or Said's analysis of it, about Europeans who crossed over. In *White Mughals,* Dalrymple reveals the extent to which Europeans absorbed elements of Indian culture, with some detaching themselves entirely from their home culture to wrap themselves in the foreign.

A closer look at narrative structure reveals Dalrymple's strategies of *enunciation* in his travel histories: where is he speaking from, who is speaking to whom, and who or what authorizes what is being said? Firstly, he makes the narrative multivocal by including extensive dialogue with local postcolonial subjects, and by incorporating texts from other historians and travel writers from Europe, Persia and India. This multivocalicity extends the form of travel writing from 'sightseeing and witnessing' to a form which locates subjectivity in the ruins, mementoes and living memories of others. Secondly, by writing from India, as well as about India, Dalrymple shifts the subject position geographically. He tries as far as possible to become an *insider* by adopting a 'travel-in-dwelling' approach, to reverse James Clifford's term (1997: 26). *City of Djinns* is based on the part-fiction that Dalrymple and his wife, Olivia, live in Delhi for a year, travelling, sketching and historicizing while ensconced in the tragi-comic atrium of the Puri household. In fact, they had lived in Delhi for about four years before the book appeared, so he actually underplays his immersion in the city (Youngs, 2005: 42).

Nevertheless, Dalrymple is a Westerner continuing to represent the Orient for consumption by dominant Western cultures. Despite the undoubted success of Indian writers, and writers with Indian origins, such as Iyer, Rushdie, Naipaul and Ghosh, it would seem that there are Westerners still claiming the authority to write about the East. To see if he evades the problems identified above, and of reiterating Orientalism as Said defined it, we need to examine more closely his formal strategies of 'self-making' and 'self-unmaking' (Dissanayake, 2002: n.p.).

Dalrymple 'self-makes' the narrator as a British Indophile traveller in *City of Djinns,* and as a quick-footed British investigative historian in *White Mughals.* He 'self-unmakes' these narrators by deferring to other witnesses and texts. The second half of *City of Djinns* is predominantly *told through* earlier travel texts, Indian literature and through dialogue with Dr. Jaffery. So, as well as incorporating textual evidence of the past, he extends narrative authority to the other through these conduits. Local knowledge is thereby privileged, but is there yet a *structural* imposition of Western knowledge on Indian history and culture? As a Western travel writer and historian, we might expect Dalrymple's narrative authority to stem from the legacy of Western rationalism and science. Despite his undoubted empathy with Indian culture and his extensive local knowledge, behind his presentation of local legends and the paranormal, there still lurks Western thinking. The *djinns* and the many other supernatural elements of Indian religion and culture are therefore cast in a realistic frame. We know *he* will never actually see a djinn, although he reports many sightings and sensings by others. It is possible then, whether Dalrymple intended it or not, for such moments to be read as exotic interludes in an otherwise Westernised history designed for a Western market. We could say that he is not only a traveller *from* the West, but he is also travelling *in* the West, because the structures of knowledge through which he mediates the non-Western world are essentially Western.

This is not to say that Dalrymple's subject position is entirely monolingual or monocultural. Through various strategies, rhetorical, epistemological and ontological, he is able to modify the Western-centric position. Epistemological manipulations generally involve the reinsertion of non-Western and marginalized Western travel writings and histories. These are sources which for one reason or another did not constitute colonial history. Dalrymple is at pains to display his depth of knowledge of the culture that he is dealing with through a display, not only of his understanding of the language, history and social structure of India, but also of the processes by which he has come to acquire this knowledge. In both *White Mughals* and *City of Djinns* there is a determined studiousness which highlights Dalrymple's personal quests for knowledge. And by seeking information which contravenes established colonial history, his research leans towards the counter-discursive.

Ontological intervention comes from Dalrymple setting up home in India for long periods at a time, learning local languages, interviewing people from different ethnic and racial backgrounds and studying Indian history *in situ*. As already mentioned, his narrative authority is to some extent localized by using the travel-in-dwelling form to describe shared social and cultural experiences between himself and local subjects. He tends to do this self-consciously, sharing with us these journeys of histori-cal enquiry as he sets about tracking down local information. Although the process of embedding himself in Indian culture is a prominent strand in the narrative, we do not learn much about Dalrymple himself here. We do, however, learn a lot about his method. Unlike colonial travel narratives, where the observer maintains a privileged space outside the socio-cultural space of the observed, there is a more symmetrical relation-ship here. To reinforce this, Dalrymple often reports dialogue in which he is the observed, the interrogated, and sometimes the local guide. For example, in Karachi, he is asked by one of the Delhi exiles, 'Have you ever been to Gulli Churiwallan? ... The *havelis* there are the most magnificent in all Delhi'; but Dalrymple knows the place better than the ex-resident, informing us this is 'a dirty ghetto now full of decaying warehouses' (1993: 61). Similarly, he tells us that superficially Delhi has been in decay since Mughal times, but 'if you know where to look' (1993: 270), you can still find the past penetrating the present. This 'knowing-where-to-look' proclaims the authority of the traveller-in-dwelling. Yet if he claims authority to tell us about the present, the authority to describe the past always lies with the exiles, the Anglo-Indians, the local scholars or the personal narratives of early travellers. The imaginative reconstruc-tions of the past in the present, which are his strength as a travel writer, stem from direct encounters with the locale, and a developed sense of the aura of places. History is explored *in situ* through palpable traces of the past and living memories, as well as through texts. This immersion in local culture, even if it is partly staged, enables Dalrymple to avoid that abstraction into oriental fantasy that frequently beset colonial travellers.

White Mughals describes Europeans who crossed over into Indian culture and cast off their European subjectivity. It reconstructs the turn-ing point in the history of British involvement in India: that pivotal moment at the end of the 18th century when British administrators were forbidden from dressing in Indian garb, taking Indian wives and converting to Islam, all of which had characterized their residences previously. The book tells the family history of the Kirkpatricks (British) and a Shustari family (originally from Iran, but later settling in Hyderabad). Connecting these personal histories is the interracial romance between Major James Achilles Kirkpatrick, 'the thoroughly Orientalised British Resident' at the Court of the Nizam of Hyderabad (1798–1805), and Khair un-Nissa, a young Hyderabadi girl. The book is introduced with two genealogical trees (the Shustaris coming before the Kirkpatricks – colonized before colonizers), and lists of 'Dramatis Personae', as if we are about to read a dramatized family saga, an idea further prompted by the subtitle for the book, 'Love and Betrayal in Eighteenth-Century India'. This love affair seems to have been reciprocal (so not an instance of the colonizer imposing himself on the colonized), and the couple were married in 1800, causing some consternation no doubt in official British circles. Mary Louise Pratt suggests that 'transracial plots' can be seen as 'imaginings in which European supremacy is guaranteed by affective and social bonding; in which sex replaces slavery ... [and] romantic love rather than filial servitude or force guarantee the wilful submission of the colonized' (1992: 97).[2] For Pratt, the transracial romance can also stand for the 'mystique of reciprocity' in colonial situations (97). But this is only one incident among many in *White Mughals*, which together suggest a degree of cultural and racial intermingling in India that belies the official British colonial vision of ethnic and racial division: of 'East is East and West is West'. In this case, reciprocity is not a mystique but a reality, and even the norm in 18th-century India. Dalrymple introduces the book as, '[t]he story of a family where three generations drifted between Christianity and Islam and back again', but this one story clearly raises fundamental questions about Britishness and the nature of Empire:

> The deeper I went in my research the more I became convinced that the picture of the British of the East India Company as a small alien minority locked away in Presidency towns, forts and cantonments needed to be revised. The tone of this early period [late 18th century] of British life in India seemed instead to be about intermixing and impurity, a succession of unexpected and unplanned minglings of peoples and cultures and ideas. (2002: xl)

As in a three-decker Victorian novel, *White Mughals* sets a romance against a realistic historical backcloth, and includes minor dramas, interludes and intrigues. But quite unlike the Victorian novel, the central theme here is intermingling. Beginning with the Portuguese in Goa, whose enthusiastic absorption of Indian culture was interrupted occasionally by the Inquisition, Dalrymple presents a host of examples of Europeans forsaking the narrow paths of their own cultures and religions to embrace Mughal culture. This aspect of colonial encounter in India seems to fly in the face of Said's assertion that 'Every European traveller or resident in the Orient has had to protect himself from its unsettling influences' (Said, 1978: 166). Further, it was not only the hookah-smoking colonial elite who took Indian wives, dressed in Indian garb and took on the customs of the Mughal court:

> Whatever the reason, many thousands of Europeans took service in Indian courts all over the subcontinent ... At the height of the Mughal Empire, so many Europeans took service in the Mughal army that a special suburb was built for them outside Delhi called Firingi Pura (Foreigners' Town) ... many of whom chose to convert to Islam ... (2002: 15)

Dalrymple hints that for administrators like James Kirkpatrick, immersion in Mughal society was a strategy as well as the fulfilment of personal desires:

> By wearing Islamic dress, using Mughal styles of address, larding his speeches with ... Persian aphorisms ... and accepting and using Persian titles, James Kirkpatrick made himself intelligible in the political *lingua franca* of the wider Mughal world ... By mastering the finer points of etiquette and submitting to procedures that some other Residents refused to bow to, James quickly gained a greater degree of trust than any other British Resident of the period, and so was able to reap the diplomatic rewards. (2002: 127–8)

So there was political purpose in Kirkpatrick's appreciation of Mughal culture, and this ulterior motive could be construed as a prelude to a later phase of less benign colonialism. In general though, Dalrymple suggests that such examples of crossing-over were no more than staged subordination or *noblesse oblige*. The weight of evidence points to crossing-over as an expression of cultural and aesthetic preference, to the passive seduction of colonial agents into Mughal culture and Islam.

As well as converting to Islam, some British 'defectors' turned to Hinduism. General *Hindoo* Stuart, we are told, walked every day to bathe and worship in the Ganges and wrote a pamphlet in defence of Hinduism (2002: 42). These European defectors and renegades should not necessarily be regarded as exceptional characters in colonial history. Instead, Dalrymple advises that the British had every reason to defect from the East India Company in its early days in Gujerat, and to seek their fortunes elsewhere. By the late 18th century, the British arriving in India were more purposeful, evangelizing even, and colonialist attitudes hardened. Yet even then, the staged outrage at witnessing one's own 'going native' at first hand was more a reflection of the political-ideological mood of the British at home. While in the political and economic reality of the colonial front line, renegades and defectors became 'important mediators between the world of Europe and the world of India', and 'demonstrated the remarkable porousness and fluidity of the frontier which separated the two' (2002: 16). These European renegades spanned the social scale, and were involved in Indian culture at all levels of trade, military service, education and affairs of state (British and Indian). Of course, it is not difficult to believe stories of sexually disoriented Europeans embracing a culture that allowed them more than one legal wife – the European male psyche needed little prompting in this form of exotic fantasy. But Dalrymple suggests this was more than sexual dalliance. He goes so far as to normalize the phenomenon by claiming the British East India Company actually depended on its employees crossing the line:

> the traders, soldiers, diplomats and even the clergymen who ventured eastwards had little choice but to embrace Mughal India. Nor should this tendency surprise us: from the wider perspective of world history, what is much odder and much more inexplicable is the tendency of the late-nineteenth-century British to travel to, and rule over, nearly a quarter of the globe, and yet remain resolutely untouched by virtually all the cultures with which they came into contact. (2002: 17)

In the context of post-Orientalism, this is an interesting reversion. It turns defection in the contact zone into a more likely, and more natural, outcome than the binary opposition between colonizer and colonized which prevails in colonial accounts of British India and in some postcolonial theory. That idea of total segregation, of remaining 'resolutely untouched', was probably an ideological construction. As structures of domination became ingrained in the British imperial psyche, the idea of being tainted by the foreign would have become increasingly abhorrent.

I would prefer to use the term *past*-colonial rather than postcolonial to refer to Dalrymple's work, because although he does use rhetorical and narrative devices associated with postcolonial theory, his strategies are conciliatory, not oppositional. For example, in *City of Djinns*, when he finds the human remains of British colonialism in Delhi, the Anglo-Indians and Anglicized Indians, some living on and some displaced, he regards these sympathetically, but on a par with other Delhi citizens (Sikhs, Christians, Muslims and Hindus) who suffered inter-ethnic and racist strife during the Raj, and then again after Partition in 1947. Hybridity can be a cause for celebration in postcolonial theory, and it is an especially prominent theme in Salman Rushdie's postcolonial fictions on India and Pakistan, yet here it is tinged with sadness. The older generation of Anglo-Indians, who can still remember Delhi before Independence, are left behind like the remains of some grotesque experiment in eugenics gone awry. There is a gently mocking tone too in Dalrymple's descriptions of the Smiths and Browns, whose world-view is still locked in the colonial past. They are decidedly *past*-colonial, never having arrived in postcolonial India. These 'bits of stranded flotsam' are left to suffer the prejudices dealt to half-castes abandoned by history (1993: 117). There is sad irony in Mr Smith finding it neces-sary to rebuke Indians in the market place who 'get nasty sometimes', by insisting that '[m]y roots are deeper here than what yours are. Don't look at my skin. Look at my heart ...' (1993: 134). It is something to be accused of not belonging in your own home, but something else to be dressed in the garb of a nationalism that no longer fits. As Mr Smith tells Dalrymple, 'we're not Britishers ... We're something different ... Of course we sing the British songs ... And we wear English clothes. Speak the English language. But we're different. England's not our home ...' (1993: 134).

In South America, men of mixed colonial and Indian parentage like Simon Bolivar came to the fore, but in India the story was always dif-ferent. The reason Dalrymple suggests was that 'Hindus and British were both too proud of their blood for "half-castes" ever to be really successful' (1993: 130). Hybridity could act 'like a two-edged blade' (1993: 129). One prominent victim was Colonel James Skinner, whose mixed Scottish and Indian parentage made him ineligible for the East India Company. This forced him into the employ of the 'Hindu Mahratta confederacy' as a mercenary, one of a growing number of marginalized Europeans working for the principal rivals of the Company. As rivalry increased, his British blood excluded him from the Mahrattas' employ, and then with his infamous irregular cavalry he went back to the East

India Company and helped 'secure great chunks of North India for the Union Jack' (1993: 126–8). And yet his family would become the butt of jokes as prejudice and bigotry took hold in the strict ethnic, class and racial divisions of 19th-century British India. One Victorian lady travel-ler remarked on the Skinner family: 'They were very dark in complexion and spoke with an extraordinary accent ... although they looked upon themselves as English people' (1993: 130). In Delhi society, the Anglo-Indians were excluded from English clubs and commonly referred to as 'Blackie Whities' or 'Chutney Marys' (1993: 131). Through such per-sonal histories of hybridity in India, Dalrymple charts the gradual shift from tolerance to intolerance, from the celebration of difference to the condemnation of it, from inclusion to exclusion.

The Anglo-Indian community in late-20th-century Delhi are the visible, hybridized remains of what Bhabha calls the 'mimic men' (1984: 125). To Western eyes these might once have reflected distorted versions of the colonizer tinged with the colonized. This was discomforting, con-fronting Westerners with disoriented, or 'de-occidentalized', images of themselves. But how much more unsettling was the reverse mimicry Dalrymple highlights in *White Mughals*? Here, the European 'defectors' demonstrate how the *colonizer mimicked the colonized*. Such transfigured images of self must have produced complex dialectics of repulsion/attraction and conformance/transgression in the mind of the colonizer. As Bhabha says, Said's claim that colonial power was entirely the pre-serve of the colonizer was 'a historical and theoretical simplification' (1983: 199).[3] The otherness onto which the West projected the will to control was also the object of desire, and India was always a site of ambivalence and transgression.

The sources Dalrymple uses in his travel histories are predominantly personal records. He concentrates on travel memoirs, diaries and per-sonal testimony, and ignores, or is critical of, official histories (British and Indian), political speeches and English literature of the 19th century. The emphasis on the personal and the anecdotal from Western and non-Western sources helps disrupt the idea of Orientalism as an organized and organizing discourse reflecting Western hegemony. Said asserts that Orientalism 'domesticated' knowledge of the Orient for the West through a systematized ordering of the matter of the East. It pro-duced a 'simulacrum of the Orient', a copy with no original, 'converted from the personal, sometimes garbled testimony of intrepid voyagers and residents ... converted from the consecutive experience of individ-ual research into a sort of imaginary museum' (1978: 166). Dalrymple deconstructs this 'simulacrum' by reinstalling those disruptive and destabilizing individual testimonies and laying bare the 'intrepid' and the 'garbled'.

In representing the history of the East, and in particular, relations between Islam and other religions, Dalrymple is walking several tight-ropes. He might fall foul of fundamentalisms, or, through his undoubted enthusiasm for Mughal India and a 'medieval Orient', be accused of 're-exoticizing' the East for Western consumption.[4] In *White Mughals,* he does sometimes hold his gaze on dancing girls, erotic performances, concu-bines, sexual relations, circumcision and so on. Such fascination was also found in those Western explorers' tales that contributed to the idea of the Orient as an overly sexualized, and to male readers, exotic and erotic zone. Recirculating the 'currency of nostalgic images' of Empire is, however, not Dalrymple's primary aim (although it could be an unintended conse-quence) (Huggan, 2001: 77). Rather, his stated aim is to reinstall Oriental Studies in the wake George W. Bush persuading the US that Islam was an intolerant religion bent on destroying Western Christendom. It is in the context of this disastrous misrepresentation of history that Dalrymple attempts to set the record straight. In his characteristically forthright manner he has argued that '[a]t no point in history has there been more need for proper understanding and scholarship of the Islamic world than now ... Never in my life have I come across a subject about which there is so much misinformation, such total incomprehension and such a lack of will to understand' (quoted in Amodeo, 1997: 67). And where were the American Orientalists in all of this? 'Impotent' apparently:

> Hoover Institute anthropologist Stanley Kurtz in his 2003 testimony before the House Subcommittee on Select Education, said that Said's post-colonial critique had left American Middle East Studies scholars impotent to contribute to Bush's 'war on terror'. (Quoted in Young, 2009: n.p.)

Hundreds of years of knowledge about the East were trampled into the dust of the Iraqi desert. There are even reports that some of the his-toric soil of Babylon was used by US coalition soldiers to fill sandbags. Said had effectively hindered left-leaning academics from engaging in Orientalism, and a theoretical brand of postcolonialism emerged, more concerned with textuality than the content of historical texts. Meanwhile, President Bush and the neo-conservatives set East/West relations back to the time of the Crusades.

Dalrymple sidesteps the leviathans of theory to focus on 'real' histo-ries variously experienced in the testimonies of actual people. And yet through the apparently straightforward interrogation of witnesses and texts, and broad historical enquiry, Dalrymple's writing nevertheless (and perhaps contrary to intention) sometimes shows affiliation with postcolonial theory, while, at the same time, opposing Said. For example, in using the serendipitous mode of travel writing to connect a variety of actors and witnesses with place and history, Dalrymple restores Bhabha's notion of 'the repertoire of conflictual positions that constitute the subject in colonial discourse' (Bhabha, 1983: 204). *White Mughals* especially brings to light 'the colonizer' as a plural, precarious, transgressive and transmutable subject, and challenges Said's claim that colonialism operated through a singular ideological intention, maintained by a simple equation of knowledge and power. Dalrymple's array of historical evidence points time and again to disoriented (and de-occidentalized), and dislocated subject positions. He challenges the totalizing history of colonialism presented by Said through what Lyotard calls the 'petits récits', local histories that resist systematization (1984: 20–3). His preference for travel narratives shows he is willing to exploit their inherent idiosyncrasy and vagrancy.

Dalrymple's presentation of Anglo-Indian history produces markedly different effects to Said's philological approach. Said, for the most part, analyses political speeches, colonial historiography and literatures which reveal their ideological bases rather too readily. Given much wider use of raw materials (personal records, unpublished memoirs, letters and oral histories), Dalrymple presents far more intricate and intertwined histories. This deconstructs, but does not displace, Said's emphatic critique of the historicization and politicization of the East. Indeed, it shows even more clearly how resolutely the imperial machine used its ordering codes to select and reshape that history to its own ends. This Empire-making apparatus generated 'a world historical scheme that assimilated non-synchronous developments, histories, cultures, and peoples to it' (Said, 1985: 22). Dalrymple releases that Western grip on knowledge of the East in *City of Djinns* by incorporating the work of local scholars like Dr Jaffery, and narratives of European travellers quite obviously marginal to, or even directly opposed to, Western hegemony. His many sources for the history of the Mughal empire include the testimonies of the 17th-century French doctor Francois Bernier, and the 'self-confessed con-artist and charlatan', Niccolao Manucci (1993, 192–3). These accounts of life at the centre of power in 17th-century India are written by foreigners and peppered with fictions and 'malicious gossip', for Dalrymple though, they 'rescued the Mughals from being suffocated beneath landslides of silk, diamonds and lapis lazuli', which is what he finds in the 'sycophantic official court chronicles – the *Shah Jehan Nama'* (1993: 191). Here is an instance of European travellers disrupting the other's (the Mughal's) historicism – Orientalism turned inside out.

Dalrymple offers an alternative to the well-worn idea that travel produces knowledge and knowledge leads to power (as a simplistic reading of Foucault would have it). In British India at the beginning of the 19th century, it was power in the form of institutionalized systems of meaning-making, and a firm ideological grip on the colonial imaginary which helped to shape knowledge. Said's analysis of the texts and relations between texts, through which he defines the problematic of Orientalism, ignores the processes of production (editing, censorship, print economics, distribution) and reception of these texts (critical reviews, the shaping of popular opinion and so on). Power expressed as state-controlled manipulation of representation and self-censorship is not really addressed by Said, for whom there is always this assumption of the irresistible strength of colonialism transforming all in its path. By contrast, Dalrymple shows how precarious was the actual colonialist position in India, and how colonial discourse in its official guise, and in its direct and indirect control of the production of texts, papered over, or talked down, the cracks and fissures in Western hegemony. Referring to obscure letters and some of the less well-publicized events of history, he presents British and French involvement in India as a series of blunders, 'fortunate' accidents and gambles. For example, the subterfuge that led to the surrender of the largest French force in India to James Kirkpatrick at Hyderabad in 1798 (2002: 149–53) suggests a very fluid and dynamic unfolding of history. Stories of extraordinary military adventures such as this, and courtly intrigues and vacillations in Indian–European alliances, are told largely through contemporaneous accounts by participants. They offer a very different picture to that presented by Said when he insists that 'the Orient for Europe was until the nineteenth century a domain with a continuous history of unchallenged Western dominance. This is patently true of the British experience in India ...' (1978: 73).

It is Said's contention that Western writings on the East, especially travel texts, issue from a position of 'great cultural strength, and its [the West's] will to power over the Orient' (1978: 94). But surely it was a *retrospective* colonialist history which made sense teleologically and imaginatively of relations between Britain and India? For Dalrymple, one of the main vectors influencing acculturation was the seductive power of India. This operated, together with the various accidents of history, in opposition to Western hegemony, at least until Britain could impose itself through superior military force at the end of the late 19th century. The seductive power of India might have been framed and abstracted as aesthetic exoticism in colonial discourse, which would support Said's thesis by containing and marginalizing it through colonial power structures. But against this, Dalrymple presents an interracial romance as the *centrepiece* of *White Mughals*. The marriage of a British colonial administrator to a young Indian woman, and his conversion to Islam, is not presented as an exceptional practice but, in its time, the norm. It is in itself a romantic and exotic story, but it is also one with deep, symbolic resonance for the British love affair with India. Dalrymple has shown this had real, as well as imaginative, issue in the 18th century. Whereas Said's argument shows that colonial discourse was mobilized *subsequently* to excise this mongrel progeny as a matter of grave importance to the British Empire.

In exploring Dalrymple's work as postcolonial travel writing, I have looked at direct and indirect responses to Said's *Orientalism*, the circulation of postcolonial themes, tropes and motifs, and the dislocation of (Western) narrative authority. By way of conclusion, I would now like to explore a few examples of Dalrymple's use of place, through which he *positions* history. This is the advantage the travel writer has: the ability to give presence to place, and then *in situ*, to pass through the portals of time and down through layers of sedimented history. If there is nostalgia, it is not a yearning for the British Raj but for Delhi in the 18th century and earlier; for a time when history seemed not so black and white, in several senses. The juxtaposition of overlapping and intertwined histories, and the locating of the history of the Raj within an extensive *Indian history*, rather than as a truncated episode within the history of *British* Empire, suggest postcolonial revision. Delhi is presented as a vast 'graveyard of dynasties', of which the British Raj is one among many. The ambitious criss-crossings between past and present are designed to give 'a portrait of a city disjointed in time, a city whose different ages lay suspended side by side in aspic' (1993: 8–9).

Dalrymple might show more interest in Delhi's past than in its postcolonial present, but then in a postmodern world, where futurism is on the wane, past and present flow into each other. So, as he surveys the monuments of the past in Delhi, the Red Fort, the *havelis* of Ballimaran, the Mughal *tykhana*, the British Residency in Shahjeanabad, Luytens's New Delhi, he senses the aura of the past, and the flow of time that connects it with the present (1993: 223, 270, 124, 109, 83). His palimpsestic approach to history is not theoretical, but practical. In *City of Djinns* he clambers through cellars and hidden passages literally to trace his way back through the accumulated detritus of fallen Empires. This is not to interpret the past to explain the present, but to understand and inhabit the past as a dimension of the present, and to bridge that divisiveness of history which has driven a wedge between the Islamic world and the rest.

Works Cited and Consulted

Amodeo, Christian (1997) 'A Scotsman in India'. *Geographical* **75**(11): 67–70.

Bhabha, Homi K. (1983) 'Difference, Discrimination, and the Discourse of Colonialism' in Francis Barker, Peter Hulme, Margaret Iversen and Diana Loxley (eds), *The Politics of Theory*. Colchester: University of Essex Press.

Bhabha, Homi K. (1984) 'Of Mimicry and Man: The Ambivalence of Colonial Discourse'. *October* **28**: 125–33.

Clifford, James (1997) *Routes: Travel and Translation in the Late Twentieth Century*. Cambridge: Harvard University Press.

Dalrymple, William (1989) *In Xanadu: A Quest*. London: Penguin Books.

Dalrymple, William (1993) *City of Djinns: A Year in Delhi*. London: Harper Perennial, 2005.

Dalrymple, William (2002) *White Mughals: Love and Betrayal in Eighteenth-Century India*. London: Harper Collins.

Dalrymple, William (2006) 'The Last Mughal and a Clash of Civilisations'. *New Statesman,* (16 October): 34–7.

Dissanayake, Wimal (2002) 'Narrative Authority in Post-Colonial Travel Writing'. Unpublished paper presented at the Crossroads in Culture Conference, Tampere, Finland.

Fisher, Michael H. (ed.) (2007) *Visions of Mughal India: An Anthology of European Travel Writing*. London: I. B. Tauris.

Huggan, Graham (2001) *The Postcolonial Exotic: Marketing the Margins*. New York: Routledge.

Hulme, Peter (1987) *Colonial Encounters*. Cambridge: Cambridge University Press.

Lyotard, Jean-François (1984) *The Postmodern Condition*. Minneapolis: University of Minnesota Press.

Pratt, Mary Louise (1992) *Imperial Eyes: Travel Writing and Transculturation,* New York: Routledge.

Said, Edward (1978) *Orientalism*. London: Penguin Books.

Said, Edward (1985) 'Orientalism Reconsidered' in Francis Barker (ed.) *Europe and its Others*. Colchester: University of Essex Press.

Stratton, Jon (1990) *Writing Sites: A Genealogy of the Postmodern World*. Hemel Hempstead: Harvester Wheatsheaf.

Young, Robert (1990) *White Mythologies: Writing History and the West*. London: Routledge.

Young, Robert (2009) 'Edward Said: Opponent of Postcolonial Theory'. Unpublished paper presented at the University of Hong Kong, 19 March.

Youngs, Tim (2005) 'Interview with William Dalrymple'. *Studies in Travel Writing* **9**(1): 37–63.

Notes

1. William Fraser, who is likened to Conrad's Kurtz, was an oriental scholar and the leader of an irregular army charged with subjugating restless natives around Delhi. He was also, says Dalrymple, 'a forebear and kinsman of my wife' (1993: 99). Through family connections he gains access to Fraser's letters, quoted extensively in the book.
2. On transracial romances, see also Peter Hulme, 1987.
3. For a fuller discussion of Bhabha's critique of Said see also Robert Young, 'The Ambivalence of Bhabha' in Young (1990: 141–5).
4. For the problems facing writers of postcolonial texts of invoking and capitalizing on the currency of nostalgia for Empire, see Graham Huggan (2001).

10
An Interview with William Dalrymple and Pankaj Mishra

Tabish Khair

Introductory Note by Tabish Khair

More often than not, the term 'postcolonial' is applied to countries like Kenya, India and Australia: once colonized spaces that are now independent nation-states. But whatever the aptness of that designation as a historical and political term used to specify the political status of a nation after colonization and decolonization, in its larger discursive uses surely postcolonial should apply to the once-colonizing state as much as the once-colonized state? In that sense, if Algeria is postcolonial today, then so is France; if India is postcolonial today, then so is Britain. My choice to interview William Dalrymple and Pankaj Mishra is based on this perception (shared, as the various chapters indicate, by the editors of this book): in different ways, both are postcolonial travel writers; together, they should shed interesting light on postcolonial travel writing, as well as their own extensive and acclaimed travel books.

Of course, as Dalrymple makes clear in his responses (and interviews and articles elsewhere), he has serious problems with aspects of 'postcolonialism', particularly in the light of what he sees as a simplification and sweeping dismissal of the historical complexity of West–East interactions following Edward Said's *Orientalism* (1978). Mishra seems less suspicious of 'postcolonialism' per se, but even he puts some distance between his writing/scholarship and 'academic postcolonialism' (as indicated by one of his responses below). Despite this reservation – and as Paul Smethurst documents in his interesting chapter on Dalrymple in this book – Dalrymple (and, I would add, Mishra) have produced a rich *oeuvre* that runs parallel to the endeavour of postcolonialism to record and explore the multiplicity of the past, the inevitable hybridity of present identities and, more specifically, as Dalrymple puts it towards the end of this interview (albeit in another context), to challenge the 'insularity' of 'western writing on the eastern world.'

Based in India for many years now, **William Dalrymple** was born in Scotland and brought up on the shores of the Firth of Forth. His first (travel) book, *In Xanadu* (1989), published when he was only 22, won the 1990 *Yorkshire Post* Best Book Award for the Best First Work and a Scottish Arts Council award; it was short-listed for the John Llewellyn Rhys Memorial Prize. His second book, *City of Djinns* (1993), a book on Delhi published six years after he had moved to the Indian capital, won a number of awards, including the 1994 Thomas Cook Travel Book Award. Other travel books have included *From the Holy Mountain* (1997), a highly acclaimed study of the demise of Christianity in its Middle Eastern homeland, and *The Age of Kali* (1998), which won the French Prix D'Astrolabe. Dalrymple's subsequent historical books, *White Mughals* (2002) and *The Last Mughal* (2008), also won much acclaim and various prestigious awards. Dalrymple is a Fellow of the Royal Society of Literature and of the Royal Asiatic Society; in 2002 he was awarded the Mungo Park Medal by the Royal Scottish Geographical Society for his 'outstanding contribution to travel literature'.

Pankaj Mishra was born in North India in 1969, and studied in Allahabad and Delhi. His first book was *Butter Chicken in Ludhiana: Travels in Small Town India* (1995), one of the first travelogues to attempt to trace the social and cultural changes in India in the new context of globalization. His novel *The Romantics* (2000), which contains many narratives of travel and desire, was published in a dozen languages and won the *Los Angles Times'* Art Seidenbaum Award for first fiction. A subsequent book, *An End to Suffering: The Buddha in the World* (2004), a *New York Times* Notable Book, mixes memoir, history and philosophy while attempting to explore the Buddha's relevance to contemporary times. His recent book, *Temptations of the West: How to be Modern in India, Pakistan and Beyond* (2006), describes Mishra's travels through 'Bollywood', Afghanistan, Kashmir, Tibet, Nepal and other parts of Asia. Like his previous books, it was featured in the *New York Times'* 100 Best Books of the Year. In 2005, Mishra also published an anthology of writing on India titled *India in Mind* (Vintage) and he has contributed introductions to various books, including new editions of Rudyard Kipling's *Kim* (Modern Library), E. M. Forster's *A Passage to India* (Penguin Classics), J. G. Farrell's *The Siege of Krishnapur* (NYRB Classics), Gandhi's *The Story of My Experiments with Truth* (Penguin) and R. K. Narayan's *The Ramayana* (Penguin Classics). He has also introduced two volumes of V. S. Naipaul's essays, *The Writer and the World* (2002) and *Literary Occasions* (2003).

As is evident from the above summaries of their careers, both authors have written texts that cannot be called travel writing in a narrow generic sense. Pankaj Mishra is the author of a novel, *The Romantics* (2000), and collections of political and introspective essays. William Dalrymple is the author of historical studies, such as *White Mughals* and *The Last Mughal*. In the context of this interview, such texts – as the last question suggests – add to their *oeuvre* as travel writers, for travel writing, as a genre, is a notoriously hydra-headed and oceanic thing.

The two authors were interviewed separately, with the questions merging or diversifying on the basis of their responses. Towards the end, they were both provided with opportunities to access each other's responses in writing and, if required, add to their commentary.

The Interview

Tabish Khair: *We will start with a general and personal question. Both of you have penned (individually) travel books in a generic sense (*In Xanadu, Butter Chicken in Ludhiana*) and also books that are not travelogues but still seem to be marked by the trope of travel in all its senses, such as* White Mughals, An End to Suffering: The Buddha in the World *(2004) or the novel,* The Romantics. *Why this fascination with travel and writing about it?*

Pankaj Mishra: There are many answers that come to mind, but if I were to put it very simply, travel for me has been primarily a way of learning things that I did not learn at school or college, that I did not inherit from my class or nationality or religion; it is the most effective way I have of allaying my general ignorance about large parts of India, the world. *Butter Chicken* describes that process of discovery; so does the Buddha book at a deeper level. And I still choose to go to places – China, Israel, Japan, Turkey – about which I know very little, and against whose intellectual and political and economic backdrop I might learn a few more things about my own life, add to what I know about India and the West in general, deepen my preoccupations and so on.

I could never think of myself as providing a vicarious experience to the reader, or even a portrait of another society. For that I would have had to know a lot about myself and the world, be very confident in my own assumptions, and it is a difficult pose for me to maintain. So travel writing as such – as it has mainly existed in the modern West – has never attracted me as a reader. I still travel to places first and then read about them afterwards, comparing my experience with those of others, and in a larger sense comparing the experiences of societies I know about. Exoticism, or complete 'otherness', doesn't appeal to me. As both reader and writer, I like a degree of familiarity to exist between the reader and the page. A book like *Butter Chicken*, for instance, assumes that the reader will recognize its characters and places, and the mixed emotions of its narrator-observer.

William Dalrymple: I am not sure I am fascinated with travel per se – and in fact my wife maintains I am a very bad traveller who is always happier where he is and is very difficult to move. What I am interested in, and have been since my teens, is a particular quadrant of the world – the area roughly between Athens and Calcutta – and over the last 25 years have written about the past and present of that area as a historian, a biographer, a critic and a journalist, as well as a travel writer. It's true that my first three books, dating from before I settled down and had children, were all travel books, and that as a student at Cambridge I read through and loved the whole library of classic travel writers; but I read very little travel writing these days, and was surprised to find myself this year again writing a book which could just about be classified as a travel book, *Nine Lives* (2009).

What I like about travel writing is that it is a very flexible form of non-fiction which allows you to write about a huge variety of topics within a narrative structure, in an attractive and accessible way. What I think is in all my books is a sense of place and a sense of history. In some the history predominates, in others the place takes the lead. But any fascination I had with the business of travel itself – walking, catching buses and trains, getting from a to b – was pretty well exhausted after *In Xanadu*. Since then I have been using the form to write either about place – trying to catch the essence of Delhi in *City of Djinns* for example; or about an issue – the demise of the Middle Eastern Christians in *From the Holy Mountain*. *Nine Lives* is in some ways deliberately the opposite of the sort of narrator-led travel narrative like *In Xanadu*: here the narrator is almost absent, there is no description of travel, no continuous narrative, and I suppose it is as much a work of journalism or anthropology or spirituality as a travel book; and yet it is in some ways very much a classic travel book: the individual setting off with a notebook and set of questions and writing it up when he gets home.

Khair: *Will, it is interesting that you talk about your use of 'sense of place and history', which are obviously among the strengths of your work as historian, travel*

writer and journalist, and how your later work differs from the 'narrator-led'
travel narrative of your earlier In Xanadu *(as also noted by Tim Youngs in*
an interview with you). As you know, postcolonialism has been very sceptical
of travel writing (of the 'narrator-led' sort), claiming that it formulated
discourses of difference and contributed to the politics of colonial expansion.
You belong to a postcolonial generation of travel writers – I do not see why
the term 'postcolonial' cannot be applied to, say, the British and the French –
but you also belong to a long, and very rich tradition of British travel writing
about the Orient (people like Wilfred Thesiger and Robert Byron). How do
you negotiate this mine-infested and incredibly fertile terrain?

Dalrymple: Narrator-led travel writing, like any form of autobiographical writing, reflects the views, prejudices and outlook of the writer
at the time he writes them. This is true whether the travel writer is
a Chinese Buddhist monk like Hiuen Tsang, a white colonial official
like Curzon, an open-minded Indophile like Fanny Parkes, a pious
Muslim judge like Ibn Battuta or a racist Persian nobleman like Abdul
Latif Shustari. Each traveller comes from a particular culture, and goes
to others: the act of travelling may or may not change his views about
his own or other cultures.

To see the travel writing of 19th and 20th century Europeans as
uniquely prejudiced and uniquely politicized, exclusively open to
formulating 'discourses of difference' or contributing in some unique
way to the politics of colonial expansion, seems to me to be historically naïve and clearly factually wrong: Abdul Latif Shushtari and
Fanny Parkes were direct contemporaries travelling through India at
the same time, but of the two it was Fanny who was far more engaged
in and open to India; Shustari in contrast was unable to shed centuries of highly cultured Persian hauteur towards an India he regarded
as culturally and civilizationally inferior – an attitude that was again
tinctured with centuries of conquest, migration and colonial history.
Human history is more complex, and human prejudices more varied
than many of the academic acolytes of Orientalism would allow.

So the travel writer is an individual, who may or may not represent
the views of his more stationary and less adventurous compatriots, and
who may or may not be changed by what he sees and experiences on the
road. For myself, I have no doubt that my travels have radically altered
my views and outlook: the untravelled public-school boy who set off to
Xanadu in 1986 had – for better or worse – very different views of the
world to the middle-aged man with three kids who has lived in Delhi for
the best part of a quarter of a century. How could it be otherwise?

As for being part of a British tradition of travel writing, this is certainly the case, but that tradition seems to me to be more diverse and less monolithic than the more unthinking sheep tumbling along in the wake of Edward Said's flock would allow. For me, travellers tend very often to be rebels and outcasts and misfits: the very act of setting out alone and vulnerable on the road is often an expression of rejection of home and an embrace of the other – history is full of individuals who have fallen in love with other cultures and other parts of the world in this way. Then there are those whose views changed as they travelled and their horizons widened: see the prejudices against Islamic culture and civilization expressed by the young Robert Byron in his letters from India transform as he sets off on the *Road to Oxiana*.

So if as a young writer I drew sustenance from writers as diverse and different as Robert Byron, Fanny Parkes, Robert Louis Stevenson, Bruce Chatwin and Patrick Leigh Fermor, I do not see that as a problem to be negotiated so much as a valuable source of inspiration.

Khair: *Pankaj, is your reluctance to provide 'a vicarious experience to the reader, or even a portrait of another society' a postcolonial element, given postcolonialism's suspicion of travel writing as containing colonial tropes? On the other hand, it is also true – as William Dalrymple has observed – that 'cultural prejudices' about other spaces have not been simply the prerogative of Europeans. How do you relate to this complex of inter-related issues and does an awareness of it determine the nature of your travel writing?*

Mishra: I don't know if it is a postcolonial element. If you mean something formulated in universities or academic works, then, no, since my own contact with these things has been fleeting and has had little impact on me. I suppose it is another aspect of the self-exploration that travel writing is for me, that as someone journeying out of ignorance I can't pretend to superior ethnographic knowledge for the sake of the reader. And the awareness and disclosure of my own assumptions is part of this process. William Dalrymple is right. Prejudice is not a European monopoly. My travel writing, for instance, in Pakistan and Afghanistan is really shaped by my childhood memory, common among small-town lower-middle-class Brahmins, of Muslims as threatening 'others' – and there are moments when I lapse into these inherited fears. I can't write about China without discussing our national image of the 'devious' neighbour who stabbed our backs in 1962. And I can't write about Israel without bringing in the great admiration my RSS-aligned family had for the Zionists who supposedly knew how to keep Muslims in their place.

Khair: *If one cannot, as you highlight, keep the personal out of a travel text, how does one avoid what Paul Theroux claimed was the problem with most travel books: 'transparent monologuing'? How do the personal and political define and/or resist each other?*

Mishra: I don't quite see the personal as distinct from the political in the way that, I suppose, an Anglo-American writer might see it. My personality and preoccupations as a travel writer cannot be detached from my national and racial identity. How can it be? To give you an example, with an Indian passport I have to get visas for practically every country in the world, which makes travel writing a very different experience altogether. The confident aloofness of writers like Waugh was underpinned by assumptions about the dominance of their countries that they either suppressed or were unaware of. Norman Lewis stands apart because he understood what it meant to be a travel writer in Asia and Latin America from a powerful Western country, and he embraced the obligations and responsibilities that came with that awareness. Waugh could only express impatience over his inability to write about picturesque people in the old way after 1945 and the end of the British Empire. Theroux is more interesting. His early travelogues, especially the *Great Railway Bazaar*, follow in the exuberant tradition of Waugh, Robert Byron, Peter Fleming and other travel writers of the 1930s. His new book, *Ghost Train To The Eastern Star*, retracing the same terrain 30 years after, is more engaged and serious, and necessarily so; huge geopolitical shifts – the decline of and threats to Western power – have made it impossible for him to dismiss Afghanistan or Iran as a 'nuisance'; he is more unhappy about the genre of travel writing, because he knows that 'transparent monologuing' by some fresh-out-of-college writer in Asia and Africa just sounds silly in the age of YouTube and highly politicized 'native' populations.

Khair: *As you suggested, Will, cultural prejudices were never just the preserve of Europeans and that other travel writing traditions show similar trends – something I frequently confronted when co-editing* Other Routes: 1500 Years of African and Asian Travel Writing. *Though, of course, one can argue that the postcolonialist preoccupation with European/ized 'prejudices' owes much to the fact that over the past three centuries the views of a Curzon would have greater impact than the views of a Shustari. Bearing this in mind, how do you approach the issue of writing about the 'Orient' as a 'Westerner'? I am asking you this question particularly in the light* *of your trajectory as a travel writer:* In Xanadu, *your first book, might be seen as containing some faint 'Orientalist' echoes, but since then you have written against or at a tangent to many 'Western' perceptions. For instance, in your latest book,* Nine Lives, *you take up a very difficult matter (for a 'Westerner') – Indian spirituality in today's 'Shining India' – and do (if I may say so) an exceptionally nuanced and complex job of narrating it without succumbing to stereotypes.*

Dalrymple: I think the trajectory you mention simply comes from growing up and becoming a little more familiar with the world outside Europe: I was 22 when I wrote *In Xanadu*, I was a callow public-school boy, and had been nowhere. Twenty-five years later, it's hardly surprising my views are a little more mature, and I am a little more familiar with the part of the world in which I have chosen to live for so long: after all, stereotypes almost always derive from ignorance, and familiarity is always the best way to combat that ignorance.

As for dealing with Indian spirituality, you are right: this is a particularly perilous subject, given the amount of nonsense written about 'Mystic India' by Westerners, especially in the 1930s and 1960s – between Madam Blavatsky and Karma Cola, words like 'karma' and 'nirvana' have become so cliché-ridden that perhaps the only way to deal with them, and to reclaim them from the ectoplasm-seekers, dharma bums and hippies, is to do what I have done in *Nine Lives*: to let people deeply immersed in these mystical and devotional traditions speak for themselves, and to keep the narrator firmly in the background.

Finally, the issue of, as you put it, 'writing about the "Orient" as a "Westerner"'. The inverted commas you put in the question indicate your own awareness of the fluid and porous nature of these concepts. I write about the world I live in, and write it as I see it, and encounter it. Generations of my family have lived and died in India, I have Bengali blood swirling in my veins, I've lived here for quarter of a century and I think of it as home. I will never be an Indian, but like many people in today's globalized world, I am both insider and outsider: who today spends their lives in the village where they were born? To have that dualism is I think a pretty useful complexity for a writer, not an obstacle.

Khair: *Talking of the globalized world today, various critics have noted the rise of 'synthetic' travel destinations, something being compounded by globalization. Lawrence Osborn, for instance, coins the term 'whereverness' to* *describe a sense of the interchangeability of cultural experiences. Have you noted this in your travels? How do you cope with it in your writing?*

Dalrymple: I think this idea of everywhere now being alike is a huge deception. Though there may be a superficial veneer of similarity – it is true that the same Nikes are worn from Alaska to Zanzibar, the same Michael Jackson songs listened to by kids of a certain age across the globe – this masks huge differences of outlook and belief. As Jonathan Raban once wrote: 'Old travellers grumpily complain that travel is now dead and that the world is a suburb. They are quite wrong. Lulled by familiar resemblances between all the unimportant things, they meet the brute differences in everything of importance.'

One moment this came through very strongly for me was while writing about the Deorala sati – the piece is in the *Age of Kali*. Roop Kanwar was a college-educated kid; her house had satellite TV; she wore jeans and Nikes. Yet she still willingly jumped on her husband's funeral pyre, and lived simultaneously in a mind-world made up of attitudes formed in the period of the Ramayana. It is just those sorts of paradoxes – examining the world caught between modernity and tradition – that I am interested in exploring in *Nine Lives*.

Khair: *Travel writing as a 'genre' is reputed to be very difficult to define, partly because it contains almost all literary genres and is contained in almost all genres. Chaucer's* The Canterbury Tales *is just one ambiguous example. Would you define travel writing as a genre, and if so, how? And, finally, how do you see travel writing, defined as a genre or not, developing in the future?*

Mishra: I am actually more and more reluctant to define travel writing as a separate genre. The description emerged at a time in the West when few people could travel, and the occasional intrepid traveller to remote lands came to possess a unique intellectual authority. Think of Tavernier's and Bernier's accounts of India, how they helped create powerful notions of Oriental despotism. Travel writing could be a genre because it was specifically defined by the then rare act of travel, which brought to readers almost the only kind of knowledge they could acquire about other countries. (Of course, travel writing by Asians in both the pre-modern and modern era has not had the same taxonomic obsessions). But, now? In the age of mass travel, almost everyone can be an observer of native customs; the travel writer has ceded his authority to the foreign correspondent and the ethnographer, and probably won't regain it anytime soon. Travel writing has seemed more and more a form of middlebrow entertainment for readers uninterested in serious enquiry about other cultures and societies. It can only 'develop' in the future if it manages to recapture some of its intellectual curiosity; the form remains flexible and capacious and a literary sensibility capable of sophisticated socio-political analysis can still renew it.

Dalrymple: I agree with Pankaj that travel writing as a genre is difficult to define – it can be cross-fertilized with so many other literary forms that it is one of the most hybrid forms of writing in literature, and so difficult to pin down and encircle. But I disagree with any suggestion that travel writing need now see itself as a form of 'middlebrow entertainment' or that it has necessarily ceded its authority. It is certainly true that a lot of travel writing produced during the travel-writing boom of the 1980s was second rate: publishers over-commissioned, and there was a flood of mediocre and downright bad books, often revolving around silly stunts (taking a dustbin cart to Borneo, a tricycle to New Orleans or a pogo stick to the Antarctic). As a result, travel writing's moment in the sun ebbed away. Many of the writers of my generation who had written travel books moved on to new forms: Sarah Wheeler and Katie Hickman to biography, Anthony Sattin and myself to history, Philip Marsden to the novel.

But returning recently to travel writing after such a long gap made me think again about the form. Has the genre anything left to offer in the age of mass tourism and the internet? And is there anyone of real talent still at work in travel writing? I believe the answer to both questions is yes. Since 9/11 there has been a new insularity about Western writing on the Eastern world. The British in particular once prided themselves on their cosmopolitan global experience, yet throughout the Bush years our literary commentators and media, as much as the Blair government, swallowed the Neocon lies and over-simplifications about the Islamic world hook, line and sinker. Even left-leaning and liberal papers like *The Guardian* and *The Observer* regularly ran a slew of pieces about the Islamic world by writers like Martin Amis who appears never to have visited an Islamic country or talked seriously to any Muslim, but instead produced a compilation of second-hand views lifted from the usual Islamophobic Neocon primers – the works of Bernard Lewis and Paul Berman. As insular, ignorant article piled on article, one longed to bring back the dead masters of travel writing: where was Wilfred Thesiger or Bruce Chatwin when you really needed them?

Nevertheless, over the last few years there has been a slow trickle of books by younger writers which have I think been as good as anything published in the 1980s. Suketu Mehta's Bombay book, *Maximum City*, is one of the greatest city books ever written, in my opinion, while Alice Albinia's wonderful *Empires of the Indus* is a breathtaking debut by an author who writes enviably cadent and beautiful prose, but has nerves of steel and the pluck of a 21st century Freya Stark. I also hugely admired Pankaj's own collection of travel pieces *Temptations of the West: How to be Modern in India, Pakistan and Beyond*. There are probably many others.

I recently asked two writer friends, Colin Thubron and Rory Stewart, whether they believed that the age of the travel book was over. Rory Stewart, probably the most highly regarded of the younger generation of travel writers, believes passionately that travel books allow writers to explore other cultures in a slow and unhurried way that is impossible with journalism or most other forms of non-fiction. Now a professor at Harvard, Stewart is quite clear that travel writing has a more important role than ever: 'Just look what gets written about Afghanistan', he says. 'In an age when journalism is becoming more and more etiolated, when articles are becoming shorter and shorter, usually lacking all historical context, travel writing is one of the few venues to write with some complexity about an alien culture. An Obama speech, a foreign policy paper or a counter-insurgency briefing minimizes differences, and the same phrases like 'failed states' are used to link countries which are actually very different such as Yemen, Afghanistan or Pakistan. But the best sort of travel book with its imaginative empathy and depiction of individuals inhabiting a landscape helps the reader to live through and understand the possibility of cultural difference. You can deploy paradox and incongruity, and use encounters with individuals to suggest complex problems within foreign societies. Above all you can leave things unexplained, and admit ignorance and uncertainty, and stress the fundamental problems of communication in a way that is almost never seen in policy documents or journalism. What kills so many briefing documents and newspaper reports, apart from their tendency to exaggerate fears and aggrandize ambitions, is their aspiration towards omniscience, and their impatience with everything that is intractable or mysterious. Travel writing provides a space for all these things.'

Stewart is also sure that the kind of travel writing which will now show the greatest durability is that where an informed observer roots and immerses himself in one place, committing time to get to know a place and its languages. Many of the greatest of the travel books of the early 20th century were about epic journeys, often by young men, conveying the raw intoxication of travel during a moment in life when time is endless, and deadlines and commitments are non-existent;

when experience is all you hope to achieve and when the world is laid out before you like a map: think of the exhilaration of Eric Newby's *Short Walk in the Hindu Kush* or Robert Byron's *Road to Oxiana*.

Today, however, many would argue that the most interesting travel books are by individuals who have made extended stays in places, getting to know them intimately: books like Ian Sinclair's circling of the capital in *London Orbital* or Sam Miller's *Delhi: Adventures in a Megacity*. There is also Amitav Ghosh in his Egyptian village in *In An Antique Land*, or Chris de Bellaigue's magnificent recent study, *Rebel Land*, which examines the way that the ghosts of the Armenian genocide and Kurdish nationalism haunt a single remote town in Eastern Turkey.

The last word should perhaps go to Colin Thubron, the most revered of all the travel writers of the 1980s still at work. He is also clear that travel writing is now more needed than ever: 'Great swathes of the world are hardly visited and remain much misunderstood – think of Iran. It's no accident that the mess inflicted on the world by the last US administration was done by a group of men who had hardly travelled, and relied for information on policy documents and the reports of journalists sitting interviewing middle-class contacts in capital cities. The sympathetic traveller who takes time to immerse himself in a country may gain not only factual knowledge but also a sensuous and emotional understanding, and convey a people's psychology and their response to things in a way that can never be accessed by studying in a library. A good travel writer can give you the warp and weft of everyday life, the generalities of people's existence that are rarely reflected in academic writing or journalism, and hardly touched upon by any other discipline. Despite the internet and the revolution in communications, there is still no substitute for a good piece of travel writing.'

Index